One of
Us
Knows

ALSO BY ALYSSA COLE

Runaway Royals

How to Catch a Queen • *How to Find a Princess*

Reluctant Royals

A Princess in Theory

Once Ghosted, Twice Shy (novella)

A Duke by Default • *Can't Escape Love* (novella)

A Prince on Paper

The Loyal League

An Extraordinary Union • *A Hope Divided*

An Unconditional Freedom

Off the Grid

Radio Silence • *Signal Boost* • *Mixed Signals*

Other Works

In *Fit for the Gods: Greek Mythology Reimagined*

In *Marple: Twelve New Mysteries*

When No One Is Watching • *That Could Be Enough*

Let Us Dream • *Let It Shine* • *Be Not Afraid*

Agnes Moor's Wild Knight • *Eagle's Heart*

One of Us Knows

A Thriller

Alyssa Cole

HARPER LARGE PRINT

An Imprint of HarperCollinsPublishers

HarperCollins books may be purchased for educational, business, or sales promotional use. For information, please email the Special Markets Department at SPsales@harpercollins.com.

FIRST HARPER LARGE PRINT EDITION

ISBN 978-0-06-326741-1

Library of Congress Cataloging-in-Publication Data is available upon request.

24 25 26 27 28 LBC 5 4 3 2 1

For every part of you.

But the beginning of things, of a world especially, is necessarily vague, tangled, chaotic, and exceedingly disturbing. How few of us ever emerge from such beginning!

—Kate Chopin, *The Awakening*

Content Warning:
This book contains depictions of physical violence, references to self-harm, misogyny, ableism, racism, and sexual assault.

One of Us Knows

Prologue

Groupthnk: Collaborative Journal

**Collaborative Group: Bad Day System
(aka Kenetria Nash)**
Pinned Post: Members of Bad Day System
(known/verified headmates)
by: Empress
Edited by: Mesmer

Della (role: manager/caretaker [tasks], host – 65 years old – admin – she/her – active)

Solomon (role: system assistant manager – 30 years old – he/him – active)

Empress (role: teenager – 16 years old – she/they – active)

Mesmer (role: [self-]caretaker [emotions] – 20 years old – she/her – active)

Keke (role: little – 4 years old – she/her – active)

Ken (role: ~~host/persecutor~~/TBD – 37 years old – she/her – inactive)

Lurk (role: chill dude – age unknown – he/him – inactive)

Rapunzel (role: trauma holder? fragment? – age unknown – gender unknown – n/a)

Archived Post: Keke (4 years ago)
Homework: About Me

My name is Keke. I'm a good girl and very smart for my age and that's why I have to do homework sometimes which is not fun. I'm four years old and I'll always be four and that's fine with me cause adults are boring.

One thing about me is I love to volunteer at the dog shelter! Nobody cares if I act like a little girl in a big girl body when I play with the puppies. Solomon says that's cause it's "situationally appropriate."

Solomon is one of my headmates. A group of headmates is called a system, and we are Bad Day System. We all live together in a big castle inside of our head! Dr. Reese, the lady who helped us when we first came out of our rooms, said our house is in a special place called "inner world." We're the only ones that can get in here because we're special people. Not everyone shares a body and a brain with their friends, you know.

Headmates and inner world exist cause something bad happened to us a long time ago. God let us be lotsa people instead of one so we can protect each other. That's what Della told me. Dr. Reese said it's something called dissociative identity disorder and Ken said it was freeloading body-snatcher syndrome, but I like Della's version better.

In our castle, Solomon lives across the hall from me and his room is full of stuff like a museum for old furniture or the show about hoarders. Della lives in a room that has a stained-glass window with Black Jesus on it and she prays for us so we don't go to h-e-l-l. Lurk lives under the stairs and his room is so messy but only I get in trouble for not cleaning my room which is not fair. I share my room with Empress cause she's scared to sleep alone and I'm brave enough for both of us but she is mean and won't let me have the bottom bunk. Mesmer's room is full of crystals that shine like PLINK PLINK PLINK and she makes a noise like "ommm" cause she is trying to help us reach emlightenment. I don't know what Ken's room is like because she went to sleep before we could find it, but it's probably dark and full of knives.

There are locked doors in our castle, like the one to the

tower. Rapunzel is in there and sometimes they scream like they're so scared. I wish I could let them out, but I'm not allowed to.

Another thing about me is that sometimes I feel not real because our body is all grown up and I'm not. When I used to cry a lot Ken would say I was a fig mint of her imagination but I think she was wrong because I had an imaginary friend and no one else could see her, but my headmates can see me so I have to be real.

Mesmer says I shouldn't have a 'sistenchul crisis cause that's something the adults will do for me.

In conclusion, I think we should adopt a puppy, then all the headmates would want to come out and play with it and we'd all live happily ever after. That's what you're supposed to do in a castle, right?

Chapter 1
Ken

I wince into consciousness, eyes squeezed shut against the headache forking through my brain like light-ning strike. Someone is just behind me, watching.

Hazy remnants of dream, or memory—I can't tell if it's theirs, mine, or ours—wisp like curling smoke along the periphery of my mind: rough stone scrap-ing at my skin; the flame-licked hem of a white dress; the echo of a rhyme chanted in a distorted, childlike trill.

The goblin king who never sleeps,
awaits us at the stormy keep.
When all is dark, in dead of night,
The hunt begins . . .

I try to cling to the images as they dissolve and the melody as it fades, but I blink and—

I'm awake.

Fuck.

An insistent breeze scours my face with its rough caress, carrying with it a scent of outside that's more brown-green than slab gray. The air vibrates with birdsong—shrill chirps instead of the soft coo of pigeons—and a relentless rush different from the sound of cars plowing down busy streets. City sounds have a rhythm, an ebb and flow, but these noises blend into an all-encompassing, jarring drone, like the dentist's drill about to hit a cavity.

Motes of daylight drift across my scrunched-shut eyelids; even this is painful after so long in the dark. I peek between my lashes and try to acclimate to the amber light jabbing at my retinas like shards of broken liquor bottle.

Where am I?

Standing at the end of an old wooden dock. Brackish water churns beneath me, hypnotic in the way of things that might kill me if I make one wrong move.

Who am I?

My brain is foggy, my sense of self thin as a Mickey D's cheeseburger. It can be like this after a switch to the front, when I slide back into the driver's seat of the body formerly known as mine, wading through emotions and sensations that aren't my own as I take the wheel.

The only thing I know for certain is that wherever I am, I don't want to be here. I *shouldn't* be here—for everyone's sake.

My hands clench into fists as a familiar anger takes hold of me. My fingernails—which are way too goddamn long—dig into my palms, a pleasurable sting. I resist the urge to press harder, to ride the edge between painful pinch and open wound.

I review this new evidence: I'm someone with a hair-trigger temper and a penchant for self-inflicted pain.

I'm me.

Ken.

Fuck.

The multilayered ripple of distress underlying my own disappointment confirms it.

It's kind of funny in a fucked-up way. For years, I'd tried to fill the cavernous void inside of me, shoveling in nuggets of dopamine—in the form of drinks, drugs, dicks, and dildos, if you want to get alliterative—like I worked in a ship's engine room. Come to find out the void was already occupied by a whole damn castle full of other people and, after everything I'd dumped on them, they disliked me as much as I disliked myself.

That's life, I guess. Sometimes you win, usually you lose, occasionally you become public enemy number one to the people squatting in your brain. My headmates are scared of me—and they should be.

A memory of my ex-boyfriend, Landon, staring at me with fear in his eyes and blood splatter on his face after he'd pulled me off his father, flashes into my mind. The human stink of a crowded jail cell and the antiseptic burn of the psych ward mingle in the back of my throat, scent memory that never fades. The strain of muscle and slosh of bathwater as I struggled to press a blade into my wrist while my own body fought against me—

"Stop thinking about it," I say aloud, my nails finding the meat of my palms again. "Stop."

Whatever. I wasn't some Miss Hyde, sneaking out at night to ruin the life of a respectable, well-adjusted person. I was ruining my *own* life just fine before they made themselves known, but somehow I'm the problem.

I do a little two-step shimmy on the wooden planks, to shake off their discomfort and to get reacquainted with weight, gravity, and all that. A cig would be nice, a Jägerbomb nicer, but figuring out where I am, and when, is my priority.

Time is my nemesis even on a good day, but last I remember we'd been balls deep in winter—black ice on asphalt, and greedy nights that ate daylight like Pringles, leaving the can empty for the rest of us. The trees wherever I am now have shed most of their leaves, but bursts of orange and ochre dot the landscape; clusters of autumn foliage too obstinate to give in to the natural order of things.

At my side are a large pink rolling suitcase, big enough to fit like a body and a half, and an old skull-print duffel bag I've had since high school. Instead of my usual all-black outfit and leather jacket, I'm sporting a calf-length pink bubble coat over a mauve power suit that I'd randomly snagged from the TJ Maxx discount rack for job interviews during the *Ally McBeal* era—or not so randomly, since it's clearly my headmate Della's style. The look is tied together by a pink fanny pack and, in a selection as diametrically opposed to my preferred shitkicker Docs as possible, faux leather loafers that are flaking onto the planks around my feet.

I used to have a nice padding of curves, but this church-elder suit is hanging off me like a squeezed-out sausage casing. Exactly how much time has passed? The longest I've gone without fronting is a month, but clearly it's been longer. I'd pulled a Rip Van Winkle, in a way, so maybe I, too, have slept for twenty years.

I check the backs of my hands: no wrinkles or age spots, but they're ashy as fuck and the cuticles are splintering like we haven't known the moist embrace of Vaseline in way too long. The numerous thin scars I'd accumulated from X-Acto knives, hot stoves, and general lapses in common sense are still there, if slightly faded. A tendril from the twisting green-and-black medieval ivy tattoo that snakes up my left arm from wrist to elbow, placed to cover less accidental scarring, peeks out from my sleeve. I'd designed it myself, basing it on a doodle that I'd scrawled into the margins of every notebook since I was a kid. Well, I thought I designed it, but the joke was on me: despite being an artist, I can't draw for shit.

If you ever want to catch the express train to nihilism avenue, try learning that the things you'd considered the bedrocks of your sense of self had never been *you* at all. The artistic talent that had won me accolades over the years, my wellspring of knowledge, and the luck that always kicked in to save me by the skin of my teeth were apparently courtesy of my headmates. My worst attributes—stubbornness, a violent streak, and the innate ability to always make the wrong choice? All me, baby.

I force my attention back to my surroundings, swiping at my glasses again and hissing out a curse when I realize the blurriness isn't just moisture, it's the lenses themselves. This is a new pair of glasses, which is an issue since thanks to the wonders of the human brain, my eyesight is worse than everyone else's even though we have the same eyeballs. I hadn't been around for the latest trip to the optometrist, so I hadn't been able to push for a prescription closer to mine. The wrongness of it is enough to be a slightly disorienting nuisance, like having a bunch of uninvited people jabbering away at the back of your mind.

I squint to get a better view of things. Judging from the way the water in front of me snakes off in two directions, surface broken up by choppy waves, it's a river. Not the East, with bridges stretched across from Brooklyn to Manhattan like three stitches keeping the city's skin from splitting apart.

This is the Hudson, just not the part I'm used to, with crowded skyscrapers jutting out like uneven teeth and the Statue of Liberty in the background like that dangly thing in the back of your throat.

Epiglottis?

(*"Uvula."*) The unasked-for correction comes from just over my left shoulder, but also inside of my head.

Solomon.

A familiar calm settles over me; a comforting weighted blanket studded with memory-barbed nettles.

Once upon a time, long conversations and elaborate daydreams with the boy, then teen, then man, in my head had seemed normal. After reading some psychology books and learning about maladaptive daydreaming, I'd figured they were abnormal but in a crazy-sexy-cool "inventing a boyfriend as a trauma response" kind of way.

They were neither.

Solomon is entirely his own person. Unfortunately for him, I don't trust anyone but myself.

"Go away," I sneer inwardly.

(*"I can't. Have you forgotten how this works while you were off sulking?"*) His voice is a resonant monotone with bass to it, and somehow it's pitched to provoke. He knows how to push my buttons with minimal effort.

"Listen, you little punk—"

(*"It's been a while since we've seen one another, but I'll remind you that there's nothing little about me."*)

My retort gets snagged on the recollection of strong hands, soft lips, the squeeze of his arms around me— hyperrealistic fantasies that real-world sex had never lived up to, and that I'll never experience again because I crushed whatever Solomon and I had beneath the tread of my boot.

(*"You were right about us being on the Hudson. As*

to how much time has passed—you've been dormant for six years.")

Dormant? Six years?

Well, shit. I knew I was a stubborn bitch who could hold a grudge; turns out, I can even hold one against myself.

My left wrist vibrates and chimes, followed by a more subtle echoing jolt against my hip bone from something in the fanny pack. When I lift my arm, I see we've acquired a smartwatch. The pink strap of it covers the thin keloid scars that had been one of my parting gifts.

Text has popped up on the watch's illuminated screen:

Reminder

Today

New job, new start

on life!

The stress-induced pain that shanks me under my left shoulder blade reminds me how much I hate this guessing game of trying to figure out what the hell some headmate has gotten us into. I refuse to ask Solomon, so I unzip the fanny pack to search for the cell phone. A multicolored pen, a travel notebook, a small tactical flashlight, and, oddly, travel-sized bottles of Lysol disinfectant spray and hand sanitizer. The phone, a sleek, seemingly buttonless Android instead of my old reliable iPhone SE, is in an almost-hidden inner pocket, tangled in the elastic straps of . . . a surgical mask?

I run my fingers over the phone with no fucking clue how to even activate the lock screen, then my index finger presses into an indent on the side—an assist from Solomon.

My thumb swipes across the phone's screen, dismissing a winter storm alert and tapping in a numeric password; Solomon again.

It's 3:40 pm on December 1, 2022.

The screen wallpaper behind the date and time is a group drawing of everyone in the system, probably Empress's work since it's digital and leans more toward a manga style than Solomon's fine-art finesse. In the background rearing up over us is their house in the inner world, an incongruous Gothic castle that makes the scene look like a poster for a colorblind-casted *Wuthering Heights* remake.

I'm at the center of the picture. Brown skin, slim build, angular face paired with plush lips that've invited too many unwanted comments to count. I know it's *me* and not just our body because my eyes are narrowed in general annoyance behind the lenses of huge plastic-rimmed glasses. My eyelids are shrouded in black shadow, my mouth in black-cherry, and tiny glints in my eyebrow, septum, and lower lip mark where my piercings should be. My hair is how it'd been when I went dormant, a kinky wash-and-go-hawk with the sides shaved down short, not the relaxed and bumped-end James Brown bob that I see reflected on the phone's screen.

I'm wearing a black mesh tank top paired with black skinny jeans and my Docs, holding Keke on my hip. I'm leaning slightly away from her, as if I'm not quite sure what to do with her. Accurate, but fucked up since she's me, too, in a way. Me at around four years old, stubby-legged and round-bellied in a frilly floral dress and shiny Mary Janes, looking up at the older version of herself with a gap-toothed grin.

I wonder if I'd ever been like Keke, playful and open and willing to smile at someone who'd tried their hardest to hurt me. I can't remember—my earliest memory is being pulled kicking and clawing off a boy who'd been flipping skirts at recess in kindergarten.

Mesmer stands on the other side of Keke, short orange hair curling around her ears and hand clutching the little silver amulet she apparently always wears around her neck, even though I'd tossed it in the trash years ago. I'd got it at a temple visit during one of my non-Western religion fixations, which I guess was her making herself known. She's the only white person in our system that we know of, though she's a ginger so maybe that explains how she got in.

Lurk stands off to the side, wearing an oversized gray hoodie and baggy jeans. Apparently, no one knows what he looks like. I assume he's Black under there because he's the headmate that makes the bangin' baked mac and cheese that I've been complimented on so many times over the years. From what I've heard about him, he just bums around the inner world, rarely speaking and never causing problems.

Empress, short, mid-sized, and sharp featured, wearing a T-shirt with a buff green woman on it, denim shorts, and green high-top Reeboks. Her hair is in the same cornrowed style it's always been in, though it's now teal, highlighting her dark skin and bright brown eyes.

Della, high-yellow and bird-framed, is dressed like she's ready for Easter service, complete with an ostentatious mauve hat.

And then there's Solomon—brown-skinned, lantern-jawed with a close-cropped beard, and hair so immaculately waved that I have to wonder about his inner-world hair regimen. He's sporting a tailored white button-up shirt and dark denim; the small round glasses perched on his nose and tight-lipped smile hint at his annoying nature.

In many ways, like being unreasonably hot, he's the headmate most similar to me. More accurately, given our particular connection, he's the best parts of me, or the me I thought I was.

I'll never forgive him for it.

(*"We don't have time for this,"*) he says, either picking up my thought or sensing my general annoyance with him, and, as usual, he's right.

A mechanical droning in the distance differentiates itself from the racket of birds and trees, and when I squint down the river I see a ferry so old it might be breaking through the mists of time. It's moving slowly, but its direction is clear. It's coming toward the dock.

Toward me.

I put it together all at once: Ugly suit. Luggage. Meeting point. *New job, new start on life!*

Oh, hell no.

I've been handed the baton in a relay race when I haven't had time to stretch, but unfortunately for my headmates I'm only capable of a niche individual event: extreme minding my business.

"Della?" I call inwardly. *"Come out and handle this."*

We aren't genies in a bottle who can be summoned on command, but she's usually listening and waiting to extend a judgy, perfectionist hand. She's silent now. Solomon is, too, and I don't like the apprehension rolling off him, like he's watching me fumble in the dark toward a huge pile of shit.

"Della!"

I squeeze my eyes shut, listening as best I can when what I'm used to is ignoring.

Nothing.

No . . . there's something—the emotions of the others, churning below my own like the ripping current beneath the river's surface.

My headmates are calling for her too.

She isn't responding to any of us.

Chapter 2

Groupthnk: Collaborative Journal

Pinned Post: Origin Story
by: Solomon (4 years ago)

Misty asked today as I was reupholstering a chair in the back room. It was bound to come up since we'd told her about our DID a few months back. She'd found us—Keke—playing with some vintage Cabbage Patch dolls that'd come into the thrift shop.

"What happened to you, uh, y'all? What made you split?"

Singlets always want to know, and even if it's well-intentioned, it's essentially asking multiples to dredge up trauma for their entertainment. I was tempted to tell her our daycare had been run by Satan worshippers, but I gave her the boring truth: we don't know.

We were taken into foster care when we were three

years old, through one of those child protective services "misunderstandings" that often befall young Black parents. Our parents eventually got us back, but they'd had a bubbly, sweet, and intelligent toddler stolen from them and got a sullen and obstinate five-year-old who preferred daydreams to reality in return.

We may as well have been a changeling.

I don't have an answer to Misty's question. There are records, but badly kept, with monthslong gaps in our placement information. None of us remember what happened during that time—that is, none of us who've been able to answer when asked.

The literature on DID suggests all kinds of possible abuses we might have endured, but I think there doesn't have to be anything more sensational than what we already know. We might've had the kindest guardians in the world, but being ripped away from your parents for any reason, especially for no reason at all, is trauma enough.

Maybe I'm being optimistic.

Chapter 3

Ken

"Goddammitmotherfuckingshit!"

The strung-together cuss scrapes up my throat, caustic as bile. A sparrow that's just touched down on the edge of the dock wheels back into flight, away from this wolf in human's clothing.

I don't want to deal with this. At all.

I consider chucking the phone into the river and hopping in after it. Not the best solution, but the kind I'm prone to think of before coming up with more reasonable options. After indulging a quick fantasy of the sweet release of drowning, which I hear is kind of relaxing after all the thrashing, I suck it up and start searching our phone for information.

The reminder had popped up on the watch because

Della is the kind of person who thinks having two different planners, a digital calendar, and a reminder app is the bare minimum when it comes to organizing. If Solomon was the brake on my worst impulses, Della was the motor oil in my best ones—she keeps things running smoothly. I don't know what's up with her right now, but she's definitely left an easily accessible summary of the situation for whoever is fronting.

There are two widgets on the phone's home screen: "Files" and "Groupthnk Journal," as well as the usual email, phone, camera, and internet.

In the files, I find neatly labeled folders containing years' worth of past rent documentation, work invoices, scanned receipts, medical documents, and other boring shit, but nothing about a new job. I keep the search moving, checking out the journal.

The main page lists the current roster of the system, which hasn't changed since I've been gone. I look at the "inactive" next to my name and decide to leave it as-is. My presence is a temporary stopgap, a finger in the dam of whatever Della has gotten us into.

There's a lag as the posts load, the two bars of signal struggling under the load of data, but I keep swiping anyway so that when the posts appear I'm already several entries deep. I start reading, scrolling up as I go.

Empress (2 months ago)
Mood: Frustrated

Someone canceled the subscription to WeebMax before I could watch the finale of *That Time I Fell Into a Sinkhole (And In Love with a Goblin)*. My furry art commissions help keep the lights on around here! Why does Mesmer get to burn money paying some scammer for "emotional genotyping," but I can't see if Souta returns to high school in the human realm or chooses his goblin wife? 💀

Mesmer (1 month ago)
Mood: Hyperventilating

Madame Olga is an *empath,* not a scammer. The emotional genotyping results were, like, totally accurate. She said I have so many conflicting emotional blocks that they only made sense if I was more than one person! 😳 The only thing that made me doubt her was some fear blockage from 100 years ago that she mentioned. I couldn't find out more about it because the new building manager, who I knew was bad vibes, started pounding on the door and I was triggered back inside. Empress found a letter he slipped under the door about the moratorium being over, back rent, and us being evicted. Della, what's going on with the rent? Is this legal?

Solomon (1 month ago)
Mood: Neutral

I thought the rent situation was being handled, but since I can't front for long periods of time I won't cast judgment. That said, the notice is real, and even if it isn't we don't have the means to fight it. We can sell more of our stuff, but we'll need three months' rent for security deposit and proof of steady income to even submit an application at most places. And when they do a background check . . . I'll try to figure something out.

My face goes hot from anger as I stare at the phone. We'd been evicted? My apartment had been a step above a dingy shithole, but it was the only place that'd ever felt like home to me. I'd painted it in bold colors and decorated it with curbside treasures and second-hand finds that I—no, Solomon—had repainted and refurbished.

It'd been my refuge as my outer life, and then my

inner world, fell apart, and I hadn't even had the chance to say goodbye. This is the kind of shit that shouldn't have happened once I was gone; avoiding this was why I'd had to go dormant to begin with.

(*"Focus, Ken."*)

"Fuck off," I retort.

My index finger slides down the screen, not of my volition, and taps impatiently.

Della (20 minutes ago)
Mood: Blessed

We've been walking by faith, not by sight, and He has rewarded us.

I should have mentioned this earlier, but I've been contacted by an organization called the Kavanaugh Island Conservation Trust. They're restoring a historic home on an island in the Hudson River, and looking for a caretaker for the winter, maybe longer if things go well. Apparently one of us (Ken? Solomon?) submitted an application a few years back, and they thought they'd check to see if we were still interested now that they're opening. They seem really excited to work with us, which is a nice change of pace.

There's a modest monthly stipend (pay stubs!), free room and board, and basic healthcare benefits. Everything we need to get back on our feet, with the bonus of being away from all the terrible things going on in the world. The house itself is interesting; I think we'll all be comfortable there. There is one odd thing: the job only becomes official after spending one night on the island. Apparently, it's tradition. I'm not worried, though. We'll make it through just fine; we always do!

"Oh, come the fuck on," I groan. I thought Della was positive, not naïve. A job that magically appears, with all kinds of benefits and a weird catch before we can cash in? Either this is some kind of financial scam, or we're going to get our organs harvested—maybe both.

Though . . . there's a slight chance it's legit.

I'd read a *New York Times* article profiling historical home caretakers years ago, around the time my "art block" had started to kick in. It'd seemed like a dream job, and one within my reach because the positions usually went to regular people with the most important skill of all: luck. I'd rapid-fire applied to a bunch of places in one hyperfocus session, not expecting to hear back from any of them since positions rarely open up. Kavanaugh Island vaguely rings a bell, so it might have been one of them.

If this is real, then we just might be set for life. I'd fucked up our lives with my impulsiveness, but maybe

I'd unwittingly provided us a safety net with it too. Optimism laps around the ankles exposed by the too-short hem of these pants. The water feels fine, but I step back onto the pessimism peninsula before I can get sucked in by the inevitable undertow.

I'd spent my life chasing: acceptance, purpose, a definitive success that could be measured against my countless failures. Every time I had one of them in my grasp, I squeezed too hard, too fast, either crushing it into a mangled mess or watching it slip from my greedy fingers like a *Valdez*-greased penguin.

Della set us up with the perfect job, bounced instead of sticking around to enjoy it, and left only the barest scrap of information to fill the rest of us in. Even someone who isn't a paranoid bitch would be suspicious.

I run my tongue over my teeth in agitation, giving in to the unavoidable.

"If you're gonna backseat-drive, be useful. What the fuck is going on?"

Solomon's voice is louder, closer, when he speaks. (*"I was trying to, but you were ignoring me. And we're currently somewhere between co-consciousness and co-fronting, so it's more accurate to say I'm in the passenger seat, with my hand over yours on the throttle."*)

I press my thumb to the space between my brows, massaging at the headache that threatens to flare up again from sheer frustration and from the unwanted image of his hand on mine. I know how his hands feel everywhere, even if it'd only ever happened in my mind.

Our mind.

"I'd really missed your need to correct everything I say," I gripe.

(*"And I'd missed your aura of turbulent negativity that makes being co-con with you feel like doggy paddling in the Pacific garbage patch."*)

Well, damn.

Since we can't connect like we used to, in order to fight Solomon I'd have to punch myself in the face. I've done worse to myself and with less compelling reason, but it wouldn't be worth it since it'd give him an in to lecture me on my anger issues. One of the differences between us that'd become apparent when we realized we'd been hit by the DID stick is that he has said stick shoved up his ass, while I'm more likely to use it to swing on someone.

I slide the phone back into the fanny pack, my gaze locked on the approaching boat. *"Just sum up what I've missed. Quickly."*

(*"It's not possible to sum up six years quickly, but I'll try. Trump became president; climate disasters are an everyday occurrence; the global rise of fascism is rocking like it's 1932; the rights of women, minorities, and* queer people are being stripped away; and then there's the pandemic that's killed millions around the world and everyone is pretending is over. Will that suffice, or do you mean what you've missed in our system?")

"Trump? Fascism? Pandemic??" Everything he's listed is horrifying, but I latch onto the imminent threat. "Like . . . a plague? Is that what the mask is for?"

("And the hand sanitizer, and the Lysol. It's a virus called Covid.")

I pat my hands over my body again, feeling how much weight we'd lost with renewed concern. "Did we get sick?"

("No. Della was cautious. Exceedingly so.")

"Then why are we so skinny? I worked hard for that little bit of ass, and now it's gone like everything else!"

He goes icily quiet, and yeah, I guess now isn't the best time to stress about our medical-grade no-assitol, but I deserve to be informed of at least one fucking thing going on with me right now.

The ferry engine grows louder, close enough that I can make out the silhouette of the driver through cloudy glass.

"Shit. Just tell me about this The-Shining-on-the-Hudson situation."

("I know as much as you do.")

"How? Only one of us was dormant."

("*I'm not usually in control of the body,*") he reminds me, tone dry as twice-baked clay. ("*I'm not even usually fully co-con. Getting filled in as an afterthought is normal for me.*")

"*Tell me what you do know, then.*"

("*I woke up fronting and realized I'd been inside for at least a week, maybe longer,*") he says stiffly. ("*The apartment had been cleared of all our belongings, except for the air mattress we were sleeping on and these packed bags. A reminder popped up on the watch telling me to put on the suit that had been set out and follow the directions in the maps app. The destination was labeled 'pickup point.' On the way here, I checked our phone for information but there was nothing.*")

"*But the entry I read—*"

("*—popped up a few minutes before you arrived; presumably it was pre-scheduled. She knows tech tricks with the apps.*")

"*Where's our laptop? Did you check there?*"

A pause.

("*Della dropped it two days—no, two weeks ago. We didn't have money to replace it.*")

"*So you just followed her instructions and came here, with no idea what was going on?*"

("*I didn't have a choice,*") he says, and though his tone doesn't change, I can tell he's pissed. ("*There's not enough signal to google, so I was waiting here for . . . I don't know what, and then you shoved out in front of me."*)

"*Shoved? If anything, I was pushed.*" Wait . . . was I? I try to remember how I'd woken up, but can't, even though only a few minutes have passed.

I guess it's normal, but one thing I'd learned the hard way is that it's the tiny amnesia holes in the fabric of a day that can unravel everything.

I open the web browser and see that he's searched Kavanaugh Island Historical Home. No thumbnails have loaded, but the first result is a web page for the historical home. The second is a link to some .edu web page post, the preview text reading: Kavanaugh was a paradoxical mix of businessman and social reformer, and like many during the period, he found a way to convert his staunch beliefs into money in the bank . . .

I shake my head. "*Della is queen of documentation. There should be a file with pictures, floor plans of the house, water depth around the island.*"

(*"I gave you the briefest recap of what the last few years have been like. None of this makes sense to you, but an isolated island is her idea of paradise right now."*)

"*I don't care how hard things were. She set this up, so she needs to come handle this herself or at least tell us what the fuck is going on.*"

I snap my fingers.

My own brain has thrown up a force field keeping my annoying ass out of the inner world, so he understands that I'm trying to send him on an errand.

His frustration washes over me in a frigid wave. (*"I'm not being clear. You and Della are the only hosts in our system; the only ones who can front for long periods of time. You disappeared for six years, and Della hosted that entire time. Now Della is . . . n't here, and you're back."*)

"She's gone dormant?"

(*"That's one possibility."*) There's a hesitancy in his tone. (*"The only other headmate who's been dormant is you, but since you don't live with us, we don't know what the warning signs are."*)

A pit of dread opens in my stomach.

I'd had a lot of reasons for wanting my headmates gone, but one of them is as simple as it gets: hosting is exhausting. People who have one "self" get tired after a day of wrangling their neuroses. Dealing with multiple selves, each with their own thoughts, desires, neurodivergences, is overwhelming even in a world that isn't a garbage fire burning higher than usual.

When I'd been the primary host, Della'd been in the background along with Solomon and the others, keeping our train on the tracks even when I occasionally gave in to my impulsive thoughts and tried to derail it. When I needed to rest, I'd unknowingly clock out and jokingly chalk up whatever work got done or social events were attended or bills got paid during those blank spaces in my memory to "autopilot" or "fugue states." Without another host, even if it was a fuck-up like me, Della's been handling everything alone without the ability to tap out for longer than a few hours at most.

I'd been thinking of this situation as a handing off of the baton during a relay race, but tag-team wrestling might be more apt, with my teammate already changed and gone from the locker room.

My jaw clenches at the sound of the approaching engine. The ferry is here; the words CAPTAIN JOHN'S ISLAND TOUR are painted along its side, faded with age. Della could be gone for hours, days, or if she's anything like me, for years.

I'll have to handle whatever it is she's gotten us into, but we all know that I'm not made to host. I can't be trusted not to ruin everything—again.

Chapter 4

Groupthnk: Collaborative Journal

Folder: Documents Pertaining to the Incident (Scans)
Added by: Della (5 years ago)

Dear Ms. Kenetria Nash,

I am writing to inform you of your dismissal from the Master of Arts in Historic Preservation Program. You are hereby barred from future enrollment in any other programs or courses, related or unrelated to this discipline, at Benson College. You are also banned from Benson College school grounds, both main and satellite campuses.

This decision is a result of your conduct during the event "Preservation in the Twenty-First Century: The Past Lights the Way to the Future." We at Benson College have a zero-tolerance policy for violence, and though Assemblyman Pearson has refused to press criminal charges and encouraged the prosecutor to do the same, we must take the safety of students, staff, and property into consideration.

Although your time at Benson has come to an end, we hope you are able to move past this regrettable moment in your life and live up to the potential that was the reason for your admission into this prestigious program.

If you wish to contest this dismissal, please respond within ten business days of receipt of this letter. Be aware that doing so may have legal and financial repercussions for you.

Sincerely,
David Slater
Dean of Student Conduct

Chapter 5

Ken

W e'll figure things out once we're settled,") Solomon says, voice further from me as he retreats to the inner world.

I roll my shoulders, steeling myself for my first external human interaction in years as the ferry slides alongside the dock and slows to a stop.

The driver looks like Nicolas Cage doing a cameo in a movie where he's trying to play a normal old man but can't because he's Nicolas Cage. He moves with an assuredness born of experience as he hustles out to tether the ferry bouncing on the rough waves.

I size him up before I even think about setting foot on his boat, gaming out whether I could take him in a fight if I had to. Maybe, but he's got a solid build under his cable-knit sweater and probably has some of that Greatest Generation spunk in him. I'll have to keep my guard up.

Solomon's presence fully recedes, and even though having him around is like sand in the crotch of my swimsuit, I feel abandoned. Loud noises stress him out, so the engine is probably what's driving him away, but still. He's comfy in the inner world while I'm out here about to get dragged into a *National Treasure* sequel.

"I'm looking for the new caretaker?" the man calls out, though it shouldn't be a question since I'm the only one on the dock.

The irony of this situation finally hits me when I hear the job title spoken aloud. Dr. Reese had made us take some quiz to figure out our "roles" in the system. Della is our *literal* caretaker, whose main "function" is watching over the system. Me? I'm the problem she wanted to get rid of.

"That'd be me," I say as I haul the duffel bag onto one shoulder and grab the handle of the suitcase.

"*You're* the new caretaker." He stares at me as if debating whether to let me aboard.

My annoyance blooms, each petal of aggravation unfurling with a languorous stretch that's familiar and satisfying amid all the unknowns I'm navigating. "That's what I've been told. There a problem?"

"Nope, no problem from me. And you're not waiting on anyone? A boyfriend?"

Eight years had passed since Landon, and I'd been dormant for six of them, but the barb of that shame is still hooked into my skin and apparently hurts like a bitch when someone tugs at it. Not because I'm still carrying a torch for the jerk, but because of how things had ended. Brutally fast, by my own fists, and with a resultant sonic boom that'd blasted everything else in my life to pieces.

"There's just little old me. Are we good, or is there going to be a full dockside inquisition?"

His brow furrows, then he shrugs, opens the gate, and beckons me toward him.

"We can head out," he says. "Hope you weren't waiting too long. I wasn't told that the pickup date had changed until the last minute, but the folks at the trust think everyone is at their beck and call so that isn't unusual."

I give him a tight nod, noting the resentment that crept into his tone. The first thing I've learned about my new employer is that they don't respect people's time.

"I haven't been waiting long," I say. "I'm Ken. I'm assuming you're Captain John, unless you boat-jacked someone."

He gives me a sidelong glance, then beckons me onto the ferry. "Let's get going, since this storm is . . ."

His words briefly drop into background static as my thoughts crowd in, reminding me that there's a pandemic we're supposed to be navigating, but old buddy is happily raw-dogging the air like nothing is amiss.

"Do I have to wear a mask?" I call inwardly to Solomon, reaching for the comfort of his opinion like I had before everything went wrong. I cringe in embarrassment, hoping he's too far in the inner world to hear me, but he's there as always.

(*"Della always wears one, but I think it's okay not to right now,"*) he says, his voice dampened by distance. (*"We're outdoors, our vaccinations are up to date, and spread is currently low."*)

"But there's still a risk?"

(*"Everything has a risk. But focusing on risk has its risks too."*)

I don't know what he's talking about, but I awkwardly pull the heavy-duty mask over my nose and mouth, snapping myself in the cheek with the elastic band before tugging it over my ear, and then march toward the ferry's entrance.

John reaches for my suitcase as I approach, but I ignore him and hop over the gap between dock and ferry, feeling the vibration of the engine in the soles of my loafers as I plant myself on the deck.

My gaze sweeps the interior of the ferry, looking for familiar orange donuts.

"Where are the life preservers?" I ask as he passes me on his way to the steering wheel.

"Under that bench," he says, pointing to a metal box. "Can't swim?"

"A little. I never got the hang of it," I say.

I'd graduated from the Overcome Your Fear swimming course at five different YMCA locations. I should be Michael fucking Phelps at this point, but someone else had fronted each time, once again stealing something that should have been mine and leaving me in the lurch.

It's then that I catch my reflection in the scratched window on the other side of the boat and, okay, I may have overreacted a bit to his initial confusion. I don't look like a person waiting to be picked up to go do a job on an island, unless that job is discussing our Lord and Savior.

As usual, I'd jumped the gun at a perceived slight.

The boat shakes like a dog waking from a nap as I shove my bags under the bench next to the life preservers, then we're pulling away from the dock, the swirl and suck of the river at the hull clear as soon as we're away from the shore.

John glances back at me.

"You can sit up here," he calls out, lifting his elbow toward the navigator's seat beside him, separated by a flimsy sheet of Plexiglas.

I walk over carefully, but just as my ass brushes the bucket seat, the ferry crashes against a hard wave. My feet lift off the ground for a sickening moment before I grab onto the dash in front of me.

"Christ!"

I pin John with an accusatory glare and he holds up a hand in apology, then quickly returns it to the wheel. "Sorry! The river is rough with the nor'easter coming in. We're only getting the edge of this one, but it's a doozy."

I drop firmly into the seat and look straight ahead, reminding myself that attacking him while he's driving would only up my chances of ending up at the bottom of the river.

"Hope you packed a raincoat," he says, making small talk to steer the conversation away from the fact that he almost launched me from his boat like a Roman candle.

"So do I." I shift jerkily in my seat, taking in the view from the water.

I know that there are houses and highways just out of sight, but there are no other craft on the water. It feels like we're pressing through an invisible veil of wind. The hills and mountains lie on either side of us like some sleeping creatures waiting for nightfall to awaken. The late-afternoon sun had been warm on the dock, but it's already starting to sink behind the mountains and wind blows steady and cool down the river.

Back when I'd believed I was an artist, one whose skill was my own, I'd taken a free class at my local library on women painters of the Hudson Valley on a whim. This place reminds me of one of the works I'd liked best, all turbulent muddy green and close-crowded trees along bluffs and ridges.

The wind blows steadily, rustling the tenacious leaves that have refused to follow nature's marching orders. Every autumn I wonder if the trees know they'll awaken in spring. Maybe some of them don't, and fight until the wind and snow strip their branches bare. I drag my gaze from the landscape with an eye roll. I need to be getting more information, not indulging in daydreams about the inner turmoil of flora.

"Do you live on the island too?" I ask John.

His gaze flits toward me beneath knit brows. "There's only the one house on the island, and since the Kavanaughs left, only the caretaker resides there when it's habitable. You didn't know that?"

I hesitate, unsure if Della had asked anything before

accepting the job or had really just handed Jesus, and then me, the wheel.

"This is my first time doing a job like this. There's so much to remember about the island that I forgot for a second. I know everything that I need to, though, don't worry."

He whistles. "You chose a heck of a first-time caretaking job."

"I'm a quick learner," I say, and that's kind of true. "I'll be able to handle anything that comes up."

"Sure. We'll see if you last the night," he says cheerfully, smiling like we're both in on a joke even though I don't see what's funny.

"What's up with that? The whole 'lasting the night' thing?" Della had mentioned it, too, and like whatever virus this mask is protecting me from, it's a hovering threat that I need explained ASAP.

"I thought you knew everything you needed to," he says. "Surviving the night on Daybreak Island should be number one on that list."

I lean back in my seat and fix him with a hard look, the buddy-buddy energy that had been flowing abruptly running dry. "I must be on the wrong ferry, because I'm supposed to be going to *Kavanaugh* Island."

It occurs to me that this man rolled up without even having our name or any documentation and I'd willingly hopped on board just to show him up. Is this old-ass ferry really still in commercial use? How do I know he's associated with this job at all?

I begin to reach for the blade in my boot, then remember I'm not wearing them and Della isn't the "carry a weapon on your person at all times" type like I am. Not ideal, but if I have to choke him out using the sleeve of a puffy jacket, so be it.

"Same island, different name," he says quickly, one shoulder lifting defensively as if he senses that I'm plotting the most efficient way to end him. "Man, they really didn't tell you anything, did they? The trust likes to pretend Kavanaugh raised the island itself out of the river. He was a great man—a great one—but its history started long before he bought it. In colonial times, the Dutch called it Daageraad, or Daybreak, Island. Got the name because ship crews used to haze sailors by dropping them off on the island overnight; if the sailor was still alive when they came back for him at daybreak, he was welcomed aboard."

So this is the "tradition" Della had mentioned. I still don't like it, but it makes sense for people running a historical home to try to shoehorn links to the past into every aspect, even when they're kind of disturbing. "Is there any reason why a sailor wouldn't be alive?"

"The natives thought the island was cursed," he

says, his voice dropping into a spooky-tour-guide-tales drawl. "That's why they didn't live there. The Dutch paid that no mind, but *they* believed these mountains were full of goblins."

I squint at him. "Goblins?

"Just local legend," he says, his hands on the wheel as the ferry struggles against the current surging around a bend in the river. "People even held goblin hunts, back in the day. Sounds silly to outsiders I guess, but I'm a local."

"You ever catch one?"

"Would you believe me if I said yes?" His brown eyes flash with mischief as he grins, but then he points his chin ahead of us. "Island is around this turn. Makes a nice picture at this time of day."

"Thanks."

I pull the phone out of the fanny pack to document our arrival in the journal app. Della might not follow her own rules, but I will. I don't mind doing what I'm told when I have petty enough reason to.

The Hudson spreads before the prow of the ferry on the screen, the image approximately a million megapixels crisper than what my old phone was capable of.

The last rays of afternoon sunlight slip over something jutting out of the water up ahead and my stomach turns as I imagine the worst—a sinking ship. I reverse pinch my thumb and middle finger over the screen to zoom in and the bulky object comes into focus: it is, improbably, a turret, like one you'd find on top of a castle. A drowned one. The realization doesn't ease my initial reaction because there's something even more unsettling about it than what I'd imagined. Ships belong in rivers; this is a childhood dream randomly toppled into the indifferent waves.

I pinch to zoom out and see the island itself rearing up in the distance. I'd imagined something flat, and manicured, like Governors Island, or Roosevelt, but some islands make it clear that they're the product of tectonic plates and grinding glaciers, and Kavanaugh Island is one of them. The shores are rocky and wild, bathed in white foam from the surging waves. Densely treed slopes veer sharply upward, as if mimicking the surrounding mountains.

Sunlight against glass blinks at me through a cluster of trees near the summit, like an eye that's watching me approach. The house itself doesn't become visible until we make our way fully around the bend and are heading at the island dead-on, and even then flicking in and out of sight through the foliage, making it seem like it's not quite on this plane of existence.

The setting sun slips down between the mountains

on either side of the river, throwing the sloping Victorian roof, crenelated parapets, and imposing tower into silhouetted relief against the blood-orange sky.

My fingers go slack, then grip the phone tightly to keep it from falling.

(*"Ken. That's . . ."*) Solomon says in a strangled voice as he reappears, engine noise be damned.

This isn't some quaint colonial home or gaudy Gilded Age mansion. It's a goddamned castle—an exact replica of the one in our inner world.

Chapter 6

Groupthnk: Collaborative Journal

Folder: About Us
Archived Post: Empress (4 years ago)
Mood: Nerdy
Edited by: Solomon
Edited by: Empress

Copied and pasted my post from DIDSystems forum ask me anything because we needed to add more info about our system anyways!

Empress here! I see a lot of you have questions about DID systems, and of course you do: WE'RE FASCINATING.

Some systems have dozens, or hundreds, of headmates. Others have a handful. Headmates can be different genders, sexualities, races, and sizes from the body we live in; they can even have specific mental health issues or physical disabilities that manifest when they front.

Apart from the main archetypal headmate types that are discussed in this linked comment, there can be non-humans in a system, and introjects—these can be fictional characters or even real people from the outside world who get copied and pasted into your system, so to speak. This can be really cool if it's someone you like, or a character from your favorite anime (omg, I once wrote this amazing fan comic for *Sinkhole*, where instead of being transported to St. Ogrine when the sinkhole opened up beneath him, Souta showed up in OUR INNER WORLD and then he fell in love with meeeee!!). It can majorly suck if the introject is someone who abused you, obviously, and that's unfortunately much more common. 🙁

Some systems have gatekeepers, who are kinda like the Watcher in the Marvel Universe, but instead of sur-veilling the multiverse without acting, they're giving *Age of Ultron* and interfere all the time, whether you know it or not. I don't think our system has one, except for Solomon, who wouldn't tell me what restaurant he bought those bussin' birria poutine fries from. Keke said yes when I asked if it was her, but she also says she's a puppy. It'd probably be Lurk if we did have one, since he's always just hanging around quietly observing. I'm kinda glad we don't—no one headmate should have all that power, you know?

Okay, unsurprisingly, I strayed from my original point. Thanks, ADHD! In *our* system, there are at least seven of us, and for sure others that we haven't met yet—some who maybe don't want to meet us ever. One day I saw this lady all in white chillin' in a hallway. I was like, "Um, ma'am? Can I help you?" but then she just . . . disappeared?! Everyone acted like I was buggin' when I mentioned it, as if that would be the weirdest thing we have going on at the Bad Day Home for Wayward Headmates. This is a whole castle, *inside our mind*, besties. Expand your idea of "possible."

I posted more here about our inner world, with drawings, but to sum it up: We got a castle up in here. No one knows where it came from, and even though we can't go outside, we all just kind of know what it looks like from the outside. I guess it's like how you don't have to look in the mirror to remember what your face looks like. It's part of us.

In here, we have our own rooms, our own belongings, our own bodies. What happens in here is real to us—and for those of us who don't front very often, it's more real than what some of you would call reality.

Some systems have no physical inner world, no matter how many headmates they have, while others have neighborhoods, towns, countries—galaxies! And everything I've described is just a by-product of electrons firing in a sac of jelly. How are we not screaming about how amazing our brains are all the time? People out here talking about multiverses and switching timelines—there are thousands of us with that going on inside of our head all day every day.

Like, eff a Marvel movie, we legit contains multitudes.

Edit: Solomon

You posted this on a public forum? This is a lot of personal information that you've shared without our consent. I don't want to stifle you, but in the future you should change our names and identifying information if you feel a need to express yourself in this way.

Edit: Empress

Sorry! I didn't think about that because I have so many friends in that subreddit and everyone shares this kind of stuff. I went back and deleted it! Don't stress. Nobody will judge you for gatekeeping the birria fries. 😊

Chapter 7
Ken

The castle continues to blink through the trees at me, as if sending a Morse-code message that reads "Can you believe this shit?"

Maybe this is some extreme therapy that Della's set up. Or, if it's like one of the movies about people with DID that I'd binged after diagnosis, this could all be in my head, and John is another one of my headmates that I hadn't met yet, ferrying me to our castle. Maybe I'd believe that if not for the whole "too big of an asshole to access my own inner world" thing.

Whatever the cause, the shock of seeing the castle brings a paradoxical wash of clarity. My suspicion that fuckery is afoot has been confirmed. If everything had been as cut-and-dry as Della made it out to be, I wouldn't know what to do with myself; now I'm in my element.

I turn to John, who's watching me with a bemused expression, reminding me that I've made a misstep. As caretaker of this place, I should already know what it looks like.

"No matter how many times I see it, I can't get over how striking it is," I say, my voice breathy because I'd forgotten to inhale for a moment. "Who's the architect? I forget."

There's a chance they'd built similar structures elsewhere, which would explain how their work ended up inside of me.

"Kavanaugh's wife, Grace, in a way. Grace Castle. I don't know what the trust told you, but story goes that she dreamed about it and painted it. Simon Kavanaugh gave her art to the builders. They worked from that instead of a professional blueprint, which wasn't the best idea; you can see how it isn't as well made as other mansions from the time period. She was an artist."

"An artist? Really? I'm an ar—" The word gets caught in my throat, stuck on the bitter pill of truth lodged there. I'm not an artist. I never was one. I try not to sound sullen about it when I'm able to speak again. "So this is Grace's dream house, literally. That's cool."

That also means it's one of a kind.

Maybe I'd seen it on TV as a kid. Seems like something that would have a PBS special or two hitched to it. LeVar could have visited it on an episode of *Reading Rainbow*, or given how creepy it looks, it could have been featured on *Unsolved Mysteries*.

A horn blares from the shoreline and a silver cylinder rumbles through the almost-bare branches, another reminder that I'm not as far from civilization as I feel. Could I have seen it from a train? I don't remember traveling this way as a kid, but searching for specific memories is like spinning a roulette wheel with seven-to-infinity spaces on it. One of us could have seen it through a train window, connected with it, and turned it into some kind of inner refuge.

A castle has meaning to a kid, after all.

A plausible explanation. It makes sense and requires no further digging on my part, but it leaves me with the same irritation as wearing a turtleneck: no matter how loose it is, or how many times I tug at it, the air between throat and fabric crackles with the itchy, invisible menace of asphyxiation.

Della had googled before accepting the job—I'm certain of this. Both of us are "let me look that up real quick"–type bitches, me to discover, her to verify. She had to have seen a photo of the castle and known it for what it was. There's no good reason why she wouldn't have mentioned that it was our castle's doppelganger, which means there's maybe a bad one.

The engine noise quiets with a sudden shudder as the ferry slows to a crawl. The waves feel stronger now, the force of them jolting us back and forth a stomach-jolting reminder that I'm aquatically challenged.

"What's wrong?" I ask, already routing the most direct path to the life preserver I'd spotted earlier.

"There are old breakwaters just under the surface around here. Sunken paths that lead out to a turret on either side, like that one there," John says, tilting his head toward the drowned fairy tale I'd seen earlier. "Boats who don't know these parts get caught by 'em all the time when they come to get a closer look at the island."

"Bet you've never had that issue," I say, injecting a little flirtatious flattery into my tone. I'm not exactly charming, but I know an in when I hear it.

He smiles, his gaze trained on the rough river and his grip on the steering wheel tight. "Been navigating these waters since I was a kid. Had some close calls, but haven't been caught high and dry yet."

"Hey," I say, as if I've just had a wild idea. "Why don't you give me the spiel that you do for tourists?"

He shakes his head, putting up token resistance.

"You don't want to hear from an old coot like me. The trust has their pamphlet with the version of history they like to share. I'm sure they want you to stick to that."

Again, that flash of resentment when he brings up the trust.

"But you're the one who grew up here," I say, leaning toward the Plexiglas between us. "I'll have to come up with a program for visitors, and I want to get input from locals. Come on. You know this place better than anyone from the trust."

His cheeks were already red from the cold wind, but his whole face goes pink now. "I do. Maybe better than anyone from the area, if I'm not being modest. My dad used to bring me here in his fishing boat, take me around the ruins and talk about when his father used to bring him, back when the Kavanaughs actually lived there."

"So this is a family thing for you. A tradition."

"Yeah. It's always been like a shrine to the all-American success story." He leans back into his seat, settling into the story he's probably recounted in some form every tour. "Kavanaugh's family immigrated to the US and endured all kinds of hardships, but he was able to build an empire after the Civil War. He was no Rockefeller, but he got wealthy enough to move north and buy a whole damned island."

I raise a brow. "Buying a cursed island to build a lopsided castle on a goblin-infested hill doesn't seem like the best use of his all-American fortune."

Still, I can see what had attracted him. There's a savage beauty in the rocky coastline smattered with bushes and in the trees surging toward the summit where the castle sits, a defiant treasure. It would appeal to a certain kind of guy, one who sees himself as a conqueror.

John snort-laughs. "'Happy wife, happy life.' Grace wanted her castle on an island, and she got it. By all accounts, she had him wrapped around her little finger."

If you have even a passing interest in historical structures, you know that a rich dude building an extravagant home for his beloved wife is the deadlier version of getting her name tattooed on his chest.

"Remind me: did she die right before or right after it was completed?"

"A bit after they moved in," he confirms with a nod. "She got sick with the Spanish flu and just never fully recovered. Kind of like that long Covid. My neighbor used to run marathons and can't even walk up a flight of stairs without getting winded now."

I nod, though I don't know, or want to know, what long Covid is.

Something occurs to me, and I shoot him a narrow-eyed look at odds with what he probably expects after his recounting of the romantic tragedy. "How exactly did he make enough money to buy an island? Because pretty much all ways of getting rich in the South back then had a common denominator: one of my ancestors."

"He fought for the Union," John says, lips suddenly pinched. "Believed in decency, and a world where we judged people on the content of their character."

He's already reaching for the King quotes, so I really should have saved my question for the Google search awaiting me as soon as I get a better signal on my phone. "I see," I say with a decisive nod. "So about the castle—"

"Just look at how he treated his wife. Grace apparently really appreciated her fellow female artists, if you know what I mean," John continues, his tone heated and his eyes wide. I realize in this moment that he isn't just a Kavanaugh fan, he's a *stan*. He's not letting this drop until he thinks he's converted me. "And she wasn't particular about mixing with, uh, people of different backgrounds. In Harlem and places like that. I don't always include this in the tours, but there were rumors that she was passing. Like the book? She wasn't white, even if she looked it. Kavanaugh loved and supported her, despite all that. The castle was his way of protecting her, I think. That's the kind of man he was."

I'm tempted to ask if he thinks I should dig up Kavanaugh and give him a cookie for banging a Black woman, but that would only lead to another impassioned defense.

I placate him with a neutral "How interesting," and I do kind of mean it, despite not giving a rat's ass about Kavanaugh.

I'd gone into my historical preservation program hoping to focus on Black historical sites, inspired by places like the Lewis Latimer House in Queens and the United Order of Tents mansion in Brooklyn. Despite my irritation at being awake, I start envisioning the programs I could build around Grace Kavanaugh, queer Black artist. A deep dive that explores a version of the American dream that isn't entirely centered on a rich white business magnate.

If what he'd told me is true, we have more in common than I ever would have thought possible. I try to imagine how Grace must have felt, cruising down this same river toward this same island a century ago—

(*"Possibly in this same boat, given how old it looks,"*) Solomon pops up to add dryly as we pass through another rough patch and the ferry shudders ominously.

—looking up at her very own castle and preparing

for the life she would live in it. She'd made a dream into reality, and then lost it all just when everything was finally coming together.

I can relate to that.

(*"She died here,"*) Solomon says tartly. (*"Try not to relate too much."*)

My cheeks tighten as I suppress a grin. I'd forgotten that Solomon does have a sense of humor, even if he isn't trying to be funny.

"And this place was a ruin until the trust renovated it? I don't get how something so much work went into can just fall to the wayside. What happened after Grace died? Did Simon die of a broken heart or something?"

"Oh, no. He remarried not too long after. The family lived here off and on for years, but they moved away after a big fire in the '50s," John continues. "The island's been bought and sold a few times since then, but something or other always goes wrong. Fires. Drownings. Slip-and-fall injuries. Don't forget the curse." He waggles his eyebrows in faux menace. "And the goblins."

"I'll happily forget both of those things since I'm going to be living here alone. At least it isn't haunted."

He laughs. "Oh, it's haunted. One of the first deaths on the island, after Grace, was a cleaning woman who fell down some stairs while clearing out Grace's tower studio. Some swear they heard her cry out 'Mrs. Kavanaugh!' just before she fell." He looks at me with the slightly sadistic grin of someone who loves telling creepy stories to a captive audience.

Though I'm not thrilled at this new addition to the list of reasons we shouldn't be on this damn island, I'm not worried. My parents used to tell stories about how I talked to spirits wherever we went when I was a toddler, but I don't remember it and haven't had even a hint of contact from the other side since then. Whatever sixth sense they'd seen had apparently disappeared during my time in foster care. I'd tried to resurrect it as a teenager during a "reading Poe, hanging in cemeteries, and playing with Ouija boards" phase that likely had my ancestors rolling in their graves, but none of them showed up to ask what the fuck I thought I was doing.

Ghosts seem to have the same aversion to me as living beings.

"You ever seen her?" I ask, not giving John the satisfaction of sounding scared.

"Nope, and not for lack of trying. When we were kids, we had a séance and all, but she never showed up. I think we got lucky."

He squints as he carefully maneuvers the ferry around what looks like a normal patch of river to me—a breakwater only reveals itself as we pass just beside it.

"You really don't have a boyfriend?" he asks out of nowhere.

"This is the second time you've asked. You trying to get a piece of this, Captain John?" I run my hands down the front of my jacket, dealing him an Uno reverse on uncomfortable questions.

"No! I mean . . . not that I wouldn't, if I were younger and single but—" He squeezes his eyes shut, doing some kind of internal factory reset, then continues. "This is a hard place to be by yourself, even if it isn't far from shore. It'll just be you and the groundskeeper over there, and even she'll be scarce once the river starts icing over. Heck, maybe you'd be better off completely alone than trying to squeeze a conversation out of her." He lets out an uncomfortable laugh as he steers the boat around some unseen obstacle. "I can't tell you how many times she's scared the snot out of a tour group by appearing out of nowhere and glowering at us."

"Strong, silent type works for me," I say. I have enough unwanted company in my head; the last thing I need is a chatty Cathy following me around an island I can't leave.

"More like strong and scary type." He grimaces like he's adjusting dentures with his tongue. "Don't worry though. She's rough around the edges, and has a—a past, I guess, but she's not dangerous."

I lean back in my seat and smile at him. "That's okay. I am."

He gives me an indulgent dip of his head, and yeah, I guess I don't look intimidating at all in this getup.

A weathered stone archway stands sentinel at the end of the dock we're pulling up to. It's supposed to be a welcoming structure, but it looms ominously, the architectural equivalent of a doormat with the words "*Fuck off*" embroidered on it.

There are two smaller boats tethered to the dock. One that resembles something out of *Miami Vice* and a rowboat that looks old and battered and, unlike the dock, actually is.

I hop down from the navigator's seat to get a better view as we approach.

The emotions of my headmates surge and recede under my own wariness, like the waves jostling the ferry. Childish excitement; teenage cynicism; earnest positivity; a mishmash of worry and relief. I can generally guess which headmate each feeling is coming from, but then an unknown fear pushes its way to the forefront. A spike of it so intense that bile rises in my throat, eliciting a dry heave as I grab a guardrail to keep from dropping to my knees.

Anxiety that isn't my own suffocates me like a

plastic bag pulled tight over my head, blotting out everything else.

(*"We promised!"*) An almost inhuman voice grates through my mind.

"Who is this?" I yell back internally. *"What promise?"*

Frantic emotions bombard me: panic, rage, betrayal. The scent of smoke and cheap perfume floods my nose and the sense memory of an ice-cold hand clamping over my mouth startles me. I rip my mask down, forgetting why I was even wearing it as I scramble beneath the onslaught of sensation.

(*"We promised!"*) Their voice is so damn loud that it borders on painful, and I wonder how agonizing this must be for Solomon if it's this bad for me.

"Shut up! It's not like we can ignore you, so stop yelling."

The headmate who's blasting their fear like buckshot focuses on me. I can't always feel a headmate's presence, or differentiate who they are if I do, but I'm certain this is someone I don't know. I think back to the communication skills Dr. Reese had tried to teach me, but can't remember shit because I'd told her she could fuck off and so could my headmates.

"Just talk to me," I say. My inner tone isn't gentle, but the best I can do given the circumstances. *"What*

promise? And if you guys made one, what do you expect me to do about it?"

The urge to take the wheel of the ferry from John seizes me. To veer wildly away from this island, and not look back. To jump into the freezing waves, even if I won't emerge from them.

Anything to get away.

For the first time since I'd tussled in my bathtub with Solomon, I'm having to actively fight for control of my body, and the dissonance of it pushes my already-low patience past its limits.

"Okay, fuck this. I don't care what your deal is. Back the fuck up off me. Now!"

The sounds of the engine and the river and the wind fill my ears all at once—the strangling plastic bag of the headmate's presence is gone. My throat feels raw, like I've swallowed a scream, and my hands are wrapped so tightly around the guardrail that they're tingling. My mask dangles from one ear, slapping me in the face before being whipped away by the wind.

I suck in a breath that gets stuck in my suddenly too-narrow windpipe, choking me instead of calming me down. I'm smack-dab in the middle of the great outdoors, but all this fresh air can't do shit if it doesn't reach my lungs.

(*"Calm down. Breathe in,"*) Solomon urges, his presence suddenly all around me and his voice a calm counterbalance to the lingering panic.

I sigh out every ounce of air in my lungs instead, petulant even mid–panic attack, and somehow it works. The constriction in my chest eases up and slowly but surely, my body remembers how the old pulmonary system is supposed to function.

(*"Are you all right?"*) Solomon's voice is low and thin with concern. This is how he'd spoken to me after I'd made an executive decision on the conclusion to the Kenetria Nash project, and almost sealed the deal. Cautious, as if I might crack from the slightest pressure, but not like he thinks I have good reason to.

"I'm fine but what the fuck was that?" I ask, still catching my breath.

(*"What was . . . what?"*)

My stomach sinks. He's one of those can-hear-a-pin-drop-in-a-noisy-room mofos; he should have zero questions about what I'm referring to. Either he's fucking with me, or he didn't hear it at all. Both possibilities make me want to crawl back into the darkness of dormancy, where I didn't have to worry about shit like whether my headmates were trying to make me crazy or I actually was.

"You guys didn't make any weird promises while I

was gone, did you? Offer up a firstborn child or something?"

(*"The only promises we made were to follow certain rules that would keep us safe from Covid."*)

Maybe that's what the headmate was yelling about? That doesn't change the fact that I was seemingly the only one who'd heard it.

I glance up at the tower, where shadows play over the window, making it seem as if someone is standing there, watching our approach.

"I really don't think we're supposed to be here."

(*"This is our best option at the moment even if I wish it weren't,"*) he says, his voice starchy instead of soft now. (*"Please don't make any rash decisions."*)

Of course he assumes I'm just being difficult because that's the only thing I am to my headmates: a problem. And that's why I'm not saying shit about what PTSD McGee had yelled at me, or that I'd heard anything at all.

"Rash like signing everyone up for a new life on Goblin Island?" I snark, giving him what he expects from me. *"Don't worry, I'm going to do exactly what Della told us to. Remember that later."*

I'll follow Della's lead, even if it goes against my every instinct. Not because I trust her, or even because I maybe owe her for leaving her to host alone for so long.

I've spent years sleeping off the shameful stink of my bad decisions; if shit hits the fan this time, it's on her.

"You okay over there?" John calls out. When I turn, concern deepens the wrinkles on his brow and bracketing his mouth. "Looking a little green around the gills."

"Just seasickness. And maybe some new-job jitters." I try to smile but can't manage more than a grimace.

He looks at me, his eyes filled with worry. "I can just turn us around if you're not sure about this. Take you back home. This isn't a job you should do unless you're certain."

His concern, and the fact that he'd even offer, is almost enough to make me give in, especially with the mystery headmate's fear still tingling through my nerves. Problem is, we have no home to go to.

"I'm not sure, but I'm here," I tell John, and myself. "That'll have to be good enough for now."

Chapter 8

Solomon

I'm worried about Ken's odd behavior but even if something is really wrong, there's not much I can do about it. I can't be a host for our system like Ken and Della because I can't front, co-front, or even be co-con for long stretches of time, nor can I control when that time runs out, as it does now.

One moment, I'm with Ken as she shakily jokes with the ferry captain, and the next I'm standing in the foyer of our inner-world home.

Like most of the castle, the entryway is appointed with muted early nineteenth-century elegance. It looks how we, or mostly I, imagine a castle interior should: Floral wallpaper stretching up to the high ceilings above rectangular wooden panels. Fine furniture, some of it since we came out of our rooms and some of it that I've "brought in" with me from my work in the outer world.

The parquet floors had been gleaming this morning— I'd anxiety-cleaned as I combed through the house looking for Della. They're dirty again now, covered with dust as if it's been weeks since the last sweeping.

I pride myself on my calm but the sight of this mess is dangerously close to igniting the emotional tinder that's been accumulating since this morning. I'd already awoken to our empty apartment, with all of our belongings "in storage." We're heading to a temporary refuge that will be even less stable than the threat of eviction because it's dependent on our job. And now our home—our *real* home—is as filthy as it's been since our doors unlocked.

No.

I run a fingertip over the counter of the buffet and bring it to my nose. Not dust.

Ash.

A tug at my pants startles me, but I don't give in to my instinct to kick at it. Pause. Think. Act. That's what separates me from Ken, and why Keke, whose hand is sticking out of the cabinet clutching me tightly, isn't on the receiving end of my vintage leather boot.

When she's frightened, she hides in small spaces, and this is one of her favorite spots.

I crouch until we're at eye level, forcing my mouth into a carefully balanced smile. I'm an expert at pretending everything is okay for my headmates' sake, especially for her. "What's this? A mouse in the cabinet!"

"I'm not a mouse, I'm a puppy." She offers up an accurate imitation of a dog's pitiful whine.

"Sorry, puppy."

I expect her to ask about Della again but when she turns toward me she asks, "Is Ken still mad at me? Like before she went to sleep?"

Ken's return is, for me, a deep inhale of fresh air after a breath held for six years. But that doesn't change the fact that our other headmates might be readying their gas masks.

My smile almost falters, but I catch it, shore it up. "She was never mad at *you*. She was just mad. Are you scared of her? Is that why you're in here?"

She shakes her head. "There was a earthquake."

"Earthquake?"

"The castle was shaking," she says, picking at the lace edging her dress. "Not a big shaking, but like when a car is playing loud music."

That might explain the ash, and why I was suddenly back in the inner world, but in a way that leads to more disturbing questions.

I flash my fake smile again.

"Don't worry. I'll figure out what's going on. Want to come with me?" I reach in to pick her up, but she shakes her head and burrows into the cabinet.

I squeeze her puff ponytail and slide the carved wooden door shut, then head to the pantry under the stairs—Lurk's room. The door is open, but if he's in there among the piles of books, canvases, and accumulated items, I can't spot him. My propensity for collecting has a dark mirror reflection in his hoarder's delight. He's not in the kitchen, standing in the fridge with the door open, or in the living room, in his usual spot on the couch.

"Lurk?" I call out, but I'm met with silence.

He has a habit of slipping away, disappearing and reappearing at his leisure. I have no idea where he goes; I don't really know much about him compared to my other headmates because he doesn't talk much. He hasn't said anything about Della's disappearance, just like he hadn't commented on the changes in her behavior during the pandemic. How had he felt about it? Would he have it in him to do something to put a stop to it?

The sound of dragging heels echoes from the hallway to signal his arrival, as if on cue. He's shorter than me, and his hugely oversized hoodie hides his face entirely. The hem of his baggy jeans is frayed from his signature heavy-heeled shuffle.

"Hey." He drops into the indent he's made in the cushion of my velvet chaise longue with a contented sigh. "Is Della back?"

"Unfortunately not." I feel silly for my suspicions as I watch him swing his feet back and forth and rub his fingers over the couch's soft bristles. He's never so much as raised his voice and I was trying to make him a suspect like a cut-rate Sherlock Holmes, when, at heart, I'm not even a bootleg Watson. If I were, Della wouldn't have been so overwhelmed that she'd uproot our lives like this, and Ken wouldn't have gone away.

I'm the support beam that's left standing after the house crashes down: well built, efficient, but ultimately useless.

"Have you seen anything?" I ask. "Or heard anything? This morning or over the last few days."

His hood tilts to the side and stays that way for a long moment, then he says, "There was a sound upstairs. Somebody moving furniture, maybe." He pauses, and I can tell he's sifting through his thoughts again. "Someone humming a song. Paintbrush on canvas. Glass breaking. I heard that one . . . three days ago. It was loud, but no one said anything so I didn't say anything."

"Three days ago? Are you sure?" I hadn't heard any of this, even though I usually hear, well, everything.

His hood tilts to the side even more, almost touching

his shoulder. "I think so. I can't be completely sure of anything though. No one can."

He's right. Time can get hazy in here, especially when things are chaotic. My recollection of the last few weeks, the last several months if I'm honest, is gauzy. This isn't surprising given that we've been stewing in Della's diffuse stress since early 2020, but it's disturbing to realize just how unsure I am of certain details.

"I'm going to go check her room again," I say. "Or see if it's open at least."

He nods and goes back to sitting in silent contemplation.

The house shakes as I step into the hallway, like a truck has gone by outside, except there is no outside in our inner world. The vibration rides on a low, hideous wail—our headmate in the tower. This could have been the "earthquake" Keke had felt.

"Rapunzel is back at it," Empress says, falling into step behind me. "They've been quiet for a good two or three years and choose today to get back to yelling. Interesting."

"So I hear. And feel. The shaking is new. Just what we needed on top of everything else."

"Everything like your girl Ken returning from parts unknown?" Empress's curiosity pushes at me from behind as she trails me. "You good?"

"She was gone. Now she's back. Let's not make a big deal about it."

"Come on, bruh. I know you've been waiting for her, it's okay to admit you're happy," she says, and I can feel the judgmental eye roll in her tone.

"Della is missing. I don't have the energy to throw a welcome-back party."

"It's kind of romantic," she goes on. "Like . . . when Souta thought Trista had been cooked in the goblin stew served at Lord Mantis's ball, but then she showed up after having dug out of the kitchen cellar and traveled across the deadly swamp to get back to him!"

"It's not like that, at all." Ken hadn't come back for me. She treated my presence like an intrusion, like all of our years together had been a one-sided fantasy instead of a shared one. "We're headmates and nothing more."

"Okay, keep telling yourself that. Have you filled your headmate-and-nothing-more in about Della's weird behavior?"

I don't think Ken would understand how we'd watched as Della became odder and more isolated as the pandemic pressed on. There was a time to step in, and I'd missed it, thinking my bit of help was enough to take the load off, like a child who carries a pint of milk victoriously while the grown-up behind them struggles with three shopping bags in each hand.

I won't make that miscalculation again.

"Telling Ken before we have all the information will stress her out. We need to figure out what's going on first."

"Keeping secrets isn't a good idea," Empress says as we reach the door to Della's bedroom.

"Overwhelming her for no reason isn't either," I say, my tone sharper than intended. I grab the handle to Della's room in frustration, turning it as I have countless times since waking up this morning. Each time, I'd been met with the resistance of a locked door—this time, it eases open without a sound.

Empress squeals, then pushes past me in excitement, flipping on the light. "Della you scared us! Why were you ignoring us? We were worri—"

She stops short, her words following suit.

"Della?" Her name is a rasp in my throat.

The bedroom is clean and tidy, fastidiously so, as it always is. Bedsheets tucked tight enough to cut off circulation, clothes hung neatly in the armoire, toiletries lined up just-so on her dressing table. The only thing different is the jagged remains of her stained-glass window. In front of it, where Della used to kneel and pray, there's a pile of shattered glass: brown of skin and blue of sky and red of the blood of Christ.

Most crucifixion scenes are painful to look at, but

her window had shown a Jesus who wasn't in pain, and looked down at her with vigorous love, his arms spread in protection. With only the darkness of the void filling that space, a preposterous thought comes to mind: whatever he was protecting her from had gotten in.

Empress walks carefully around the room and I follow, my expression pulled into a mask of benign curiosity. I feel Empress waiting for me to react; to either follow me off the precipice into panic or be reassured.

"This looks bad, but Della is probably fine," I say. "There's an explanation for this. This is our inner world, after all. No one can harm us here."

Empress's eyes are glossy with worry, but she nods.

"Three days," I murmur. If Della had been gone since Lurk heard glass breaking, one of us should have woken up fronting, and it likely would've been me. Maybe the broken glass has nothing to do with her being gone. Correlation isn't causation, after all.

"The glass is inside the room." Empress is standing over the multicolored shards. "Doesn't that mean it was broken from outside?"

"That's possible," I reply, kneeling to touch a shard of glass. We don't bleed in here, and despite what I said to Empress, I'm not sure that means we can't get hurt. If something had happened to Della, there'd be no blood splatter to show it.

I glance at the dressing table and try not to react—from this angle I can see that the last few bottles of perfumes and lotions, the ones closest to the window, have been pushed forward, a couple of them knocked over and leaning on the bottles in front of them. The way they would be if someone had brushed against them crawling in—or leaping out.

"It doesn't make sense," Empress says, and I pull my gaze away before she notices the imperfection marring Della's collection. "No one can even go out there, except for . . ."

Her mouth snaps shut.

No one—except for Ken. It's where she lives, we think; we've never been out there, just like she's never been in here. I mentally amend what I'd said to Empress. No one can harm us in the inner world, except for someone who's already inside.

I don't want to think Ken is capable of hurting one of us, but the reality is she'd done it before, in the outer world. I recall that night—the slosh of water in the bathtub and the stinging slice of her sharpened boot blade against our fingers and palms as I struggled with her for control of our body. The anguish—seeking release by any means—that I'd been enveloped in as we fought, and the seething rage she'd felt when I was able to overpower her.

She hadn't succeeded then; is it possible that now she's trying from the inside?

"Maybe Della threw something, and the rebound of the impact is why there's glass inside? It's not like we can tell if there's any glass outside." Empress is rambling, trying to find any other possibility than the one that has apparently sprung to both of our minds. "I read that in a book once, where someone faked their death. But then in this manga I read, the killer made it look like the person had faked their own death and—"

"Empress. Hush." I raise a finger to my lips.

She looks down, expression wounded. "I'm just trying to help."

"You're being very helpful," I add quickly. Snarky as she is, words bruise her easily. "But listen."

She'd been right when she said that there was nothing outside. Our windows look out into darkness—the lack of anything at all. Similar to the void of space, there isn't any sound, or there shouldn't be. But my sensitive hearing says otherwise.

"Rustling?" Empress whispers, her hand cupped around her ear and her head tilted toward the window.

Filtering in through the darkness is the steady brushing sound of wind passing through leaves. It would be soothing if it weren't so out of place.

I reach for the window; the soft cotton of one of

Della's scarves draped on the vanity's mirror is pushed against my hand by a slight breeze. The shock of it pins me in place like an upholstery tack through soft pine.

The void is still dark, but it isn't empty. Wind is blowing through something we can't see.

"What is going on? Is Della out there?" Empress pushes past me and leans toward the window, but I grab her by the shoulder.

"Let me deal with this," I say. "Keke is in the foyer cabinet. Go check on her."

She nods and hurries off, too dazed to argue with me, not noticing the dark droplets glimmering wetly on the windowsill. I touch a fingertip to one of them and it comes away dark maroon, almost black. I don't mistake it for blood. I can tell by the texture, the slip of it between my fingers.

It's paint.

Chapter 9

Ken

I steel myself as we prepare to dock, wondering if this is what Hansel and Gretel felt like when they spotted the gingerbread house in the distance. It'd been the answer to their prayers when they'd been lost in the wild, a place where they'd find shelter and sustenance— but there's always a price to pay. I'll have to figure out who the witch is on Kavanaugh Island and be prepared to knock them the fuck out with their own cauldron.

My gaze catches on something in the underbrush along the shore: a person kneeling, not in supplication but like a hunter in a blind.

I tense, then unclench a fraction in relief when I make out that it's, improbably, another Black woman, her natural hair slicked back into a puff ponytail with some length to it. She stands, revealing a short and sturdy physique clad in green coveralls and a thigh-length camo utility jacket that's a size too large. This has to be the "scary" island supervisor: a woman who probably comes up to John's torso.

I lift my chin at her in recognition, and she stares for long enough to give me pause, then mirrors the action.

"I spotted the groundskeeper," I call out to John, voice still shaking a bit.

"Yeah, that's her," he grumbles, going about his docking procedures.

She walks toward us, heedless of the high river lapping at the dock's edge and sending spurts of foamy water onto the planks and her boots. There's a swagger to her step that reminds me of a neighborhood tomcat that used to pad heavy-pawed down our street, looking to fight or fuck.

When she reaches the ferry, she stops directly in front of me, expression probing but not at all receptive. Though her mask covers most of her face, I can see that it's heart-shaped with wide cheekbones and a flat button nose that just keeps the mask from slipping down. She has soft features that don't match the hardness of her dark-brown eyes. A tiny star, small enough to pass for a beauty mark at first glance, is tattooed on her right temple.

She reaches a callused palm toward me, revealing the thin crescents of dirt beneath her fingernails. She has the hands of someone who can take me in a fight—if it's a fair one. I could probably knock her out with a heavy object or yoke her up from behind.

(*"Please don't plot attacks on our new coworker."*) Solomon's voice is still distant but I don't miss the accusation in his tone.

"Chill. Stay ready and you don't have to get ready."

"Bag," the groundskeeper says in a raspy voice that rides the line between sexy and seventy-five-year-old smoker. I decide to play nice, mostly because I think it'll piss her off but also because I'd started off on the wrong foot with John by misreading him.

"Hi, Bag. I'm Ken." I extend my hand toward hers and she yanks her arm back, then snaps and points at the duffel.

"Your bag. Hand it over. I don't have all day."

"Dock to door service?" I needle as I hand it over to her. "I like this place already."

Her brows draw together over her glare. Other people might find her overt hostility unsettling, but I'm not even welcome in my own mind, so it takes more than this to faze me.

"You look familiar," she says, her gaze sharpening despite her disinterested tone.

I shrug, nonchalant, like I'm not fighting the desire to shove her to the ground before she bridges whatever connection is trying to form in her mind.

"People tell me that all the time. I just have that kind of face." The kind that was a mug shot featured on the front page of the *New York Post* and *Daily News*. A weirdo Black woman attacking a local politician at a liberal university is a daily rag's wet dream on a slow news week. I might have been plastered on the front page for days if some sexual harassment allegations against Pearson that cropped up while he was on his forgiving victim tour hadn't redirected the public's ire, and the newspapers' attention, toward his crimes instead of mine.

"Not sure if she wants you to play some Rumpelstiltskin guessing game, but her name is Celeste," John says.

She grunts. I grunt twice just to get the last word in.

John's gaze jumps back and forth between us before he shakes his head and unlatches the ferry's gate to let me off. "You two will get along just fine."

I step onto the dock in my flaking loafers, the rolling suitcase clattering behind me.

Passing cloud cover and dusk creeping in make the island feel like a different world from the dock I'd woken up on. The sun isn't showing its face here, and, unlike me, the humidity thought better than to make the river crossing. It's cool enough to be uncomfortable, with the steady wind shivering through the branches almost as loud as the waves coursing around the island.

"I'm going to head back now," John says as he tugs the ferry gate closed behind me. "Hope you make it through the night."

"I will," I say, then throw a couple of shadowboxing jabs. "Goblins don't want none of this."

He casts one last wary look my way and a moment later, the boat pulls off.

"So they just dumped you here with no one from the trust to show you around," Celeste says in that smoky voice. "The island is closed for the season. What would you have done if I hadn't been here?"

It's a good question, and one I don't have an answer for.

"I don't mind having you as my welcome party," I reply, sidestepping. "You can give me the lowdown about this place. How long have you worked here? Is it dangerous? Am I gonna wake up missing a kidney?"

She sucks her teeth, the sound long and pronounced; I'd admire the tongue dexterity required to pull it off if it weren't directed at me. "I'm not Human Resources. I'll show you up because I'm already here, but don't expect anything else from me."

She turns in a fluid motion and starts up the stone steps that lead to the summit of the island. I grab the handle of my suitcase and follow, eyes trained on the tower that juts out above the trees.

As the house comes into view during the torturous climb, I begin to see that the story about it being built from sketches and paintings is likely true. The angles are subtly off, like a half-assed DIY drywall subdivision in an illegal apartment. The tower has a slight tilt, as if considering making a run for it, and the oculus windows dotting the second story of the building are cockeyed. It looks like someone smashed together a Gothic manor and a medieval castle and the result is being precariously held together by the ivy crawling over the walls.

There's an uncanny quality to it, enough to make you wonder if it's real at all.

(*"It's giving isekai, purrrrr."*) Empress's voice. Faint, like she's keeping her distance but is too nosy not to butt in.

"What are you talking about, and why are you purring?"

A pause. I wonder if she's scared to talk to me, but then I hear an aggravated sigh.

(*"Isekai. 'Other world.' Portal fantasy, bestie. Our hapless protagonist gets hit by Truck-san or stabbed by Knife-kun and then—"*)

"Knife-kun? You're fucking with me. I'm not in the mood and I'm not your bestie."

(*"—and then gets transported to a strange world where they have to start their life anew. But fine, I'll keep my encyclopedic knowledge of random ish to myself since you wanna be rude."*)

"Wait. So is it like purgatory? Who is Truck-san?"

She's gone, but her suggestion has reinforced the sense of unreality. I refuse to believe this is some kind of *Jacob's Ladder* scenario, but that's what it sounds like to me.

I'd dreamed of the inner-world castle sometimes; like my maladaptive daydreaming with Solomon, I'd thought it was a dreamscape my brain had constructed that I could only visit while asleep, and I wasn't too far off. The dreams weren't like this though. I'd been in the house and my headmates had been outside of my head, not disembodied voices jabbering at me. Couldn't even escape those motherfuckers in my sleep, though I did get to push Solomon down a flight of stairs once.

(*"Bestie is a term young people use for everyone these days,"*) he says tartly. (*"And I'm still waiting on an apology for the stairs push, by the way. You knew it was a dream, but I didn't, and I felt every one of those steps."*)

"And I'm feeling every one of these ones, so let's call it even."

I'm wheezing and sweating, the burning in my thighs reinforcing the fact that this shit is very real.

As I stumble up toward the house, I get a flash of déjà vu: the stairs stretching up and away from me, and the sense memory of arms holding me tightly. It's gone in an instant and I'm too busy trying to breathe to divert cellular energy to chasing the dreamlike flash.

Celeste stops when we reach the halfway point on the stairs. My lungs are attempting to fold in on themselves and I can't remember why I'd ever thought that being in charge of this body was something to aspire to. No thanks. Della can have these muscle cramps and swamp ass.

I stop a couple of steps below Celeste, leaving us at eye level, and manage a grin between gasps. There's curiosity in her gaze that crystallizes the fact she's going to be the person I see most over the next few months.

It wouldn't hurt to be friendly, and not just to piss her off. After all, if I'm Gretel lost in the woods, she might be the witch—in which case I wouldn't mind being eaten.

It's been six fucking years since, well, fucking.

(*"You shouldn't plot attacks against our coworker, and you shouldn't plot to seduce her either."*)

"Let me live," I scoff. *"And lick."*

Solomon's bristling annoyance at my response delights me. I smile wider at Celeste, then give her a flirty wink.

"You good?" she asks.

Damn. Guess I *don't* still have it.

"People had shorter legs back in the day," I say, placing a hand on my hips instead of bending over and clutching my knees like I want to. "Lower centers of gravity. These stairs were easier for them."

Her brows raise. "Is that so? Guess my stumpy legs are why I'm not the one about to pass out."

"Short legs are great," I say, backtracking. "Sometimes I wish mine weren't so long and shapely."

She doesn't check out my gams or otherwise acknowledge my attempt at flirtation. Instead, she juts her chin toward the sharp incline that's going to finish what the stairs below us started.

"They built it this way on purpose. The windows look down on the stairs from the high ground. Most people who made it to the front door would be at least a little winded and disoriented."

For a moment I wonder if she's picking up what I was laying down because her sudden detour into historical nerdiness is effectively asking me if I want to bone, but I don't think she's aware of my niche turn-ons.

"Most rich-people houses from this time would only have the veneer of a defensive seat. What was his deal that he made his wife's castle into a hard-to-reach stronghold?"

"I have no idea why rich old white men wasted their money on shit like this, and I don't care." She rubs at her neck. "Give me your suitcase; I'll carry both bags. We need to get up there before it gets dark because I've got work to finish up and, despite what you think, my plans don't revolve around you."

"The bag is almost as tall as you. I've got it," I grumble. I'm used to people being dicks, but I haven't even been rude to this chick. Her attitude is starting to wear thin.

"Let me rephrase that," she says. "I'd prefer if you didn't have a heart attack or get dragged down the stairs by your bag. The nearest hospital is by boat or helicopter, and I have to fill out a stack of paperwork when someone dies here."

When, not if.

"I hate forms too. You have my permission to hide my body if I croak," I joke halfheartedly, trying to keep it light even though her attitude is flapping like a red cape in my peripheral vision.

"You know what? I'm not going to be nice anymore. Let's go." She snatches the suitcase and starts walking again. I start up the stairs behind her, now with a building headache in addition to burning thighs.

"That was you being nice?" I ask.

"Yeah. And I'm still being nice when I say this: you should leave." She's moving up the steps like a mountain goat, propelled by her desire to be away from me as soon as she can. "You shouldn't have come here at all."

"Why do you say that?" Since we've just met, she doesn't pick up on the way my voice is tightening like a string on a cheap ukulele. The only reason I'm holding back is because I'm erratic, not foolish. Warnings from a strange voice screaming in my head are one thing; from a coworker who has the lay of the land are quite another.

"Because I don't want you here. You can barely make it up the stairs by yourself, you have no idea what the job entails, and I didn't sign up to be responsible for you." She turns and looks down at me, her eyes blazing with unexpected anger. "Tomorrow morning you're going to use the CB radio in the office to contact John and tell him you want off the island before the storm arrives. Understand?"

Heat rushes to my flushed and sweaty face; I feel like a thermometer in an old cartoon, about to burst. I don't even want to be here and I have to deal with some bitch talking to me like I'm an idiot? Fuck this.

"Don't let this suit fool you. These loafers might be cheap, but they're sturdy enough for me to kick your—"

(*"Ken!"*) Solomon's presence slides right up against me, as if he's ready to yoke me back into the void—or try to. (*"Calm down."*)

"Why should I?" I snarl inwardly as I glare at her.

(*"Because this job is all we have right now."*)

"You know I'm going to fuck up eventually. Why not let me get it over with and save us all the suspense? Who knows, maybe it'll make Della wake up, just to have the pleasure of telling me that I should have stayed gone."

(*"Please, Ken. I know you're upset but just . . . ignore her."*)

I can feel him struggling to keep it together, and that more than anything he says makes me cool my heels. While fuckery is my comfort zone, structure is his, and from his recollection of events today has come as a complete surprise to him too. Despite that, he's still trying to be what he's always been to me: a support, so solid and dependable that when I became aware of his existence, I lost myself entirely.

"I'll try," I say, and despite my peevish tone I feel him relax a bit, like he's actually taking me at my word.

I roll my shoulders and refocus on Celeste. "Did you want this job or something? Or is this some kind of hazing? The whole 'no one lasts a night on Daybreak Island' thing?"

She scoffs. "Do I look like I give a damn about that?"

"Then what's your problem? I'm here to do a job. If you're not HR, then stop acting like you have a say in that."

She works her bottom lip with her teeth and then after a moment, nods. "All right. I gave you advice, you don't want to take it. I'll stop."

We stand there awkwardly; I'm not sure what to do, since she's actually respected my request.

"Thank you. I hope we can put that behind us and move forward amicably," I say, sounding like someone's suddenly shoved a stick up my ass because it's Solomon speaking, not me.

"Cut it out!"

Celeste walks off with the suitcase, not bothering to slow her pace. I scramble behind, with the occasional assist from Solomon when I take a misstep, not looking up until we reach a portico littered with fallen leaves. In a real castle there'd be a portcullis ready to box me in, and a murderhole above for guards to rain death on me from above. This place has neither, but I still have the sensation that I'm walking into a trap.

The front door is impressive: oak planks fastened together with lengths of brass and fitted into an arched doorway lined with gray stone. Lancet windows bracket it, revealing only darkness on the other side of their smoked glass.

"It's the same in there, right?" I ask Solomon, even though I already know this from my dreams and my headmates' drawings. There's no way we saw this from a passing train.

"I don't have the keys to the main house on me," she says, shooting me a look. "Like I said, I'm not HR."

She keeps walking instead of stopping at the door, the suitcase bumping loudly as she turns the corner of the house, passing from smooth stone to a tiled walkway.

When we leave the awning of the portico, a thick coat of ivy grows over the wall, being ruffled in the wind, and I can't resist the urge to run my hands over it as I walk. I don't exactly like nature but there's something about the slip of the leaves between my fingers that I find calming. My hand runs into something, and I grab hold of it. A broomstick? No. I feel around a bit more; it's a ladder, eaten by the leaves and branches. I tug my hand back, not sure what else might be hidden by the greenery. I glance up and let out a snort at the gargoyle rainspout peeping down from between the ivy growing on the house. Like the rest of the castle, it's not quite right, discombobulated in a way that seems to say "I'm doing my best here."

Me too, buddy.

Ahead of me, a newer portion of the castle juts out, its gray brick exterior chosen to blend into the original stone construction from a distance.

"Caretaker's quarters. I figure you'll want to see this first though," Celeste says as she drops my bags in front of the door and continues walking. She undoes a thin metal chain attached to a No Trespassing sign at the end of the cement walkway and heads down a small flight of stairs.

The ground seems to be made of the same natural stone as the island itself, and the outer perimeter of the area is edged by a low brick wall. Trees sway in front of the opening, taking some of the brunt of the wind but not blocking out the rising howl of it.

It might be the pre-storm heaviness and the lack of natural light, but the space is oppressive. Dank. I feel like it could collapse in on us, not from any structural weakness but simply because it wants to.

(*I feel it too. This place has bad vibes,*) Mesmer says, then retreats as quickly as she came.

The wall around the space serves as both guardrail and viewpoint. Walking along the perimeter of the space reveals the side of the island I hadn't seen during my arrival. The trees are sparser, and there's a reason for it; where the front of the house has stairs, this side has a sheer rock wall. I'm not one to get vertigo, but my vision starts to swim as I look over the side, and I take several steps back.

"Watch where you walk around here." Celeste taps

the stone with her boot, and a hollow echo sounds below. "False floor. Used to be a koi pond or something. People who snuck in to explore the house and underestimated how deep it is have drowned over the years, so they covered it."

"Great. Not sure why a booby-trapped zone was preserved in an open-to-the-public historical home, but I'm intrigued."

"This is the prayer grotto. Closest thing to a church on the island," she says, and as she watches me, I realize what she reminds me of: a hawk. Clear-eyed, focused, and kind of cute for something that could rip you to shreds. "Heard you were religious?"

This catches me off guard. I'd assumed she knew nothing about me but Della had spoken to someone enough to impress her general personality upon them, and they'd shared that with Celeste.

"Yup! Love me some Jesus." I tap the toe of my loafer against a stone seemingly modified for prayerful genuflection. "Perfect place to get down on my knees and, uh, worship."

She rolls her eyes.

"I'm not quite sure what they were praying to in here," I say, my eye catching on an inset niche along the inner wall, protected with iron bars. Behind it, instead of a Bible or religious relics, sits a large gilt-framed black-and-white photo. A group of people standing in front of the castle—several men dressed in suits, but not fancy ones; the pants balloon a bit at the thighs, and are tucked into knee-high gaiters. Hunting outfits. They remind me of pictures I'd seen of Theodore Roosevelt doing old-timey good-ol'-boy shit.

The women wear loose white dresses under their open coats, and everyone stares at the camera with the focus of people trying desperately not to blink for however long it takes the photo to develop. There's something off about the scene: a smugness that doesn't pass the vibe check in the men's faces, while the women's expressions are completely blank.

I lean in to examine one man in particular, older than the others, with a weak chin and heavy brow that make him look a little ratlike. There's something in his demeanor that's unsettling; he's the kind of dude who, if I saw him walking behind me on an empty street, I'd jaywalk and make a U-turn because I wouldn't want him at my back. There's a flatness to his stare that can't be accounted for by the type of film or age of the photo; it raises my hackles, even though this mofo has been dead for decades.

"Is this Kavanaugh?" I ask, a grimace pulling at my mouth.

"Yeah." Celeste is lingering behind me, close enough

to cut the brunt of the wind sweeping through the grotto.

"Yikes," I say. "If I keep this job, I think we're going to have to talk about switching in a less creepy photo."

His fingers wrap around the arm of the woman—barely more than a girl—next to him; his grip on her is possessive, tight, with the fabric of her wide-sleeved jacket bunched around the top and bottom of his fist.

"He got over Grace quick enough," I mutter.

"That *is* Grace," Celeste says.

I jerk my gaze away from the photo, confused.

"This is Grace? Is there really a rumor that she was passing, or was John just fucking with me? I mean maybe there's something there in the cheekbones . . ."

"The rumors were an insult." Celeste flips the collar of her jacket up and shoves her hands in her pockets. "She was white, from a family of plantation owners, but when she started doing things like wearing pants, dancing with Black women at queer jazz clubs, and saying everyone deserved the same rights, the rumors started—to slander her, and her rich father. Marrying Kavanaugh fixed that."

"Ohhhhh. Damn." It's silly but I feel actual disappointment and, as I look into Grace's blank face, anger. The main thing that'd excited me about this place hadn't been a secret history for me to explore but a lie meant to degrade. And the love story schtick wrapping it up in a bow was just a cover-up for an old geezer taking advantage of a young woman in a precarious situation. "John really tried to make Kavanaugh sound like some kind of romantic hero, but he's just a creep."

He'd also made it seem like Grace was a strong-willed artist and political force, such a match for Kavanaugh that he'd built a castle to keep her. The woman in this photo looks brittle, fragile; like something inside of her has broken. Though she isn't the Grace I imagined, maybe we still have something in common.

"He was no hero. He was born poor, but once he made it out above the rabble he decided they didn't need help, they needed regulation. He was all about enforcing virtue and eradicating vice. He came to New York because women, Black people, and poor people were getting too many ideas about freedom. He knew he could use his influence—and make more money—shutting that shit down. Of course, it was called 'weeding out vice' back then."

Wind funnels through the grotto, rattling the glass candleholders in the niche.

"I listened to a podcast about this," I say, squinting as I try to remember the details. "It's like that Comstock guy, right? He could call anyone a ho, get them locked up, and make a buck from it."

She gives me a cool look.

"I'm not judging. I'd definitely be thrown in jail again if that were the case."

She maintains the same expression except for the lift of a brow. "Again?"

I wince—I'm supposed to be avoiding reminding her of my front-page spread, not sparking memories. "Eh, just had a wild weekend a few years back."

"I wouldn't judge," she says, and I'm this close to asking about her tattoo but decide to have a scrap of decorum.

"Anyway, given that I'm already a criminal, I'll be sure to indulge in as much vice as possible while I'm here to avenge my historic hoes. You down?" The sly smile I give her isn't *just* a distraction.

She shakes her head. "You're a mess."

"And you're a liar. You acted like you didn't care about any of this Kavanaugh stuff, but you know more about this place than John does."

Her mood dims abruptly, and I pretend I don't notice. Everyone thinks I don't pay attention to people's feelings because of my general assholery, but I can sense a downshift from forty paces.

When she doesn't answer, I talk to fill the tense silence. "Maybe he built the place like this because he thought the people he busted would come after him? Those vice busts messed with mob money, too, I think. But he was running an extortion racket himself in a way. . . . Do you know if he built this place to protect himself and not his wife?"

Celeste looks up at the ceiling of the grotto, but I know she's really looking at the house, sitting heavy above us. "I have to go. I'll drop you off at the apartment and head out."

She's already heading back in the direction we came from, her departure meaning I've lost my windscreen. I shiver and then walk after her, slowing my pace when I get the urge to bolt out. I'm tired of scurrying behind her like a toy dog.

(*"Dog?"*) Keke's voice, but her presence recedes before I can respond.

"You're doing the creepy-groundskeeper thing again," I say to Celeste when I catch up to her by the stairs. "One of these days you're going to have to answer my questions."

"A smart person would have had answers before they got here."

Fun time is over, and we're back on this bullshit.

My frustration throttles any smartass comeback I could make—she's right. I shouldn't be having to ask questions like this. I stew in my anger and embarrassment as we head back around the house, then she breaks the silence.

"I'll answer a question. You asked me if this place was dangerous," she says. "The last person who died here was the director of the trust's wife. She fell down these stairs. They came here during the lockdown to escape Covid because she was immunocompromised, and this place killed her instead."

"Damn." I look around at the ground as if there'll be the remnants of a chalk outline beneath my feet.

She stops at the door to the caretaker's apartment and I squeeze past her.

The small space is nicely appointed, and after having seen Kavanaugh, better than having to live in the castle itself. This space is newer, not built by a creepy dude who could activate my fight response through a daguerreotype. The walls are painted eggshell in the living-room area, bright yellow in the tiny but efficient kitchen with a pass-through opening, and a deep orange-red in what seems to be the bedroom. The door frames, windowsills, and floor skirting are all a uniform beige. There is a hodgepodge of vintage pieces; different from my old studio, but close enough to make me homesick for it.

"So this is where people stayed during the lockdown?" I catch myself before asking when exactly it was, and what it entailed. Solomon can fill me in later.

"Yeah. Kept themselves safe and did some of the minor renovations while they were at it."

"Nice. *The Masque of the Red Death* meets *This Old House*."

The bedroom is small, with the bed itself an intricately carved four-post daybed, with a thick velvet curtain, fitted into an alcove, and a door directly next to it that looks too ornate to open into a closet.

As a card-carrying member of the before-bed maybe-there's-a-monster-in-the-closet-and-demon-under-the-bed collective, I'm not thrilled about a weird door directly next to where I'm supposed to knock out for several hours per day.

"What's this?"

"Leads to the main house," Celeste replies from outside the door, where she still stands.

I eye the brass knob and plate, and the darkness of the empty keyhole, then make my way to the small kitchen, where the fridge and wooden cabinets are fully provisioned: cheese, bread, cans of soup, boxes of pasta and jars of sauce, preserves of various kinds. Someone has even been thoughtful enough to provide an actual assortment of spices.

Celeste clears her throat. "If you need anything

and I'm not around, let the trust know on the CB and they'll arrange a delivery. Packages go to a PO box in town. Your office is in the house." She pauses, then adds, "It'll be full dark soon, and I know you don't like being told what to do, but I highly suggest you don't go exploring until tomorrow morning."

"Why not? Will the goblins get me?"

For the first time since I saw her crouched in the grass, an expression other than annoyance grips her features, drawing them taut with concern. "Because if you hurt yourself in the dark, I won't find you until morning, and that's if you don't fall into the river."

I give her a nod; her worry seems real but she's probably stressed imagining the paperwork she'd have to deal with.

I drift around the room, giving a couple of testing slaps to the small counter fitted into the pass-through that separates living room from kitchen, two bar stools pulled up so it serves double duty. Sitting on the counter is a plaster gnome in a red hat, the kind you usually find decorating a garden. Cute, kitschy decor, if not for the fact that its face has been smashed in, leaving an uncanny white void where a white beard and rosy cheeks should be.

"The fuck is this?" I mutter, picking it up to examine it more closely.

There's something about the total obliteration that makes it clear this wasn't caused by mishandling.

I turn to ask Celeste if this is part of the hazing, but she's already bounced. The only response to my question is the trees swaying dark against the dusk.

"Good night!" I shout through the open door, but the wind eats my words before they can travel far. The last rays of the already-out-of-view sun sneak through the wind-shivered branches to create ominous shadows in the ruins. It's unsettling but also beautiful, and I once again feel that almost painful urge to sit in front of a canvas and channel the feelings the scene evokes.

I close the door, against the dusk and my desire, and lock it.

The windows are barred, with clunky ironwork that looks more like a jail cell than a way of keeping intruders out—and the apartment is secured, except when I turn around I realize it isn't.

The door next to the bed.

Curiosity lodges in my throat as I walk toward it, a familiar knot of impulsive tension that won't dissipate until I give in.

The knob is cool against my palm, and when I turn it, the door bounces softly, freed from the restraint of the locking mechanism.

I unzip the fanny pack, my fingers closing around

the cool metal barrel of the flashlight inside. Celeste had said I shouldn't go out, but she hadn't mentioned anything about going in.

I tug the door toward me and peer into the darkness. What's out there? Or who?

While I generally wouldn't explore an old castle, on a possibly cursed island, alone, in the dark, I don't see any way around it. I'd rather seek out trouble than wake up to it standing over my bed.

My first step through the door is slowed; Solomon isn't actively trying to stop me, but he's so opposed to this decision that it's bleeding into my motor skills.

(*"What are you doing?"*) he whispers, as if anyone outside of the doors would hear him.

"Investigating."

(*"That can wait until morning, like Celeste said."*)

"I don't think so. We've been dropped on a random island in the most shady way possible, in a castle that shouldn't exist outside of our mind. I'm not trying to piss you off, but I need to know if someone is waiting to harvest our organs out there."

(*"This doesn't seem like an ideal organ-harvesting location."*) Solomon pushes the door closed a little. (*"Carrying valuable hearts, livers, and kidneys down those stone stairs is inefficient and risky."*)

"Don't you want to know if the castle looks the same as

the inner world on the inside?" An image, probably from one of my dreams, pops into my mind. *"If this house has a stained-glass Black Jesus, I'm gonna lose my shit."*

His resistance falls away suddenly. (*"You've seen Della's bedroom window?"*)

"I think?" The image of it is in my mind, bright light streaming through a Jesus who looks suspiciously like Morris Chestnut with locs.

(*"When did you see it?"*)

"I guess in my dreams. Like when I—"

(*"Yes, when you pushed me down the stairs. Have you had other dreams like that? Where you came into the house? And hurt headmates?"*)

I ignore him, flick on the flashlight, and step into the hallway. The first thing that hits me is the smell—dust and damp and decay. The second is the distinct sensation that I shouldn't take another step forward.

Another headmate shifts behind me along with Solomon. I can't tell who it is, or if they're the one who'd yelled at me, but they definitely don't want me to continue. That's all well and good for someone deep in the inner world, but I have to deal with real-life shit.

A long hallway stretches before me as I walk farther into the castle: wooden floors, crown molding with an indecipherable design, chandelier, banister.

"If someone is in here, come out now!" I shout. "You should know that I'm insane and will beat your face in if you try anything."

My response is a gust of wind that passes me with a low moan.

The light is surprisingly dim, barely making a pool around my feet. I tap the flashlight against my hand, and Solomon makes a staying hiss. (*"That'll just break it. Press the button and it should get brighter. There are different settings."*)

I follow his instructions and activate some kind of strobe-light setting, suddenly changing the vibe to a Webster Hall Halloween rave. The darkness throbs rhythmically, closing in and retreating with an almost visceral curiosity.

That's when I see it—feel it more than see it—at the end of the long hallway, where the pulsing light just reaches. A sinuous textile ripple that might be a curtain but seems more like fabric draped over a human form in motion.

It's a dress. A white dress. The thought comes to me as a fact, not a guess, disturbing in its clarity.

In the next bursts of light, the movement disappears—and then everything does because the flashlight's died.

With the light gone, I might as well be standing at

the edge of a chasm. The air is cold but not bracing—it feels heavy, sticky, like the beam of my flashlight had been cutting through the residue of time and now it's closing around me. Goose bumps ripple over my skin, as if my hair is trying to flee in advance of whatever is coming our way.

"Fuck." I turn on my heels and cross the threshold back into the apartment in two long strides, my neck crawling with the sensation that something is in pursuit. As I dash into the room, catching myself on the door then pivoting to shut it behind me, a gust of wind barrels down the corridor, slamming into the solid wood like a linebacker.

Solomon is so damn close behind me that I can feel his anxiety crawling over my adrenaline spike like ants on a log. (*"What are you doing? Close it!"*)

"I can't!"

I brace my legs and lean into the door, but the sudden wind is persistent and sustained. The moan of it coursing through the house rises into a plaintive wail, sounding enough like an actual human to make my stomach lurch. It's a wild thought, but it feels . . . personal.

Chastising.

Pissed-off.

A loud creak sounds from somewhere in the house; it

could be anything, but sure as hell sounds like a heavy footfall on stairs.

Shit, shit, shit.

I'm pushing so hard that the meat of my hand aches, but the wind presses back, defiant. Another footfall.

"I don't know if that's you, Grace, or some damn goblin, but you better go back up those stairs! Don't come over here!" I shout, fumbling for some appropriate rebuke to a supernatural being. Since Della isn't around to offer suggestions, I latch onto the first thing that pops to mind. "The power of Christ compels you!"

Solomon makes a sound of frustration. (*"Now you're dragging us into an impromptu exorcism? I told you not to go out there!"*)

"Not helpful!" I lean my shoulder against the door, bending my knees and trying to push back against the wind. These damned cheap loafers have no tread and slide on the tile.

(*"Let me do it."*)

"I've got it. Just a little more—"

He shoves me unceremoniously out of control of the body and leans us into the door with a grunt, finally managing to press it into the jamb until the catch holds. The wind pounds against the door for a few seconds longer, and by the time Solomon has stepped away from control of the body there's silence on the other side of the thick wood.

("*You can't just do whatever you want, Ken,*") he says. The sentence starts off harsh, but finishes tight, like he's reined himself in.

"*We almost got Amityville-horrored, and you're lecturing me like this is my fault?*"

When he speaks again, his words wear soft slippers made for walking on eggshells that you really, really want to stomp on. ("*Your actions, no matter how you justify them to yourself, have consequences for all of us.*")

He withdraws without even a "fuck you" for me to hold against him, and I stand there breathing hard and feeling the familiar shame that comes after I've done something that seemed logical to me, only to be reprimanded for it.

Man, fuck that.

What had just gone down proved that something is up with this castle, and this job. I guess this is why these trust fucks had added that "you have to make it through the night" clause that Della had mentioned; what had just happened might have scared the life out of someone with a weaker constitution.

I'd pack my bags and leave, if I could. But there's no way off this island unless I hot-wire a boat and figure out how to drive it in the dark over a rough river full of secret breakwaters waiting to sink me.

Christ, Della had a terrible definition of "miracle" if this was her idea of one.

I bound over to the chest of drawers and push it, surprised at how easily it gives after the resistance I'd just experienced, until it's firmly in front of the door. Something falls to the floor as I'm struggling with it, but I only give it my attention after I've listened out for more footsteps and heard nothing.

On the floor I find a thick sheet of paper edged with dust. It's a watercolor painting of the island in autumn, trees ablaze with color. I stare at it, trying to figure out what seems off, despite the beauty of the painting and the clear talent of the artist.

There's no tower. Without it, the castle looks charming and welcoming, less like a challenge to all who pass and more like a home.

GK, Spring '18. That would be 1918, I imagine, not 2018. GK would be Grace. Some presence in a house supposedly haunted by her had just tried to get in, and now I've found work by her own hand? Yet another coincidence.

I turn the paper over; at first it looks blank, but when I peer more closely there's a sketch, faded by time and the moisture from the watercolor on the other side. A woman's bust, a side profile, evocative despite its simplicity. The bare shoulders and chest make it seem like an artist's model, but it's her features that strike me: a fullness of the bottom lip and wideness of the nose. The quickly rendered curlicues of hair indicate a tightness to the curl that few white women would have.

If John was wrong about Grace, then who is this?

I squint at the barely visible pencil strokes, which must have barely scraped across the page when first drawn, as if the artist had not wanted the permanence that slightly more pressure would have rendered. There's a word scrawled delicately beneath the sketch: "Lottie."

As I stare at it, an ache builds behind my eyes and I close them, rubbing at the space between my brows.

(*"Ken?"*)

"What?" I respond aloud.

(*"You've been standing here for a while and it's been a long day. Eat something and get some sleep."*)

"Okay." The fact that I don't fight him is evidence of my exhaustion. I place the sheet on the nightstand and then drag the bags into the bedroom, the sketch engraved on the back of my eyelids every time I blink.

Who is she? Despite the overwhelming amount of shit that's happened since I woke up on the pier, and everything that'd happened while I was gone, something about that delicate portrait is stuck like a pebble in the folds of my brain. A discomforting sensation that I can't dislodge.

A pair of flannel pajamas are folded neatly atop everything else when I unzip the duffel bag, along with a toiletry kit and what looks like a few boxes of pregnancy tests.

"*I guess Della isn't as uptight as she used to be. Noice.*"

(*"Those are Covid tests,"*) Solomon says. (*"We take one every day or two, sometimes more if we've been around strangers or don't remember where the body's been before we switched in."*)

"*Are you guys still losing time? I thought that was supposed to stop when you communicated and shit.*"

That was part of why I'd had to go. I'd been the one holding the system back from their perfect future where they didn't have to worry about waking up hungover, scuffed-up, or in jail.

(*"The sample collection is going to be uncomfortable—you have to swab inner cheek, back of throat, and your nasal cavity. Your lack of a gag reflex should make it easier, but you should brace yourself."*)

I roll my eyes at his slick little comment, though it's his evasive reply that pisses me off. I guess when you're hoping that someone goes back from whence they came, it's easier to brush them off rather than waste time explaining things to them.

I try reading the instructions for the test myself,

sulking, but have to restart every few sentences, since lists of instructions are one of many banes of my existence and the tiny print is giving me a headache with these damn glasses.

I drop the instructions in frustration and Solomon takes over, then I carefully align the packets I'd dumped on the floor and set up the testing station like some kid's laboratory playset.

After having my brain gently poked at, followed by a sneezing fit, the test is done. I head to the tiny bathroom to wash the sweat and stress of the afternoon off of me while waiting the fifteen minutes for the results.

(*"I'm going to rest. Will you be here in the morning?"*) Solomon asks stiffly.

"Not if I can help it," I snap. *"Don't worry, you'll be rid of me again soon enough."*

(*"That's not what I . . ."*) He sighs. (*"Good night."*)

I wrap my hair and then shower at 4x speed with my glasses on and the ugly plastic curtain of the tiled cubicle pulled open so nothing—human or supernatural—can get the jump on me. Apart from a crack in the tile that I briefly mistake for a silverfish, I wash my ass uneventfully.

By the time I sit down at the counter and drop a dish towel over Smashface the Gnome so I can eat my Cup Noodles in peace, there's a dull ache banding around my skull. Fronting is more draining than I remember. The stairs had taken me out, physically, but simply existing is exhausting.

I pull out the phone, hoping the scrap of signal from the pier has at least enough to carry some data, but even that has disappeared. We're in a dead zone.

"Fuuuuuck!"

A quick glance around the room reveals something as shocking as no service: There are no books in the apartment. Not even the standard coffee-table photo collection that's strictly decoration but can be picked up as a last resort.

Instead of sitting and stewing, or reading the ingredients on my noodles, I retrieve the little notebook and pen from the fanny pack. When I flip past Solomon's sketches, I find one of Della's Bible verses that I hadn't seen earlier.

He shall bring forth your righteousness as the light, and your justice as the noonday.
Psalm 37:5–6

I roll my eyes and flip the page.

"Della, I know you're supposed to be some paragon of perfection," I scratch out, confident I won't be around whenever she reads this, "but you're a raggedy bitch. Here's why:"

Chapter 10

Groupthnk: Collaborative Journal

Archived Post: Della (6 months ago)
(Hidden by Admin)

I noticed a special feature in the admin dashboard when we downloaded this app, and today I'm going to use it. Hiding my real entries feels wrong, but I think after these past couple of years, I deserve a space just for me.

All my time is spent staving off the disaster of one wrong breath. I'm trying to hold on. The others are worried about me, and if they knew how slippery my grasp on things actually was, it'd cause chaos in the system. So, they get semi-functional Della; I get this space to vent.

It's not much, considering that everything else is being taken away bit by bit.

During our session this week, Dr. Bryant insisted that we meet in-person, saying that I need to "re-acclimate to post-pandemic life." I told her it was best we part ways. I wish Dr. Reese hadn't had to retire, but she lost the long Covid crapshoot. I wonder how many systems will suffer because she won't be there to help them like she did us.

The business I was doing remote data entry for told me I have to start coming into the office once a week, as if they need to see my face while I do the same job I've had for two years. I quit.

I've been to too many Zoom funerals, been asked to pray for too many people in the hospital or ailing at home, yet everyone is acting like life is back to normal, like I'm the strange one for still taking precautions. No one else seems to jump when an ambulance wails by, or to look at refrigerator trucks parked on the street wondering what else has been stored inside besides food.

Never forget, except this, even as it continues.

Is this what happened when the water from the Great Flood began to recede—did they toss the animals from the Ark before the ground was even dry?

It is so hard to slog through this mud. I am covered with it.

I do not feel clean.

I did force myself out of the house today, after two weeks. Only one other person was also masked on my walk. Our eyes met briefly, and a knowing look passed between us. Maybe this is what it felt like to be a believer in ancient Rome, catching glimpse of a symbol that gave you the comfort of solidarity.

I sat on a bench at the little park—thankfully Ken's background made us eligible for the monkey pox vaccine, so I didn't have to lie—and let the heat burn away my fears, my anger, and my uncertainty. I baptized myself in sweat and imagined that it washed away my worries. I prayed that I be given the strength to believe things will get better. Believing is different than pretending, which is what everyone else seems to be doing.

Just as I was starting to feel better, hopeful, a stranger stopped to ask me why I was still wearing a mask now that we know Covid was a hoax. I told him it was because I could smell his stank breath from fifty paces.

I've never been some carefree young thing, since I was "born" older and set in my ways, but I used to see the good in the world. It sparkled at me beneath the surface of grime covering this earthly realm: order beneath chaos; light to balance the dark. It's why I couldn't understand Ken and her rage and how she only ever saw the bad, except when she had to hold herself accountable for her actions.

I can humble myself enough to admit something: she was right to be angry all the time.

She was right.

Chapter 11
Solomon

I wake up fronting in the middle of the night, releasing my hand from its grip around the handle of the kitchen knife Ken had tucked under the pillow, and then sliding from under the blankets and off of the unfamiliar bed.

For a moment, I think a train is passing by outside, but it's the wind rattling the windows. A precursor to the storm to come.

While I enjoy nature, I'm not a fan of metaphoric weather.

The lights are on, since Ken hates the dark, somewhat ironic given where we think she lives in the inner world.

The void—the place where someone might have come from to attack Della.

Someone. If not her, then who?

A space heater fighting valiantly against the invading cold drones beside the bed, and panic wrapped in grim focus vibrates at a low hum in the back of my mind.

The feelings aren't mine; Ken is dreaming.

I can't see her while she sleeps, for obvious reasons, but I imagine she looks like one of the scrawny dogs Keke and I sit with during her trips to the animal shelter, growling and twitching as it fights imaginary battles that, even in its own mind, are stacked against it.

Nighttime is when I usually front, even if I'm co-con at points during the day. Empress has joked that my inner clock is set for demon time, whatever that means, but I think I simply structured my life so as not to interfere with anyone else's.

Ken had spent years trying to figure out her sleep issues, researching circadian rhythm disorders and melatonin resistance, and had at one point even resorted to attaching herself to her headboard with fuzzy handcuffs to prevent "sleepwalking." What she saw as a nuisance quirk was actually me. She'd wake up to muddy boots and new blisters, annoyed with herself about yet another odd behavior, after I'd enjoyed a night of observing the quiet, and not so quiet, city streets. She'd also find pieces of furniture I'd saved from the curb on garbage nights, designs for new projects she'd been thinking about in her sketchbook, or, later when we got into grad school, dozens of browser tabs open to the exact information she needed for her preservationist courses.

She'd thought all of these things were her own work, and I had never thought of them as solely my own.

That's the crux of our problem.

As I pass the kitchen counter, I replace the towel that's blown off the disturbing gnome figurine, tucking it under the object's feet to keep it in place. I notice that the counter beneath it is clean, like the rest of the apartment. Someone had made the decision to leave this malevolent thing here instead of putting it where it belongs—the bottom of the river. It might seem hypocritical, coming from someone who sees other people's trash as my treasure, but one thing you learn is that not everything can or should be saved.

I sit on the couch and pick up the pen and notebook, flipping past Ken's words so I can idly doodle through my thoughts. It's the only time I draw these days. Though I have the talent and the execution, Ken was the one with motivation and vision, and though she claims to be talentless, I can't paint without making a muddy mess. I'm as useless without her as she is without me, though she's never bothered to ask me.

My pen scratches over the textured paper, the thin

lines huddling together to form the trunk of a tree, hatches and whorls giving depth to the bark. I'm lost in the woods, unable to see the forest for the trees, and need to zoom in for perspective. This tree, spindly and thorned—who are the trust?

This sapling over here, with the shredded bark—why did they choose us for this job when they would have been inundated with eager and more qualified applicants?

This gnarled and bent one—why didn't Della leave a paper trail, when she's so fixated on detail that she'd once made a spreadsheet tracking toilet paper usage?

The magnificent oak, branches heavy and dangerous if they catch you unaware in a brisk wind—how is it possible that Grace Castle is exactly the same as the home in our inner world?

This should be my biggest worry, but it isn't.

The sugar pine, towering over all the others—if Della really was taken by force, the only possible perpetrator can be one of our headmates. If I accept the evidence of what we'd seen in her bedroom, it will mean that something in our system is irrevocably broken; I don't see how we'll be able to move forward. If Ken did it . . .

I search for an explanation that could justify it to the other headmates. When she'd ceded most of the hosting and system management to Della and me, Ken had come to the front in particular situations, like when a stranger had "accidentally" rubbed his crotch against us every time the crowded train car swayed, or the time a drunk man had stumbled out of a bar and tried to pull us into a bear hug.

Misguided as her behavior had been, Ken had come barreling back to the front when we were in some kind of danger. If she *had* attacked Della, could it have been done to protect us from her?

(*"Solomon!"*)

Empress doesn't have to shout my name twice.

The apartment fades into the background and then I'm in the inner world, standing in the foyer. I nearly slip on the fine layer of soot covering everything as I run to the parlor, where I find Empress and Mesmer at the window.

"Something is happening out there," Mesmer says. Her trembling fingers tug at the metal amulet around her neck. "It's, like, I don't even know. Just look."

When I peer out, instead of the nothingness that I'm usually greeted with, I can discern the shadowy outline of tree branches and, above them, the silhouette of storm clouds, as if the darkness were a wash of velvet black over some hidden image. Or maybe the image isn't hidden, but in progress, like developing film or . . .

"Underpainting," I say, remembering the drops of acrylic on Della's windowsill.

"Oh em gee, you're right," Empress whispers. "I see it now. What the eff?"

"See what? Under what?" Mesmer tears her gaze from the bizarre view outside.

"It's a base layer some artists use when painting," Empress explains. "Sometimes they sketch first, then they cover the canvas in a base color and build on it. Dark to light."

Mesmer nods, less in understanding and more like a bobblehead doll that can't stop.

I lean closer to the window, picking up the low rustle I'd heard earlier. "I'm guessing that if I looked out the window of the caretaker's apartment, the view wouldn't be very different from this."

"For some systems who have an inner-world house, they're the places they lived when they were kids." Empress hugs her arms around herself. "Places where . . . you know."

"Where bad things happened to them," Mesmer finishes quietly. "The places where their systems were born."

"None of us have any recollection of a castle," I say.

"Um, none of us remember a chunk of our childhood, either, bestie," Empress says.

"None of us who are able to share it," Mesmer adds.

The castle shudders, and ash sifts down like black snow.

In the outer world, I stand from the couch and start pacing the room.

The forest, the trees, this house that reflects our inner world—they hold something in their shadows, and I'm not sure that we're prepared for what will happen when it comes to light.

When I glance toward the kitchen, the gnome is uncovered, the towel gone. I can't remember if it had been turned in my direction before, but it is now.

Even without eyes or a face, it somehow watches me.

Chapter 12
Keke

I'm in a dream with Ken!

When we first met, she used to yell at me all the time and tell me to go away, but now she's holding my hand so tight, like she wants me to stay with her! We're both wearing white dresses, like a matching pair.

"Where are we?" I ask.

Ken shushes me, and when I look up at her, I can see the white parts of her eyes, like something called whale eye; that's what the dogs at the shelter do when they're scared.

"We have to be quiet," she says. "Quiet and careful. You know that better than anyone."

"Quiet and careful," I whisper. The words are

familiar in my mouth, and they taste like something burnt and nasty.

I can hear them now—the monsters. They're coming for us, singing a song that I know but don't know, and laughing. This isn't a fun dream, like the time I was swimming with mermaids that were half puppy half fish; it's a nightmare.

"Shit." Ken starts to run and I get dragged behind her like one of my rag dolls.

The monsters run too. Their footsteps fill the darkness around us like something big and terrible, and I want to scream but my voice doesn't work right. My legs feel like jelly and they don't listen when I try to make them move.

Ken picks me up and looks at me. I know what she's thinking: she can throw me to the monsters, and then she can get away. Even a little kid knows what adults will do to escape danger.

"Don't leave me again!" My voice comes out like a little squeak even though I try to scream, and she pulls me against her and starts running again.

"Thank you," I whisper. "I'll be a good girl. I promise."

"Shut up," she says, but she pops me on her hip so she doesn't drop me.

My head is on her shoulder, so I can see the monsters

as they chase us—the monsters are men. One is right behind us. I know him, even though I'm not supposed to. Sometimes I see things the adults don't want me to.

He jumps with his hand out and grabs Ken's ankle and she almost falls! She kicks back and tries to keep running, but he won't let go. I feel her body turning to face him, and her start to let me go even as I cling to her.

"Don't let her see him, Keke," the whispering lady says from behind me. "Not yet."

"Wake up, Ken!" I'm not whispering anymore but it's like she can't hear me, even though I'm shouting and shaking her.

"Keke, darling," the lady whispers. "Be good and do as I said."

Good. I'm a good girl. I think of what a puppy would do, and then bite Ken's shoulder, hard.

Chapter 13
Ken

S hit, motherfucker, ow!"
        I jolt awake on the couch in the living room, shoulder tingling uncomfortably and pain shooting through my big toe. I've kicked myself out of a nightmare right into the coffee table.

What the hell?

I'd knocked out in the bed with a knife under my pillow and my back to the wall, not three-sixty exposed and weaponless on the hard-ass couch in the middle of the living room.

"Solomon! You got something against sleeping comfortable?" I gripe. When my fingers brush grit and grime on the soles of my feet, I add, *"And wearing socks?"*

(*"Sorry,"*) he replies faintly, barely paying attention to me.

Reaching out to his presence had been natural, something I'd done without thinking for years, but his tepid response is a reminder that everyone was hoping I'd slip back into whatever dark crevice I'd been hiding in. I hold on to the thing that makes it bearable: they don't want me gone more than I want it for myself.

"Is Della ready to slide back in here so I can go about my business?" I ask.

(*"Still no sign of her."*)

Annoyance rears up in me at the distress in his voice. I don't give a fuck about how he feels about me—I don't—there's just something infuriating about him treating me like an interloper while moping over the person who'd been neglecting and mismanaging my body while I was gone. She's lucky I didn't wake up and knock her—

My thoughts crash into the wall of a terrible possibility. I can hold a grudge, and petty isn't just my middle name—it's my nature. Conjuring up the worst, most paranoid possibilities is my nature too.

Could I have somehow done something to Della? Noticed she'd landed this sweet gig I'd applied for and then took it for myself? I'd lost my artistic talent.

Control of my body. Six years of my life. Would I tolerate losing this job too?

An image rams its way into my mind: Della kneeling on the floor in front of me, surrounded by broken glass. Her eyes are wide with fear, and I hate her for it—she has no idea what fear is. Just as quickly it disappears.

It's just an intrusive thought. Just a thought. Thoughts aren't reality.

I pinch the fragile skin of my forearm hard, a reflexive defense mechanism. Pain is sharper than the negative thought trying to dig into me, and a superstitious sacrifice to ensure that my dark musing doesn't come true.

Solomon's presence blurs my own as he moves closer to me. He's observing—ready to step in to protect me from myself if needed, as always.

I tell myself that I'd remember every detail of it if I'd hurt Della, just like I remember hurting Pearson and other people I'd fought with, even if I didn't always know what started the fight. If my memory is good at anything, it's preserving those moments I'd rather forget.

A jittery presence inches closer to me.

(*"Can I, ah, do our morning routine? It will help ground us. If that's okay with you."*) If I'm a floating garbage patch, Mesmer is a washing machine at spin cycle, trembling at 400 rpm. It's a familiar and mundane terror, like the random bouts of uncharacteristic social anxiety I'd get out of nowhere.

"Do what you need to do," I mutter, searching for the scarf I'd wrapped my hair in that's disappeared at some point in the night.

(*"Is that a yes? It helps if the person fronting gives their consent to a switch."*)

This is new. For me and Solomon, communication and co-fronting had been natural, like two vines clinging to each other as they grew, communicating innately. With everyone else it had happened whether I wanted it to or not. In both cases, I hadn't truly been aware of it.

"Yes, you can do the stupid morning routine," I say, annoyed, and brace to be shoved aside. That was how it had felt once I became aware of the others and switching became a power struggle. Instead, Mesmer kind of . . . glides past me, Empress in her wake but staying behind me. I'm pushed back, but not into the darkness. Though I don't have full control of my—our—body, I feel the change in it as she takes over. The way our breathing deepens so that my chest and belly stretch and expand, and the precise posturing of my limbs as she moves through a slow, fluid tai-chi routine.

My hands start to tingle pleasantly, and my scattered thoughts begin to settle. For just a moment, the anger that's always stalking behind me comes to heel. Deep breath in, glide of hand through air. Deep breath out, push of palm and bend of knee.

I'd learned a routine like this from a group of older women at a park in Chinatown, after stopping to sketch the pavilion behind them and being invited to join. I'd gone every Saturday for three weeks, then dropped it after growing frustrated that it didn't immediately make me a different, better person. Mesmer has kept it up and, without me around, she's seemingly mastered it—I can feel how in control she is, her movements and breath striking that sweet spot of precision that comes only when you no longer have to think about what you're doing.

Art was the only thing I'd stuck with, the only thing that I'd been able to feel fully in command of in this way; because that talent wasn't mine, I'd never actually been good at anything at all, except for being bad at everything.

As if sensing my growing agitation, Mesmer wraps things up with a flowing movement and a deep exhale and then recedes back into the inner world. I feel calmer and more clearheaded, though that doesn't help with understanding why we're here and why I'm still fronting. My mind jumps to the sketch I'd found—today I'd make it my mission to find out who that woman was. If I'm going to be stuck here, I'll at least make it interesting.

After showering, I go through the travel sacks, surprised that some of the clothes are things I would've packed myself.

I pull on a white tank top, black Henley, black skinny jeans, and a black oversized zip-up hoodie before finding a surprise: a clear plastic bag containing my Docs. They'd been grody the last time I'd worn them, but they've been cleaned and buffed; bright yellow laces have replaced the shredded ones that I'd refused to get rid of. I give the tongue of the right boot a squeeze and nod when I feel the unbending resistance there—my knife.

I slide one of the boots on, the leather supple from care I'd never given it. Something pokes my toes as I tug on the second boot, and I pull my foot out expecting a spider or some other unpleasant surprise when I shake it out. Instead, a folded piece of paper falls to the ground. A note, in Solomon's precise handwriting:

Welcome back. Your presence has been missed.

I crumple the paper and shove it into the key pocket of my jeans. It has to be a joke because what was there to miss? Schadenfreude and suicidal ideation? I pretend I didn't see it and distract myself with the jackpot I find in the makeup bag—a pot of black eye shadow and a tube of black-cherry lipstick. I brush the shadow onto each lid with my pinkie, smudging it out at the corners so that it looks almost as good as the winged eyeliner style that I'd been sporting since high school. I tap it along my lower lash line too—this is the good stuff that won't leave me looking like a raccoon in a couple of hours.

A smear of the lipstick, shiny black that deepens into blood red when the light hits it just right, completes the look. I comb out my wrapped hair, which has flattened out so I look more Fall Out Girl than falling-out-from-the-Holy-Spirit.

I should probably go for a more conservative style, since this isn't Della's vibe at all, but when I look in the mirror I finally see me and it's more grounding than caffeine or tai chi.

"Hey, bitch," I say with a grin; my reflection doesn't answer back because that shit only happens in movies.

Solomon moves closer to me; his presence isn't jittery like Mesmer's, but a nervous tension escapes from his generally airtight demeanor.

"You told me this island would be like paradise for Della. Why?" I ask. *"Because of the lockdown stuff Celeste mentioned?"*

(*"There were periods of semi-lockdown at the beginning of the pandemic to avoid spreading or contracting it, and Della took it very seriously."*)

"As she should have. Why is that a bad thing?"

("Eventually most people stopped taking precautions and people who continued to were treated like they were hypochondriacs.")

"Wait. While the plague was still happening? I mean, it's still happening. I think most humans are ignorant motherfuckers, but I must be missing something."

("It's a whole political thing. Maskers and anti-maskers. Vaxxers and anti-vaxxers. Most people just wanted to pretend it was over. It's hard to explain, but it made it difficult for Della to keep a handle on things. She likes to plan things, to know outcomes, and that wasn't really possible with everything going on. So she started to lean into controlling the only things she could.")

A series of images pops into my mind: standing at our front door, hand on the knob, terrified to leave; abandoning our cart at the checkout line of the supermarket as the person in front of us pulls down their mask to sneeze; sitting in at our gouge-covered table with a container of takeout in front of us, wanting desperately to eat it but feeling certain I'll get us sick if I do.

Those were memories, ones I don't think he purposely shared, and even those brief flashes of the situation with the accompanying emotions stripped down to almost nothing was enough to make my fight-or-flight instinct kick in.

Fuck.

Would she have gone that far off the deep end if I'd been around to take the burden off? Do I have some responsibility for whatever had happened?

I hate these insidious dandelion musings—they seem like passing fluff, but they can drill right through all of your defenses and take root.

"That sounds tiring. Maybe she knew she was going dormant and was trying to set up a safe place for you guys before she did," I say. *"I didn't know I was going to be dormant but . . . I didn't want to deal with being part of a system anymore, so maybe I'd triggered it even if she had wanted me gone. It'd be just like her to plan her departure out, complete with a dramatic move, while I'd just dipped without a word."*

(*"Maybe,"*) he says. (*"If she's dormant at all."*)

That was a quieter thought that I don't think he meant for me to pick up on, like the memories—he's tired and his boundaries are slipping. I refuse to acknowledge that he's worried that her disappearance is something other than garden-variety deep sleep mode. If it isn't, then what are the alternatives?

I actually had done research when diagnosed with DID, even if I acted a fool in Dr. Reese's office. So I know that headmates can go missing in a few ways. They can go dormant. They can fuse with one another, creating a new headmate or leaving a few personality traits behind as a parting gift. And, in some systems, they can go dormant for so long, that there's no emotional difference for their headmates between that and death.

I brush the thought away; dormancy of unknown duration would be unbearable enough. Her being gone forever-ever isn't something I can process, so I don't.

A heavy knock on the door jolts me from my thoughts.

"You in there?" Celeste calls out.

I jog over to the door and find her on the other side wearing rust-brown coveralls paired with her camo jacket. Her mask is off, showing a face that's surprisingly sweet, and a mouth that seems like it smiles more than it frowns, which I wouldn't have guessed. Her eyes are bright, and her cheeks scrubbed dusky rose by the wind. If I'd met her today, I wouldn't have been able to imagine the sullen hostility that'd been rolling off her in waves yesterday. The wind carries the scent of a perfume that's floral with a musky note; maybe vetiver or bergamot.

Behind her, the trees that looked creepy and malevolent last night now seem not exactly friendly in the dim morning light, but at the very least morally ambiguous. The sky is shifting layers of gray, like cubist color blocking, and the water is a murky gray-green carpet with a pattern of cresting waves. Lower clouds roil on the tops of the mountains on either side of the river, a view both stunning and foreboding.

"Look at who it is. For someone who isn't HR, you sure are here bright and early to check on me," I say, leaning against the brick entryway and being reminded that stone retains cold. "The goblins didn't get me. I guess that 'survive the first night' bit was the same kind of rumor as Grace being Black."

"I guess. You look different though," she says, examining my clothing and makeup so intently that I squirm a bit. This is closer to how I'd looked in my mug shot that'd been plastered everywhere, but I remind myself that had been close to a decade ago. My worry from yesterday had been of someone who forgot six years had passed her by, fading most of the events that felt like still-bleeding wounds to her.

"So do you," I say with an approving nod. "Glowing and not glowering."

"I had a date last night; it improved my mood," she says, glancing off to the side as if remembering something salacious that I'd be interested in hearing more about, but I don't pry because I do have some home training.

"So that's why you left without saying bye yesterday. You were heading out to get some."

Her brows draw together. "I said bye. I told you I'd stop by when I got to the island this morning."

My immediate thought is that she's lying, but why would she? I'd been looking at the gnome, and then she was gone . . . it's possible that I'd zoned out. Even on a good day my brain has a few record skips, and yesterday I'd been just trying to stay on the turntable.

"Right, right, I remember now," I say quickly. "Want to come in? You can tell me more about the ghost that tried to bust into the apartment last night."

She blinks a few times too many, too fast, before replying, "No thanks. Can't help you out with that anyway."

I bat my lashes at her, feeling playful for some reason. A fine woman is a great distraction from the weird-ass situation I've been dropped into. "Come on. The best part of waking up is mediocre instant coffee with the coworker you're determined not to like."

She shoves her hands in the pockets of her jacket. "Anyone ever tell you that you're weird?"

"Weird is among the nicer things people have called me," I say, jutting my hip out in the hopes that optical illusion will make up for my lost curves.

A gust of wind barrels by the door and she shivers

against it, her smile losing some of its brightness. "I already had coffee, and yeah, I'm determined not to like you. Glad you noticed."

I wait for her to crack a smile, but no. She really means that shit.

"Got it. All right, well thanks for making sure I'm alive, I guess," I say. It's not like I'd argue with her for not liking me when it's the most common reaction to my existence.

She heaves a sigh that frosts the air between us and when she tilts her face up toward mine, her gaze has a weight to it like a firm grip on my chin. "Don't take that the wrong way. 'Determined not to' implies effort. It's a compliment."

I'd been boasting about my ho-ness but she really has me out here blushing like a damned amateur. I swallow, then lick my lips. "So . . . no coffee. Herbal tea? Nesquik?"

She presses her lips together, shaking her head and taking a step back, and it's more satisfying than if she'd let herself laugh.

"I have things to do before the storm arrives. Here are the keys." There's a jingle as she holds out a key ring, holding it by the end of the large skeleton key and letting the other smaller keys, a mix of older and newer design, dangle. "This one is for that door."

ONE OF US KNOWS · 143

I catch her glance at my makeshift barricade.

"Okay, well, that's settled. *Bye.*" She says the last word pointedly, so that there's no mistaking either her departure or dismissal of me.

I'm about to step back into the apartment when someone calls out, "Come check out the castle with me!"

That someone is me.

"Who did that?" I growl inwardly.

(*"We haven't had a megabyte of Wi-Fi or a sliver of cell signal to our names since yesterday,"*) Empress says, voice firm as I've ever heard it. (*"No Netflix, no TikTok, no Twitter discourse! I need to get my dopamine fix from somewhere. You can be my K-drama—Ken Drama. Get it?"*)

"Why would I do that?" Celeste asks.

Empress answers for me again. "Because I'm scared of the ghost. I didn't make it through the night in the Haunted Mansion ride just to get unalived by the Babadook."

Celeste doesn't smile, probably because, like me, she has no idea what Empress is talking about.

"All right, you've had your fun. Cut it out."

(*"I'm trying to liven things up. You'll thank me later."*)

"Let's go." Celeste turns smoothly. "Don't expect me to hold your hand."

Empress laughs mischievously.

(*"She's already thinking about holding your hand. This is one of those fast-paced K-dramas! Let me get some popcorn before you're thrown inextricably together by some outside force."*)

"You have popcorn in there?" I ask. The question is genuine, since the inner world is mostly a mystery to me.

(*"Wouldn't you like to know?"*) she taunts. (*"Are you sure you can't come inside to check?"*)

I dash across the room to grab our coat, which I can tolerate because even though Della's taste is 180 degrees from mine, there's something kinda punk about a hot-pink bubble coat that brings it around to 360.

My movements slow as I pull on the coat. Her taste wasn't only different from mine, it was judgmental of it.

She hated these fucking boots; said they made her feel like Frankenstein's monster. She didn't wear skinny jeans, or Henleys, or hoodies, opting for trousers and blouses and cardigans. She thought black makeup was satanic and red lipstick was for hussies, yet my favorite eye shadow and lipstick had been in the makeup bag. Not the old and dried-out ones I'd left behind; the makeup I'm wearing is smooth and creamy—brand new.

An image flashes in my mind—paying at the register of a Sephora store. A mask over my mouth hiding the fact that I'm frowning at the maskless cashier even if I'm faking it by crinkling my eyes. A small black-and-white bag being handed to me, with a receipt dated November 2022.

This isn't like the glimpse of Solomon's memory that I'd gotten; he'd been co-con with me. This came out of nowhere; it has to mean Della's around somewhere, and maybe that she had more control than I thought. I hadn't planned my dormancy, but if she could plan for hers, did that mean she could have actually been responsible for mine, too? She was the one who'd always been pulling organizational strings that I'd had no idea existed, like I was a marionette. How far did that control go?

I'm halfway through locking the door when I remember a fun nature factoid: Bears don't stay knocked the fuck out for the entirety of a winter hibernation. They can wake up and wander around if they want something badly enough.

What I'd wanted more than anything six years ago hadn't been to make myself disappear; I'd wanted everyone else gone. Dormancy had been the runner-up prize. What I don't know is whether bears remembered their hibernation jaunts or if they faded like dreams— and popped up as stray memories.

I pinch the back of my hand, bite my inner cheek for good measure, then jog after Celeste.

Morning birds chirp in the trees around us as we walk but are mostly drowned out by the rush of the river and the wind, which have both picked up since we arrived.

Celeste heads toward the main entry of the house and I take my position behind her, resigned to the fact that for the time being, I'm the follower. One of the gargoyles poking out through the ivy catches my eye. The one I'd seen yesterday had been cute in its misshapen glory, but the stormy sky casts this one in a different light. From this angle, the gargoyle doesn't look like a kneeling sentry, teeth bared in whimsical warning—it looks like it's being pushed, tumbling forward with its mouth agape in fear. I look away from it with a shudder, then move closer to Celeste.

"Where can I get signal on the island? I need to check my email and stuff." To double-check whether there's any correspondence about this job, even though Solomon hadn't found any, and to do some googling. Not about Simon and this island; there was a research rabbit hole on Grace and Lottie begging me to tumble into it. Something about the photo of the brittle woman standing next to her husband and the sensuous sketch

I'd found last night is bugging me—maybe this isn't the story of a Black woman's dream castle, but there's still more to this place than the story John had told me. A woman forced to marry a man who, given his job, would have seen her queerness as a vice to be purged from her.

Celeste huffs a sigh. "There isn't signal on the island. Anywhere."

"How? We're not that far from land." I scan the hazy mountains on either side of the river for signs of a cell tower. I'd assumed there'd be a little scrap of signal somewhere—it's not like this place is the great outdoors. It's a fancy house that will probably have events for fancy people once it's up and running.

She stops and shoots me an annoyed look, her earlier glow gone.

"What do I do in an emergency?" I ask. "Raise a white flag and hope a passing ship sees it?"

"There's the CB radio in the office," she reminds me, and I kick myself for never cracking open the *CB Radio for Dummies* book I'd bought back in 2012 when I was brushing up on apocalypse survival skills. "You're lucky you have electricity and hot water. They only put the generator in because the members of the trust holed up here."

"I should be grateful then," I grouse.

"I don't want to hear it. You're the one who—" Her eyes widen with anger, but she turns away instead of laying into me. When she speaks again she has her tone back under control. "Who's intent on being here. If you want to complain, save it for the people paying you."

I follow her around the house toward the main door, where I'm met by a frigid gust that slaps into me hard. "I'm starting to think the wind here has some kind of beef with me. It hits like it means it."

"That's where the goblin legends came from," she mutters, once again reluctantly sharing her knowledge of the area. "A goblin king in the mountains who sends wind down to sink boats and mess with people."

(*"I wish. That would mean Souta was here!"*)

I once again have no idea what Empress is talking about.

(*"Empress's favorite anime takes place in a world with goblins and goblin wives and, trust me, we've heard all about it,"*) Solomon says wearily.

(*"Actually, you haven't,"*) she says. (*"This Daybreak Island thing reminds me of a goblin fact: they only come out at night in the folklore. Kinda like vampires, but less 'sexy blood-drinking' and more 'taking dumps in your shoes.'"*)

"What does that have to do with the island?" I ask.

(*"If the Dutch believed goblins existed and left sail-*

ors on this island overnight, it's because that's when the goblins were out doing goblin business. They turn into stone when the sun rises, so you'd only have to make it to daybreak. In some of the stories, humans trick the goblins into staying out until daylight, and then they gang up and smash them. Like in episode 3 of Sink-hole, when Souta stopped a pre-dawn raid—")

(*"Please,"*) Mesmer chimes in. (*"Do you not remember that you made us watch that episode five times?"*)

(*"But it's so romantic! Right as Lord Mantis is about to smash Trista to smithereens, Souta runs out and . . ."*)

I stop listening, frustrated by the maddening sensation of a memory circling the periphery of my mind like a roulette ball bouncing without ever landing in a niche.

Sailors had to last on the island until morning to get their job, and so did I. And then there was a goblin king . . .

Keke had been humming a song earlier. I can barely remember the melody, but the lyrics are part of that itchy brain sensation.

The goblin king who never sleeps . . . awaits us at . . .

"Watch it!"

Celeste's warning is an instant too late. Whatever thought I'd latched onto is knocked out of me along with my breath as pain jangles through my knees and palms as they collide with the stone walkway. The rest of my body doesn't follow through on the consequences of our pact with gravity because Celeste yanks me up by my hood.

"Shit!" I exhale sharply as I dangle. My heart is thumping an EDM beat in my chest and the chatter in my head rises as my headmates react in alarm.

Celeste pulls me up, helping me to my feet with surprisingly little effort.

"If you insist on being here, you can't just space out like that," she says, her voice rough with frustration. "I'm not always going to be around to catch you."

I want to snap at her, to vent the sudden influx of fear and embarrassment, but I just nod stiffly. "My bad. I wasn't paying attention."

She takes both of my hands in hers, rotating my wrists and glancing up at me to see if I react. Her touch is a surprisingly gentle contrast to her work-roughened fingertips and her constant annoyance with me. There's a tenderness in her dark gaze that slides past my defensiveness and unfurls itself with a flutter in my belly. The urge to lean into her and pull her close surges through me, a shocking intimacy to the desire that I've never felt for anyone but Solomon. He was the only one who'd ever touched me with this kind of competent care, but that had been in our shared fantasies. Because my brain is determined to fuck up my shit on every possible axis, I of course imagine what it would be like to have both of them touching me at once.

"I'm fine!" I shout in Celeste's face, tugging my hands away. "Totally fine and thinking chaste thoughts."

She gives me a knowing look, then keeps walking. I feel like a teenager again, all pinballing emotions and racing hormones.

Empress scoffs. (*"Aht, aht, those are grown, almost-forty feelings you're having, bestie."*)

I pretend I didn't hear her for both of our sakes, and because Solomon's suspicious silsilencece means he'd possibly picked up on my feelings, too, or worse, my actual thoughts.

"You coming or not?" Celeste calls out, looking at her wristwatch. My shitty coordination makes another appearance as I hurry over to the front door and fumble with the keys she'd given me, acting like I've never opened a door in my life. I finally manage to get the right key into the lock, and hear the click of the tumbler when I turn it, but when I push, nothing happens. I push again, harder, and then bump my hip against the door.

Then . . . I tug. The door opens, fluid as silk. A

glance at Celeste from the corner of my eye shows her lips pressed together, though I can't tell if she's suppressing laughter or the urge to rip me a new one.

Just through this door must be where I'd seen the movement in last night's disco flashlight show, and a frisson of apprehension crawls over my skin. There are no curtains on these windows.

Apart from the first few steps that are illuminated from behind me, the space in front of me is pure darkness. The scent of household cleaner overlaying decades-old must fills my nose, and a cold breeze wisps over my face.

I reach inside and feel along the wall. There's no light switch, but Celeste is a column of warmth behind me and my ego won't let her know I'm a punk.

"Okay, I guess this counts as my first day of actual caretaking. Let's go!" I step through the door with a confident stride. As my foot passes over the threshold, there's a shout in my mind, and then darkness swallows me.

Chapter 14

Solomon

I stumble as I slam into control of the body. My foot comes down on hardwood, the boot clunky and unfamiliar after years of Della's soft, lightweight loafers and my own walking sneakers. A headache blooms behind my eyes, thankfully spreading lightly like watercolor and not thick like acrylic, given how jarring the switch was.

"Ken?"

She's gone.

This sudden switch makes no sense. Darkness for her isn't like sound overwhelm for me, or everything for Mesmer. Ken's fear doesn't inhibit her like it does other people; it fuels her. I wonder if her inability to enter the house in the inner world has somehow translated to the outer world. I'm not sure that's even possible, but anything seems within the realm of probability at this point.

Weak daylight trickles in through the door behind me, but like Ken, doesn't make it far over the threshold.

"Is there a light somewhere?" I ask Celeste. My voice is deeper than Ken's and my tone more polite. I clear my throat and recalibrate for both timbre and rudeness. "Or do they expect the caretaker to be able to see in the dark."

She moves past me, the flaps of her open jacket brushing against our bubble coat with a soft *fwish*, then the wall sconces lining the hallway bathe the space in warm yellow light. Her hand hovers over a light panel and she watches me as she flicks each one and bulbs flare to light in the other rooms.

"Better?" A raised brow, but the word isn't infused with the snark it could have been.

"Yes. Yeah. Thank you," I say, and take a few halting steps before finding some happy medium between my smooth, controlled swagger and Ken's cagey but chaotic stride.

If I were a tourist seeing this space for the first time, I'd probably be impressed with Grace Castle. Instead, I'm sickened by everything that's familiar about it.

(*"We shouldn't be here. What if we rip a hole in the*

space-time continuum?") Empress asks. (*"And then we get sucked through multiverses and end up in a world with goblins and Souta—"*)

She catches herself this time, actually keeping her fanfic to herself. I walk farther into the house, trying not to show the fact that I'm both intrigued and frightened.

While our inner world feels homey, safe, and secure, this house is too big, too impersonal, too conservative—it sets me on edge. There's a hollowness, despite all of the perfectly replicated early twentieth-century furniture filling the rooms, a coldness despite the warm lighting. None of the nouveau-riche gaucheness or trophies of wealth and business acumen common in the homes of so many Gilded Age magnates.

From a distance I can make out some of the items in the display case: books, cutlery, and other preserved pieces from the original home discovered during the renovation. Empty slots awaiting description cards are mounted next to each, and I wonder if that'll be part of our job too.

To my right, a doorway opens into a parlor, and I catalog the vintage couches and chairs, the filigreed iron gate in front of the hearth, and the cream-and-green patterned wallpaper illuminated by the dim lighting.

Pocket doors on the wall facing the interior of the house reveal a dining room that's a pared-down version of our own, though the furniture is clearly more expensive. A suit of armor in the corner where the light doesn't reach.

Despite the castle being called Grace, all the portraits that welcome visitors are of her husband. Simon hauling brick as if he built this castle himself; Simon holding a huge fish, his fingers crammed in its mouth; Simon leaning over a table doing businessman activities while the men around him look on, enraptured. A shrine to early twentieth-century white masculinity that doesn't mesh with the portrait of wholesome philanthropist and everyman John had described to Ken.

There are a few landscape paintings attributed to Grace: views of the river and the areas surrounding the island that are technically well executed but flat and, I hate to say it, insipid.

One of the paintings catches my attention. It's a view of the castle from the river—maybe from the tower that capped the breakwater. The style leans more toward impressionism than realism, and unlike the other paintings, the brushstrokes are heavy, angry—there's an indentation where it seems like the artist had almost gouged through.

(*"There's no tower in the painting,"*) Mesmer says.

The painting isn't my taste, but is captivating, and somehow familiar.

"*Ken, come look at this,*" I say when I feel a presence behind me, since she knows more about painters in this style than I do. She doesn't respond, and I suppress the slight panic that's triggered by calling for her without being answered.

Six years.

"Do you know where the office is?" I ask Celeste. She chucks her chin down the hallway. We walk down side by side, her gaze jumping to me more times than is necessary before we enter the room at the end of the hall. It would have been easier to just enter through the door from the apartment, but I don't say that. I take in the office, decorated in Arts and Crafts style with dark wooden wainscotting, lighter-toned Victorian floral tapestry wallpaper, and a vintage Edwardian secretary desk. A row of large windows fills the back wall, making the space feel open to the elements.

"Thank you. I appreciate you taking the time to show me around."

"You got manners all of a sudden?" she asks, her dark gaze resting on me with a curious humor that makes my stomach clench. For the first time outside of Dr. Reese's office I feel that someone is looking at me. Solomon. I allow myself a moment to pretend, to imagine a life where I'm my own person, not just a nightshade blooming in my headmates' shadows.

But even if she's noticed a difference in behavior, she doesn't see *me*. In movies about DID, switches between headmates are comically dramatic and outsiders can easily tell who's who. In reality, we were created as a defense mechanism, and the best defense is keeping our multiplicity secret—even from one another. It's not as hard as people think; singlets have changing moods and demeanors too. The average person's changeability is our camouflage.

"I was just trying to be nice," I say. "I can go back to being rude and inappropriate if you prefer." I head over to the desk that dominates the room after the windows, running my fingertips over the smooth oak, which has been oiled to a lustrous shine. When I look up, Celeste's gaze is following the path of my hand.

"How long have you worked here?" I ask.

"I've taken care of the island for a few years. Was part of a reintegration program after I got out of prison."

She holds my gaze as if expecting a reaction, but her back story isn't what I need information about. "Did the trust hire you?"

"Kind of. They reached out to the program. Part of their whole helping-the-downtrodden philosophy. Doesn't apply to anyone on their board, of course. They're all rich as fuck."

Rich but they came here to isolate instead of going

to the Hamptons or jacking up real estate prices in the plains of Montana, like everyone else?

"The CB radio is in the bottom drawer," she says. "If you want to call John and leave before the storm arrives."

"Noted," I say crisply, still unnerved by her attention and the undeniable fact that she wants us gone.

"Why are *you* here?" she asks, the question abrupt but not rough.

"To work. Like you."

"You don't seem like the kind of person who'd take a job alone on an island for months unless they had good reason."

(*"It's giving Inquisition,"*) Empress says.

I sit down firmly in the wooden chair, opening drawers to see if there's any actual information for me. "I'm aware that you don't want to babysit me, but once I get settled in we won't have to interact if that's how you'd prefer to move forward."

"Who are you kidding? You know less about this place than the annoying tourists who show up to litter and injure themselves trying to take selfies but you think you're gonna live here just fine?"

An angry presence pushes up behind me. Ken. Her emotions overlap with mine, and I reply to Celeste as calmly as I can.

"We both have things to do, so we should end this

conversation here before one of us says something that will make working together difficult."

Celeste pushes off the side table she'd been leaning on. "All right. I'll leave you to it then."

(*"Yeah, keep walking!"*) Ken shouts after her. Thankfully I manage to maintain possession of our mouth and vocal cords so only we hear her. (*"I don't care how cute she is, she needs to back off."*)

(*"Where did you go, Ken?"*) Empress asks. (*"You can't get into the castle, but you've never told us where you are when you switch out."*)

(*"You wouldn't even tell me if you guys have popcorn and expect me to spill my secrets?"*) I'd attribute her flash of childish anger to a lingering mood after Celeste's departure, but she's always been sensitive, and secretive, about her solitary inner life.

Earlier, I'd wondered if I'd been pulled to the front because Ken couldn't enter the castle in the real world, either, but here she is. The only reason we all know she can't enter the inner-world castle is because she told us so. I believed her and I still do, except . . . that's the only evidence we have of it being true. I've searched for years for the room where Ken and I would meet when she thought I was nothing more than a testament to her creativity, but I've never found it. That doesn't mean it isn't in the castle though. Maybe even she isn't aware of it.

I'm debating whether to push this—to ask her flat-out if she's been in the castle and be done with wondering if she had anything to do with Della's disappearance—when a noise interrupts my waffling.

SLAM, followed by a low, rough scraping noise.

I stand, the movement mine and hers both, and we move into the hallway.

SLAM! Scrape.

It's coming from upstairs.

"It's probably just the wind. Or maybe a raccoon," I say.

(*"A raccoon with really strong opposable thumbs,"*) Ken adds, her voice so close that it's all around me.

Our arm reaches out and grabs a heavy pewter candlestick as we walk by the side table in the hallway. I'm holding the candlestick but not holding it, not passing it back and forth between my hands and passing it. My muscles begin to tense, not from rigid posture but as if readying to pounce.

I'm in that in-between space that comes with a switch, where Ken and I overlap, and, for an instant, I feel both diminished and whole. A few blinks later and I'm no longer fronting but still co-conscious, watching our actions from a remove. She's wrapping the fabric runner from the table over the end of the candlestick.

(*"That's a good idea to protect it from damage."*)

I'm impressed that she'd keep preservation in mind even with a possible threat.

She chuckles. *"No. It's the slip-wrap technique, like when I put a sock on my baseball bat. You cover it in fabric and if the intruder gets hold of it, the covering slips off in their hand. Then BA-DOW! Candlestick upside the head."*

She isn't afraid; her excitement and anticipation send a vicarious thrill through me that reminds me of something: art wasn't the only thing that had brought Ken joy. Creation had been the element that linked us; but Ken reveled in destruction as well.

She glances at the painting we'd seen earlier, the angrily painted fall scene.

"Do autumn trees know they're going to wake up, or do they fight the coming winter?" she thinks, a stray thought that I pick up because we're strongly overlapping. I hear it and feel a familiar desire grip her; the urge to create. The longing she feels is oppressive because I know that even if there weren't an imminent threat, there'd be no outlet for it.

SLAM!

She refocuses on the task at hand, stepping lightly onto the edge of the first stair, where it's less likely to groan or creak.

"Let's see what there is to see."

Chapter 15
Ken

The candlestick is a reassuring weight in my left hand as I climb, and I roll my shoulder as I walk, limbering it up. *"If I run into anyone up there, I'm swinging and not stopping until they're a bloody—"*

(*"You're scaring Keke,"*) Solomon interrupts, his voice firm.

"Keke is listening?"

A whimper resonates in my head in response.

This shit is annoying. There's usually some kind of barrier that keeps her from seeing and hearing things that she shouldn't, yet here she is all up in the adult Kool-Aid.

"Fine, fine. I'll chill out. The noise probably is raccoons," I say. *"Or maybe squirrels. Something cute and fuzzy."*

(*"Are you going to smash the cute and fuzzy animals?"*) Keke asks with real concern.

"I can be a dick, but I don't hurt animals."

(*"You're talking to a four-year-old,"*) Solomon chides.

Keke, on the other hand, is unfazed by my language. (*"Only monsters?"*)

"Only monsters," I confirm to reassure her—to get her to shut up—even if the truth is that I'm the monster.

(*"Ken will slay the monsters,"*) she announces with a squeal, and I'm tempted to make a dark joke—*Last time I tried that, Solomon wrestled the blade away from my wrist! Hi-yo!*—but even I have limits.

Whatever. She's a kid. She can delude herself into believing I'm a hero if she wants to.

A frigid breeze courses through the second-floor landing as I step quietly onto the gritty floorboards. The hallway is long and high-ceilinged, with windows at either end reflecting the gray clouds outside.

Even though the space looks clean and newly refurbished, this is where the musty smell I'd gotten a whiff of last night is coming from. The scent of years of dust and mold and who knows what else that a new coat of paint can't cover up. It's seeped into the particles of the castle, and not much can get rid of that.

I peek into each room—a few bedrooms designed in

ONE OF US KNOWS · 165

beige modern decor, a bathroom with a huge tub and lovely tiles that had likely been saved from the original construction. One of the rooms seems to be an actual reproduction of what the place would have looked like in its own time, a staged area for tours. A roped-off bed with lacy bedsheets and a nightstand with a Bible on it are directly under the window. Another roped-off area encircles a blank canvas on an easel, with brushes and a palette beside it. I approach it slowly, as if the easel might lunge toward me like a zoo animal that's figured out how to unlock its cage. One of the brushes has fallen to the floor and I pick it up, my throat going thick at the familiar smoothness of the barrel.

I place it back on the display, resisting the desire to run the bristles of the brush over my skin, and the following harsher urge to break it in half—to make sure that if I can't use it no one can.

There's a small bookcase in the room and I quietly walk toward it to pick up a thin booklet that sits atop the shelf. I expect it to be an old work order or something, but when I flip to the first page, I realize I'm holding a relic.

March 23, 1918

The castle is almost complete. It's all going so much faster than I imagined, like everything has since Simon and his men burst into Lottie's rent party and stumbled upon me in flagrante delicto. I would have much preferred jail time over this life sentence of marriage, but when Father spoke of trepanning to "cure" me, I decided I prefer my cranium intact, no matter the cost.

Everyone has what they want, more or less, with me having been volunteered for less. The rumors about my lineage and my appetites have died down, and Daddy's business is more successful than ever. Simon has the respect of his peers for taming one of those "fallen women," using me as an example of how effective he is at ridding society of vice. I choose not to fracture his ego with the reminder that my choices were him or a lobotomy and I'm still not sure he was the better option, but it is delectable to imagine his reaction.

I have the promise that I can go see "that woman" from time to time if I'm discreet, which is enough for me. It isn't just her sweet caress that I miss, but that deep peace that can only be found when we lie on her lumpy studio mattress, paint-stained and turpentine-scented; entwined body, mind, and soul.

Back to the castle.

Simon brought me to see it this morning.

When it came into view, I was struck speech-less. The beautiful mountains like flour-dusted loaves plumped up on either side of it. The sharp crack of Daageraad splitting the river with a strength that even these raging currents can't erode. The short, wiry stands of trees that will soon grow thick and verdant. And then—the beauty of the castle, still adorned in ropes and scaffolds. It was magical! Except . . .

"Why is there a tower?" I'd asked Simon, staring at the unsubtle phallic imposition. The shadow of it seemed to stretch down the river and crawl over me like a cloud of gnats.

He laughed. "I added it to your sketch. All castles worth their salt have towers, silly girl. They're meant to keep you safe."

"Safe from whom, silly husband? We'll be the only ones there."

He didn't answer.

I stare at the entry, my mind whirling. Lottie—Grace's lover. At least one part of the rumor was true, and I can see how the other started. I can't imagine the woman in the prayer-grotto photo bumping coochies and shading her husband, but this seems to be written by her own hand.

Who exactly was Grace Kavanaugh? And who was Lottie?

SLAM!

A creak in the hall reminds me of why I came upstairs to begin with, and I tuck the pamphlet into the hoodie's pocket and follow the noise. A thin rectangle of light at the end of the hallway widens slowly as a door is pushed open.

(*"That's the tower door."*) Solomon's voice is strained. (*"In our house, that door is locked. And Rapunzel is behind it."*)

SLAM! Scrape.

I've never understood why people in horror flicks meander toward danger. I'm not gonna be tremble-breathing and half-stepping while something or someone is waiting to take me out. Strike fast—before you can psych yourself out and before they can react.

The door creaks open again, and I run toward it, adrenaline pulsing through me, driven by an eagerness to swing, bash, kick. To bruise my knuckles and finish winded, battered, and hopefully victorious.

But when I get to the end of the hall, I slow, study the jerky push and pull of the door for a moment longer, then lower the candlestick and drop my head back with a groan of relief mixed with disappointment. "It's the fucking wind."

The door's lock bolt is stuck, hitting the frame and bouncing back each time the wind pushes it shut. I grab it, holding it in place so I can put the candlestick to some use—three hard taps and the bolt is working as it should.

I turn the knob back and forth to check out my handiwork, then peek behind it. If this area is locked in the inner world, I guess it's my duty to check it out. It's also kind of funny getting to explore a part of the castle before they do, and since it's the highest point on the island, maybe I can snag a few bars of cell service despite what Celeste had said.

Thick air clogs my nose as I walk in, dust underlaid with a scent familiar to me after years of shifts at Misty's, sorting secondhand items.

Decay. Rot.

Beneath it—the scent of smoke that has permeated the very stone.

I reach in our pocket for a mask and pull it on.

Light trickles down through one of the lancet windows despite the gray and overcast weather; it seems to run over the walls like rivulets of water in a cave. Motes of light swim against my vision, but I blink until I see as clearly as I can with these glasses.

A spiral staircase, like in my dream.

The sound of my boot treads hitting stone echoing in

the tight space is what lets me know that I'm climbing the stairs, one hand to the wall to keep myself steady.

My brain starts to get staticky as I climb, like an old TV on the fritz. My other thoughts fade, and I can focus only on putting one foot in front of the other. Voices call my name, but they seem faint and far below me, and I can't look back.

When I reach the top of the stairs, there's another door—solid wood and imposing, with carved panels: scenes from a hunt, with bucking horses and dogs chasing down prey.

It opens easily, so light despite its size, into a circular room of bare stone, kind of like the grotto but furnished into a living space. A fine wooden bed, not so different from the one I'd fallen asleep on in the apartment, sits on the far side of the room. A side table with a washbasin atop it.

An easel is knocked over onto the floor, and the canvas lies flat, a trail of dark droplets in its wake; it's been painted black, the high ridges in the paint showing the slash and push of wild brushstrokes.

All of these things could be part of a display in a restored historical home.

The woman directly across from me is another matter.

She stands at the window in a long-sleeved white

gown, a red scarf tied around her hair. The candles glowing around her give the impression that she's swaying.

"You promised," she says quietly, her voice not so different from the moan of wind outside—or the one that had permeated the house when I'd opened the door last night.

She turns to look at me, and that's when the horror hits me, dull and distant because I'm too busy figuring out what the fuck is going on to register the shock of it. Where her face should be is a writhing mass of black lines—angry slashes of paint, layering themselves over and over again.

Though there's no mouth or facial features, the paint strokes vibrate when she speaks, and thick gobs of paint splatter onto the floor as she surges toward me. "You promised!"

"No!" I shout, swinging the candlestick out in front of me, hitting nothing.

I blink a few times before realizing I'm not in the room at the top of the tower. I'm still standing on the stairs, my teeth chattering from cold, and I've stopped for a reason. Everything between where I stand and the door above has crumbled away, lying in a jagged heap. Where the intricate door had stood, buckling plywood hangs on by a few rusty nails. I could get up there, but it wouldn't be so simple as it had just seemed.

Solomon's voice is urgent in my ear. (*"Ken! Answer me!"*)

"Did any of you see that?" I ask.

(*"See what?"*) Mesmer sidles up, and I feel her attempt to take deep, calming breaths. (*"What frightened you?"*)

I'd been researching neuroscience for fun a few years back when I read an article about how everything we see is a fraction of what our eyes take in. Our brains make executive decisions about what we need to see, creating our reality for us. Each of us in this system sees the world differently, even apart from our varying levels of myopia, but that doesn't discount a simple fact: if I'd seen something solid and tangible, they would have seen it in some form too.

They hadn't, just like no one had heard the mystery headmate yelling upon our arrival.

"There was a bat," I say, tempted to sit as exhaustion kicks in. *"Freaked me out. I'm not trying to get rabies on top of everything else."*

Solomon makes a nervous sound. (*"Let's get out of here."*)

I don't look back as we head down the steps. I'd wanted to know more about Grace Kavanaugh, and I guess she'd taken me at my word and pulled up. I'm good now. Whatever secret lovers she had—or promises she and my headmate want to scream about—are none of my business.

(*"Besties, those look like scratch marks on the door,"*) Empress whispers as we reach the bottom of the stairs. (*"Are we sure we can get out of here? This is too much. I want to go home."*)

This side of the door hasn't been touched by the renovations, and so the deep, desperate gashes in the wood haven't been sanded or painted over. It's not a few here or there—there are dozens of scratches and gouges.

I pull off the mask and drop into a crouch, running my fingers over the indentations, a nasty feeling shivering down my spine, as if my body is reading some horrific message in the gouges like braille.

There's another name for a tower—donjon. Dungeon. Made to keep people safe from invaders, but serving just as well for trapping someone against their will. Fairy-tale princesses were shut up in them for a reason. Who had been locked in here, desperate enough to claw at a door no human could ever hope to get through? What had happened to them?

I remember the frenzied pulses of the squiggle-faced ghost, and the anger and fear in her voice.

What promise? If she and my headmate were talking about the same thing, I doubt it was Della's Covid contingency plans.

I see the doorknob turning but don't fully compute what's happening until it swings open. Instead of Celeste's coveralls and beat-up boots, I'm greeted by tailored khakis and leather loafers.

"What the—? Ken? Is that you?"

I scramble back until my ass hits the rough stone of the first step.

A man, blond hair short and side-slicked, leans toward me. Landon, my ex-boyfriend and the second-to-last person I ever wanted to see again. He looks like he's the one who's just seen a ghost.

"It's you," he says, "but which *you* is it?"

Chapter 16

Groupthnk: Collaborative Journal

Archived Post: Della (2 months ago)
(Hidden by Admin)

I saw Landon today.

It was one of those awkward moments when you're deep in thought and realize that you've been staring right in someone's face, made more awkward by the fact that the someone was our ex.

I'd been ruminating on the latest text I received.

Everyone has been getting these scam texts for months now: "Martha where is my invite for the wedding?" "David, my puppy is sick, please send me the number for the vet." "Hey it's Larissa. Is this Joe?"

I archive them instead of deleting, just in case. Partly because one of the scammers writes every few days, even though I've never responded.

"Terrible idea. Want me to list all the reasons why? Just ignore it."

"Call me right now. I'm serious."

Vague enough for a phishing scam designed to evoke curiosity and draw you in. Except for the message that arrived today.

"Food is on the way, make sure you eat. I'm worried about you."

A few moments after reading the text, someone knocked on the door. I didn't want to believe it, but I opened it and nearly stepped on a brown paper bag emanating a scent that made my stomach rumble: bacon, eggs, and hash browns. Someone had ordered breakfast. Paid for it. Then texted me.

That's above and beyond a simple scammer, especially because I'm broke as a joke.

I'd been thinking about what the texts might mean, and wondering if stress was responsible for my hazy memory lately, when I saw him. He was in one of those useless enclosed sidewalk seating areas that are basically disease holding pens, having brunch with a white girl—emphasis on girl, since it seems he's moved on to undergrads after his grad-school misadventure with us. Interest had flared in his eyes, until he realized who he was looking at. Then he averted his gaze, just like that; didn't even miss a beat in his conversation. He reached across the table and grabbed his brunch partner's hand. Brushed his thumb over her knuckles. Smiled as if to show that his attention was only for her.

I kept walking, wishing I hadn't given him the impression that I'd been looking at him with any kind of longing. Technically he's my ex too. Hadn't really had much choice, or known that I was someone separate and singular enough to have one. I'm pretty sure I remember how we got together with him more than Ken does. Landon caught our scent as soon as we walked into the Intro to Preservation course, then he'd pursued us until he'd worn down our considerable defenses. In the aftermath, he'd simply walked away.

I used to judge Ken harshly, for every little thing she did. I even . . . I made her disappear, I think. She may have gone to sleep by herself, but of all the things that I've ever asked of Him, her disappearance is the only prayer of mine that's been undeniably answered.

I never turned my back on her, though. She knew exactly where I stood and what I thought. He never even gave her a chance to explain—like he expected no less from her.

Landon was smart to avert his gaze this afternoon. Not from Ken; from me.

Chapter 17
Ken

The last time I'd seen Landon was after I'd attacked his father, when he'd bailed me out of jail. After a hellish long weekend locked up, my mind coming apart at the seams, I'd felt like roadkill in the treads of a cross-country trucker's tire, like I'd been smashed into the asphalt again and again for days.

All I'd wanted was, like, two seconds of support; of understanding that though I'd done something wrong, and I would most assuredly continue to pay for it, I had no idea what the fuck was going on. I'd gathered every ounce of strength I had left, held my hand out toward him, and said, "I'm really fucking scared right now."

He'd busied himself with ordering me an Uber and left before it pulled away from the curb.

I don't even know why he'd bothered coming.

It's been almost a decade for everyone else, but for me, it's only been a couple of years. Unluckily for him, that's long enough for me to have moved on from any sadness, but short enough to still be nursing a hell of a grudge.

I sit up and meet him with a cool gaze.

"It's me. Ken. What are you doing here?" I ask, tone blasé like we've crossed paths in the veggie section at the grocery store and not a cursed island in the god-damned Hudson River.

He sniffs. "Are you kidding me? You're asking me this while trespassing on private property?"

"Trespassing? I work here. I'm the caretaker."

His mouth, tight with frustration, sags at the corners.

"They wouldn't . . ." He shakes his head once firmly. "You can't be the caretaker."

"I can, and I am," I say, nudging one of the pieces of chipped stone that rest on the step with the candle-stick, just to have something to do. His gaze jumps to my hand in alarm. "You didn't answer my question. Why are you here?"

"I'm a member of the trust. I'm here for . . ." he says, then takes a step back, looking down at me like he's looking down *on* me. "That doesn't concern you. The caretaker isn't supposed to be here yet, and the caretaker isn't supposed to be you."

I stand up and start dusting myself off. "I don't know what to tell you."

"What are you trying to pull?" he asks. That perfectly combed hair that had somehow survived a march from the dock up the stairs from hell is sticking up in all angles now from him raking a hand through it in frustration. Clarity brightens his gaze, and he looks down at me with a kind of sad contempt, like I'm a worm that's tunneled toward the surface at the promise of rain. "I don't know if this is some crazy attempt to get back together, or if it has to do with whatever you were—"

I cut him off with an exaggerated snort. "We had fun, but even if I hadn't given your dad an impromptu nose job, I wouldn't be trying to get back with you. You do *not* merit the *Fatal Attraction* treatment you're fantasizing about. I'm here for work, and that's it."

I'm relieved when I realize it's the truth. I don't want the apology I'd fantasized about in the past, or the understanding. I just want to move on, and here he is blocking me from doing that.

I start to edge past him, and he grabs my arm in a swift, agitated motion, the kind that leads up to some variation of "look what you made me do." It catches me so off guard that I actually freeze instead of immediately going upside his head with the candlestick.

I'd never pegged him as the get-physical type. Even when he'd pulled me off his father, it had been with restraint.

It's been eight years. A lot can change in that kind of time, including a man's muscle mass and whether his value system includes yoking up women who piss him off.

I glare up at him, expecting him to realize his mistake and let go, but his gaze meets mine with no give at all.

"I know you think you can be all crude and quirky and men will just go along with it. That you can lead a guy around by his cock—that won't work anymore."

I bare my teeth at him. "I'm trying to leave this situation, not lead you anywhere. I'm sorry you have a hair-trigger boner and mistake a woman walking in your vicinity with one trying to seduce you."

His grip tightens a little. "You don't even realize you're doing it, do you? Women like you don't. Doesn't matter either way. It might have worked when you were younger, but now it's just tired and desperate. And I'm not stupid enough to fall for it twice."

"Are you calling me old? You do realize you're eight years older than me."

"I'm a man. My value increases while you go to seed."

"Someone has gotten bold," I say. "Last time I saw you, you couldn't even look me in the eye."

"What are you talking about?" he sneers. "Last time—"

"It doesn't matter. I'm not here to rekindle our mediocre romance. The trust contacted me and offered me the position, and I accepted. That's it," I say with an authority I don't feel. "Take it up with them."

"I'm the one who went through the applications." His voice is low, urgent, and pissed-off, and his hand squeezes my arm every few words for emphasis. "I selected the new caretaker, and it definitely wasn't you. Explain yourself."

His words finally penetrate my shield of glibness, and the grasping confusion of the system mingles with my own. Della had told us that being randomly given this job was a miracle, a chance at a new start, but Landon is saying that it was never ours.

A sick sensation roils through my stomach as I realize we don't have anything apart from Della's word. We have no contract, nothing stating the terms of employment but her journal entry.

Solomon's worry floods me, but doesn't overwhelm me, because it's no more than my own. (*I thought Della had been forgetful at worst. If what he's saying is true, that means—it has to mean she lied to us, doesn't it?*)

"You know I'd happily find fault with Della, but it could mean anything. It's more likely someone lied to her," I say.

(*"Neither of those options are great, besties,"*) Empress says quietly, her voice closer to the inner world than the outer.

No, they're not. I'd thought my initial paranoia was an overreaction, but this is beyond fuckery. This is dangerous. A headache starts to throb behind my eyes.

Shit, shit, shit, shit.

Landon senses my confidence and attention faltering and tugs my arm toward him.

"What? That smart mouth of yours doesn't work all of a sudden, or is it only good for one thing? I said explain yourself."

My fingers flex and tighten on the candlestick, ready to swing on him, and I'm pretty sure it isn't me, since I have my leg cocked and loaded to knee him in the nut sack. So much for Solomon's asking me not to be violent.

"What do you want to know? I can help."

Celeste.

She's a few feet away from us in the hallway, her gaze on Landon as she approaches a thing of icy wonder. He lets go of my arm and moves away from me, losing some of his bluster along the way, as if she's frozen the wind right out of his sails.

"She's saying she's the caretaker when I know for a fact she wasn't selected for the position." He sounds petulant, and the reminder that he's not as hard as he's pretending to be helps me to focus. I take the opportunity to push fully past him; the sensation of his grip on my arm lingers uncomfortably, a reminder that I'd been too easy on him. I walk toward Celeste who is, for the moment, Team Not-Landon. I keep in mind that it doesn't mean she's Team Ken, but I'll happily form a temporary alliance since I have no idea what to make of what he's saying.

She scratches the bridge of her nose above her mask. Her gaze never leaves him and she doesn't blink. I'm taking notes, because this is a master class in subtle menace.

"Are you a member of the trust?" she finally asks. "I thought you were just an intern, from how they treated you. Sending you on errands and such."

He bristles. "I'm an associate member, soon to be a full-fledged one."

"If you're not on the actual board, someone could easily overrule your decision. That's probably what happened," she says. She finally blinks as I come to stand beside her, and Landon jumps. "You think she's so desperate to get on this island that she'd lie about having a job here? I think your imagination is doing some heavy lifting."

"She's my ex-girlfriend," he says, "and she—"

I cut in. "*She* had no idea what this place was or that you had anything to do with it."

"Now I know you're messing with me." He lurches forward in my direction but thinks better of it after a quick glance at Celeste. "Our third date. We took the tram to Roosevelt Island to see the ruins of the sanitorium there. I told you about Kavanaugh Island. And the trust. And this castle. We talked about how cool it would be for the people who got the caretaker job, and how it was cheaper and more fun than a grad-school degree, and now here you are. What the actual fuck are you trying to pull?"

I stare, searching my memory for any scrap of this conversation. I vaguely remember being on the tram with him and having a beer at a bar on the island but have no recollection of anything else he's mentioned.

By their powers combined, ADHD and dissociative amnesia have left my memory a moth-eaten sweater, but I should have remembered learning something about this place, or the fact that Landon was connected to it—which means someone else was fronting.

"Anyone else remember that?" I ask.

I get a chorus of noes in response—but Della isn't here. It must have been her. When I think about all the cooking and cleaning and scheduling I'd done during our relationship, how my friends called it Stepford Wife mode, I have to keep it real that Della was very much present and handling most of the less-fun shit. It'd only be fair if she'd sometimes fronted for dates too, but if she knew about his connection to this place I doubt she'd have accepted the position—though if what he's saying is true we were never offered the job to begin with.

"I'm sorry that I don't remember our small talk from a decade ago, but I don't remember our small talk from a decade ago," I say, smarminess layered on thick to cover my bluffing. "Like I said, I had no idea this place had anything to do with you."

His expression darkens into a glower. "Hell. Maybe it wasn't even you. It's not like I even know who I was talking to. Did you tell Celeste about the imaginary friends living in your head, or was that just an excuse to get out of doing jail time?"

I clench the candlestick and take a step toward Landon. "Stop it."

He steps forward to meet me.

"I'll stop when you do. If you didn't remember, for whatever reason, I've filled you in. Now you have to go." He flaps his hand in an ushering motion.

"Yeah, I actually came to get her," Celeste says, her voice low, calm, and completely unaffected by the drama playing out in front of her. "We have to prep the house and do a quick circuit of the island before the storm rolls in, since it's going to be stronger than originally forecast."

"She's not the caretaker." Landon's voice cracks with frustration. "What part of that are you not understanding? The only thing she needs to do is leave!"

I've been in some rough patches before, but we have no apartment, Della'd sold or stored all of our belongings, and without the salary and perks from this job, the rent times three needed to secure a new place will never appear.

A stifled scream burns in my throat, and my heart is beating too hard, too fast. Despair drops down on me like blinders, obscuring the few escape routes that might present themselves.

Stuck. We're stuck. And I can't fix it.

I'm useless.

"First of all, if you're worried that she came here for you, let me set your mind at ease." Celeste's hand—warm-palmed and cool-fingertipped, callused in some parts and pillow-soft in others—takes my own. Squeezes once. Twice. "She's not worried about you. At all."

The victorious grin on Landon's face drops away as his brow furrows in confusion.

"Second, she's caretaker until proven otherwise. Because there's work to do in this castle and I'm sure as hell not doing tasks outside of my job description. You got anything that backs up what you're claiming?"

"You know there's no cell service here, and I don't print out people's contracts and carry them around with me." His gaze is riveted on our fastened hands. Hell, I'd be staring at them, too, if I wasn't trying to keep my composure. "Wait—why am I explaining anything to you? You're just the groundskeeper. I said she has to go, so she has to go."

"I provide a necessary service on this island. You're a gofer for the trust. You don't have the authority you're pretending to have over her, and you damn sure don't have it over me," Celeste replies smoothly. She runs a fingertip over the sensitive skin on the back of my hand, and I take back every time I'd scoffed at people stopping to bang at inopportune moments in action movies and romantic suspense novels.

Solomon doesn't chide me for my horny thoughts; awkwardly, he seems to finally be in agreement with me on something, making me miss the days when he was better at sealing up his emotions.

"You don't know her," Landon says. He shoots me a taunting glare, dangling the dirt he has on me over my head. "She's crazy. Do you really want to be alone on the island with a violent criminal?"

"Why are you here if your new caretaker wasn't supposed to show up until later?" Celeste asks. "The island is closed."

"Ken." Landon turns toward me. "Don't . . . don't make me get the police involved again. We went easy on you before, because I felt sorry for you, but I won't this time. It won't go well for you."

I want to be mad at him, but I have only myself to blame. What's happening right now is a consequence of what I'd done all those years ago—how I'd ruined everything for us. When you fuck up, sometimes you reap the consequences in one fell swoop and sometimes they gestate for a while, cropping up at really fucking inopportune times. Even if it feels unfair, especially because I didn't ask to be on this island or even part of this reality anymore, fair is exactly what it is.

My grin holds strong, but inside, the armadillo shell of anger that usually protects my more fragile emotions cracks. My bravado wavers.

I grab hold of the only thing I've ever been able to control in my life—my ability to leave any situation, external or internal, without looking back and with the appearance of giving no fucks at all.

"Okay, buddy," I say, as if he's being hysterical, then lift the hand holding the candlestick in a blasé motion. "It's not that deep. I'll get John to pick me up. Then I'll be out of your thinning hair."

Landon exhales a victorious breath as he smooths his hair down. "Good. Do that. Let's just pretend this never happened. That's best for everyone."

I try to pull my hand away from Celeste's, away from the humiliation of her pretending to want me around when no one really does, but she refuses to let go.

(*"Are we really leaving?"*) Empress, her voice so small that I might have mistaken her for Keke.

(*"We have nowhere to go,"*) Mesmer says.

Solomon moves close to me. (*"Ken, we need to figure this out together."*)

"Then one of you come front and handle this," I say, no bite in my tone. *"You knew I was going to ruin this one way or another, and now I have."*

They burst into discussion, but their words seem like a jumble of nonsense. I'm floating away from the situation, loosely tethered by a fraying cord. Behind their angry chatter, low laughter, filled with relief.

"Good thing my stuff is still packed," I say aloud, managing a semi-convincing laugh as we turn and start back down the hall toward the stairs.

"Ken?" Landon calls out.

I look back at him to find him walking toward me, hand extended.

"You can leave that with me, so it doesn't accidentally get mixed in with your things." He gestures toward the candlestick and then opens and closes his fingers in a beckoning motion.

I thwack it into his hand, hard enough to make him hiss, but he knows he's already won. He heads back toward the tower, and goes into one of the bedrooms that I hadn't even had a chance to explore before losing the job.

Just like that, everything around me goes fully unreal. As if the heft of the candlestick had been holding me down and now I can just rise up to someplace where I don't have to deal with headmates and homelessness and how all of this is my fault.

Me trying to be a caretaker *had* been a joke in the end. I'm the asshole, the jerk, and the word everyone used to whisper like it would conjure the worst of me—the persecutor. I can't help the system, even when I try. It's better that I leave now before I make things worse.

You should have just stayed gone, I think to myself. *Useless. Worthless. Della would have figured out how to fix this.*

Idiot. Fuck-up. Why are you even here?

I tense against the bombardment of my spiraling

thoughts, wishing I could pin them on a rogue headmate but knowing full well they're all me. My headmates had thought I enjoyed being mean to them, but they were just caught in the backdraft of my self-directed ire. I've never been crueler to them than I have been to myself.

Solomon shouts something to me, but it's muffled, as if his voice is coming from the other side of a thick wall. My own negative thoughts ring loud and clear, repeating over and over again. The hallway around me feels insubstantial and hazy and the sound of my boots echoes as if from a thousand miles away.

I want to leave; not this castle. The system. The body.

(*"You can't,"*) a voice whispers viciously. (*"You made a promise."*)

A deep frustration wells in me; not anger, but a kind of anguish.

Celeste is still holding my hand, grip strong and steady; I cling to it without thinking, like it's the only thing that can keep me grounded.

"I'm so tired," I say, surprising myself.

"We can call John on the CB, if you want," she says. "But first we have to get clear about something . . ."

Her grip isn't strong enough. Darkness closes in, even as my mouth opens and I respond to her.

Whatever I say is lost to me.

Chapter 18

Mesmer

"There's too much going on," Empress says from beside me, rubbing her eyes and then peering out the window. "I'm trying to see if I can catch a paint-brush drop from the sky or something, but it's like magic. I blink and a new stroke has appeared."

The landscape has been filled in more—is *being* filled in. The shadow on shadow underpainting that had appeared during the night now has another layer being built stroke by angry stroke with dark greens and shades of gray.

Treetops being blown by the wind; gathering clouds; a rocky descent leading to cresting waves. I'd always wished our castle had a view, but the sudden shift from velvet black to this wild, beautiful landscape is terrifying.

"You know I believe in the unseen hand of God, spirit, the universe, that guides the world around us," I say. "I don't think it moves quite so literally though. This feels . . . unreal."

That's what worries me the most. It had taken so much work to become even a little secure in our sense of selves. Whatever's happening right now threatens all of that.

Empress sighs. "I don't want to go there, but there's probably some connection between the fact that Miss 'My Artistic Talent Was Stolen' just woke up and someone is going Bob Ross on the void."

I glance around nervously. I shouldn't gossip about headmates, because I need to see what's loveable and kind in each of them, but only a fool ignores danger and calls it compassion.

"You heard her say that she knows what the stained glass in Della's room looks like earlier, right? The same stained glass that was broken when Della was—you know."

She nods. "I didn't want to say anything in front of Solomon because he'd just explain that Ken saw it in a dream or something. But now we know that this place is connected to her ex. That's two strikes. Or maybe even three!"

Her eyes shine with both fear and a kind of vicious glee; I'm sure mine look the same.

"And Solomon has been weird too, acting like he isn't happy she's back." My words are ugly to my own ears, but it doesn't stop me from leaning into the comfort of assuming the worst of someone. "Almost like he's trying to convince us that there's nothing between them, when we all know he'd do anything for her."

"Anything," Empress echoes.

We pause, looking at each other as if deciding how far we'll push this. I see how easy it would be for a narrative to take seed, to sprout thick roots that would burst through the foundation of trust we'd worked so hard to build.

I grab my amulet in a trembling fist and press it to my heart. "No. He wouldn't hurt Della, and I don't think Ken would either."

Empress rolls her eyes. "Of course she would. What we don't know is how far she'd go. If all Ken did was rough her up, Della would be calling for a group meeting and raising a ruckus. Instead she's gone without a trace. If this were the outer world, we'd be assuming she was . . . dead."

Her mouth squeezes shut as the terribleness of what she's saying sinks in.

"Della is dead?" Keke has crept up right behind us somehow; I hadn't even felt her presence. "She can't be! Dead people can't take you to story time or make you pancakes!"

"Della is fine. We can't die," I say, though I don't really know what's possible anymore. A few days ago I wouldn't have considered any part of this situation as feasible.

"How much did you hear of what we said?" Empress asks.

Keke's eyes glint with sudden mischief, as if she's forgotten her distress. "If you say we can get a puppy, I'll pretend I didn't hear anything."

"Blackmail is a crime, little girl," Empress says.

Keke's smile fades. "Is it?"

"Yes."

"Oh no! Wait, what is blackmail?"

"It's making someone do what you want, or keep a secret, by threatening them with something bad."

Her mouth sags into a full frown. "Friends can blackmail each other sometimes, right? It isn't always bad, is it?"

Empress and I exchange looks. "Has anyone in here done that to you, Keke?"

"No!"

I reach my hand out to her but she brushes it aside

and runs past me; when I turn, she's clinging to Solomon's leg.

"What's going on here?" he asks. His clothes, usually crisp and clean, are wrinkled and dusted with ash.

"They're being mean! Make them stop!" Keke hugs his leg harder.

He sighs deeply, and his tug at her puff ponytail is halfhearted. His expression is blank, until one of Rapunzel's screams shakes the house and he winces.

"Were you with Ken?" Empress asks. "Did you ask her what her plan is since she told Landon we'd leave?"

"No. I can't go co-con right now or see what she's doing, so I've been looking for Lurk." He doesn't meet either of our eyes, staring off into the distance. "I couldn't find him."

"We told him not to go anywhere," I say.

"I didn't find him when I looked for him earlier, and I waded through his room." Empress balls her fists and presses the meat of them against her forehead. "Two headmates are missing, none of us can go co-con, and Ken is out there spiraling with no supervision after getting us kicked off the island. Wonder what back alley we'll be passed out in when one of us can front again."

"Have you ever had to make a decision on behalf of the system?" Solomon asks, dropping heavily into the reupholstered chair he usually gets snippy about if Lurk sits in it the wrong way.

She rolls her eyes. "Of course. I—"

"Don't talk about the furry commissions. That money is a contribution, which I appreciate, but it isn't the same as having responsibility. You've never fronted during an emergency, or for a long period of time. Neither of you understands what that feels like."

I jolt as his gaze lands on me; had he heard what we said?

"I know I'd do a better job than Ken or Della have," Empress says petulantly.

"You once wrote in the journal that if we ever meet our trauma holders, we should treat them like royalty, yet you're treating your headmates forced to live in the troubles of the here and now like this." He isn't yelling, but there's something frightening about the quiet intensity of his voice. It has the dense emotion that a shout would break up and disperse, and each word lands with the impact of a heavy, solid stone instead of a pebble. "If you met the trauma holders, you'd probably thoughtlessly snark at them about what took them so long."

Her face scrunches up as she fights back sudden tears. "Get over yourself. Just because you're in love with Ken and let her treat you like crap doesn't mean we all have to do the same!"

She stomps off to her room and Keke toddles after her.

I blink back tears of my own, their anger unsettling. "You know she didn't mean to be rude. She's just scared, like we all are. Go talk to her, please—we need to stick together."

This should be the moment he regrets his actions and goes to apologize. That's what the Solomon I know would do. Instead, he meets my gaze, expression cool. "Am I the only one never allowed to get frustrated in this house? When did I sign up for that? Della is the perfectionist, not me."

He's never taken this tone with any of us, and the shock of it makes me speak before I think.

"You're the adult here, and you're handling the situation as badly as Empress. Are you mad because Landon showed up? Is that why you're acting like this? Because you're jealous?"

"Go chant a mantra or something," he says as he takes off his glasses and rubs at the bridge of his nose. "Because I'm not in the mood for this."

He keeps his energy so bottled up that we forget he's capable of real anger, but I feel it now, ready to explode from him.

He'd been alongside Ken for longer than he's been with us. I hadn't thought he'd be able to hurt Della, but maybe I was wrong. He might do whatever was necessary to keep Ken from leaving again, even if that meant harming the rest of the system.

A deep sadness fills me, along with a sense of failure. I'm so busy coming up with stories that I've ignored the obvious—if Solomon is acting out of character, so am I. I'm supposed to defuse misunderstandings, not escalate them.

I sit on the floor next to his chair, legs crossed even though I want to run from the room like Empress had.

"You asked for the mantra, don't complain about the noise," I say, trying to keep my voice steady and light. *"We are safe. We are whole. And we survive, together."*

He's quiet as I repeat the phrases over and over, and then lets out a long exhale.

"I apologize, Mesmer. I'm just . . . I'm scared. I'm not sure what Della has gotten us into or how we'll get out of it. I don't know if Della and Lurk are in danger or not. I don't know if Ken is a threat to herself right now. I'm helpless."

"I understand," I say, the commiseration not expressing how worried I am about our system's stability. "Why don't you chant with me?"

I've never asked him to before, and I expect him to say no, but he clears his throat and joins in. We repeat the words in unison, our voices strong even if they're a weak defense against all the unknowns stacked against us. Nothing has changed, but the suspicion and anger and fear give way to the truth made manifest in our joined voices: we're never alone.

Something scrapes across glass, the dissonance of the noise startling; we're both on our feet in an instant. A tremor ripples through me and I can barely force myself to look toward the source of the sound: the window.

Dark brown streaks of paint mar the pane where a spindly branch, attached to a skeletal tree that hadn't been there moments before, drifts back and forth over the glass like a beckoning finger.

Solomon strides over and tugs the curtain shut but doesn't move away afterward like I would have. He stands with his shoulders hunched and his fists clenched in the thick floral fabric, as if gathering himself. Unlike me, he hadn't been imagining some terrifying creature trying to claw its way in from the void when he'd jumped up.

He'd thought it was Ken.

Chapter 19

Ken

I hope John got your message," Celeste says from beside me, gazing out at the water, now more white-cap wave than green-gray. "River is way too rough for my little boat, so I'm gonna have to rescind that offer to take you if he can't. Mr. Associate Board Member will just have to deal."

I don't respond because I have no idea what she's talking about. I'd last been walking away from Landon in the upstairs hallway; now we're shivering in the prayer grotto. The trees dance against the slate-gray clouds that crowd ominously overhead. The occasional groan and crack of either branches or wood beams echoes around us as we pass through the creepy space, and when I glance at the photo of

Kavanaugh, he's watching us with that possessive smirk.

My head is fuzzy and achy, and my arms and back are sore. My undershirt clings to my body—sweat—though the icy air doesn't reach it through the thick jacket.

It's so dark outside that it has to be evening, but when I check my watch it's only lunchtime.

I've lost around three hours.

"Solomon? Empress? Mesmer?"

No response. Maybe they're pissed that my past actions have once again screwed them over. I'd thought I was reluctantly swooping in to save the day, but as always, my presence has ruined everything in the end.

All you do is make things worse. The thought—my thought—repeats itself over and over, and though I should be used to this kind of thing, I feel each repetition like a blow.

I hate everything.

I wish I had never woken up.

Why don't I just—

(*"Enough of this. Buck up."*)

That whisper sounds like me. Kind of. Direct and just a little fucking over it. But I'm not sure if it actually was me, and the confusion is enough to pull me out of my self-pity spiral.

"Ken?" Celeste touches my arm, then pulls her hand back. "You good?"

"Yeah," I say, looking around the space so I don't have to see her pity. "Sorry."

"I told you, no need to feel awkward. We've all had run-ins with exes, and your anger about it made securing the windows quick work."

Whoever was fronting while I was gone has worked some kind of magic on Celeste. She's actually being kind of nice, though maybe she just feels sorry for me.

"Right," I say. "Though technically I'm the shitty ex, since I beat up his father. I wouldn't be happy to see me again either."

"I stand by my belief that his dad deserved it. I mean, the political moves he's made in the last four years alone have earned him more than a beatdown. You don't remember why you did it; I think you were just prescient."

I whip my head toward her and find her studying me. I've never directly discussed that with anyone, not even Dr. Reese. Someone else had been fronting, and they'd told her about my memory lapse during the attack. Who had it been and what else had they mentioned?

"I just snapped and—"

"And what I'm saying is, I've seen a lot of people

snap like a rubber band in my life, but a rubber band always gets pulled. Know what I mean? It's like . . . physics."

I sniff and rub at the freezing tip of my nose. "I'm just like that. Pre-locked and -loaded. Waiting for trouble makes it easy to find. Been that way since I was a kid."

"You were a bully? I guess I can kinda see that. Stealing your classmates' lunch money."

"No! I was just always . . . never mind."

Most of my fights had been *against* bullies, but they were a convenient target to vent my anger at. A normal person would have just minded their business. Only a freakshow is pumped to be able to kick somebody's ass. But I'm not going to get into that with her, especially since I'll never see her again after John picks me up.

We step out of an opening on the other side that leads into the trees. I look up as we walk out onto what could barely be called a path; it's more a thin suggestion of a trail into the woods.

"This is the back way out of the house," she says, stepping surefooted over the stones. "The bridge trail gets you to the shore more quickly. It branches off a few places, we don't have time to explore all of that right now."

"It won't be necessary, since I don't work here."

We approach a wooden bridge over a deep but dry rock bed. A small toolbox sits in the middle of the bridge, with some planks of wood.

"I wanted to check this out before the storm," she says as she scoops up the box by the handle with one hand and the planks with the other. "They had some high school kids build it as a community project, but this is set to be one of those once-every-hundred-years storms that happens every other year now. Water runs fast and deep in this gully with sudden rain, as some unfortunate hikers have discovered over the years."

I reach for the phone in my pocket and then remember there's no cell signal.

"What usually happens on the island during a storm like the one rolling in?"

"Well, last time there was a storm like this with people living on the island was decades ago. None of them are around to tell us." She shrugs. "You chose the wrong day to become caretaker."

I snort ruefully.

"If there's one thing I'm good at, it's bad timing," I say, my boots loud on the bare pine planks as I follow after her. I take another look up at the sky and the dark branches whipping against it.

I don't like any of this, and even though I should be peppering Celeste with questions as I follow her on the winding path through the trees, I'm lost in my own thoughts.

A shitty thing about having terrible short-term memory and PTSD is being inured to wild shit happening in my life. A bunch of things, any one of which would have made a normal person hightail it out of here quickly, take a while to come together in my brain.

The coincidence of Della leaving no real information about the job. The coincidence of the house looking like the one in our inner world. The coincidence of Landon of all people showing up and claiming that I already knew this place existed.

And now a storm, ready to trap me here.

This is the setup to a horror movie that isn't *The Shining*, and unlike those ghosts, the one here does *not* want me to stay.

I pick up the pace, dangerously close to twisting my ankle as I hurry behind Celeste. I'm not looking around at the forest now, interested only in the winding path ahead of me that will take me back to the castle, so I can collect my things and get out of here, one way or another.

The silence in the inner world is starting to feel less like being ignored and more like being in a forest where the birds and insects have suddenly gone silent.

I go full power-walk as we pass into the underbrush

where I'd first spotted Celeste, and a burst of color alongside the path catches my eye. It takes a moment to register what the red splotch is.

Another gnome, with its face smashed in like the one in the apartment, sits in the grass. No, it's not like the gnome. It's the same one.

I step on the back of Celeste's shoe.

"What the—?" When she whirls around, she's looking me full in the face, forehead creased. "Ken? What's wrong with you?"

"I have to leave," I say. My teeth are chattering, and not just from the cold. "Now. Let's try your boat."

A viscous fear wells up in me, coating me in panic from the inside out. I take deep breaths, trying not to look like I'm losing my damn mind. Not because I think I'm overreacting but because I feel in my bones that I'm not reacting strongly enough. No one takes a crazy person seriously, even when they're right.

"You don't have your stuff."

"I don't care, I'll get it later."

"Why do you have to leave?" she asks. If she thinks my behavior is bizarre, it doesn't show on her face.

"Because I promised," I say in a voice that feels tight and angry.

"You promised?"

I tamp down the urge to shove her away from me.

It's none of her fucking business and she's entirely too calm while my heart feels like it's trying to jump out of my chest.

"Why do you care? You've been telling me I need to leave, now I want to. Just help me."

"We already talked about this," she says, expression inscrutable.

A memory flashes through my mind. Celeste and me in the office. Her standing close to me, hand on my arm. "Fine, if you really want to stay . . ."

The sound of an engine emerges under the howl of the wind, and relief floods me.

"John. I guess he got the message," I say, relieved that at least one person has done what was asked of them. I don't care if this blows back on me, or if Della or any of the others are upset. I don't care why Landon is involved or what Celeste's problem is.

I'm getting us out of here, even if everyone hates me for it.

Cold wind bites at my face as I jog toward the dock, crunching the numbers on how long it will take to go get my luggage and whether I should just leave it behind.

I stop short when I'm close enough to see the ferry as it comes to a halt next to the pier, bobbing on the choppy waves. Inside the boat a few people mill around, preparing to debark.

"Is he still giving tours, even in weather like this?"

"Tour season is over," Celeste says, not at all out of breath after catching up to me.

"Then who . . ."

I turn into the whipping wind that seems intent on pushing me back up toward the house. Strands of hair blow in my face and I squint against tears from the icy breeze funneling behind my glasses.

I can't make out the people on the ferry clearly. Then one of the passengers steps in front of the exit gate, seemingly more eager than the others.

His gaze locks onto mine and recognition sets in.

"Shit," I whisper.

The actual last person I'd ever wanted to see again—Landon's father.

The man I'd attacked in an unprovoked fit of rage, ruining my life and everyone else's in the system. My heart starts to thrash in my chest, or to beat so hard that it feels like it is, and I'm suddenly baking in my coat like a hot potato.

If he's surprised to see me, it doesn't show on his face at all. He raises a hand and waves, like I'm any old acquaintance.

"What is Winslow Pearson doing here?" I ask.

Celeste's arm brushes mine as she continues down the dock, seemingly unaware of the fact that I'm struggling to keep it together. "He's the head of the Kavanaugh Island Conservation Trust. He's the one who hired you, if the gofer didn't."

Pearson strides off the boat, his steps sure despite the water slapping over the edge of the dock. His gaze rests on me as he talks casually to the people following behind him like ducklings.

I remember some things about when I attacked him, even if not the why. The sudden surge of adrenaline-fueled rage and how it had shocked and overwhelmed me—and I remember that even as my fist had connected with his nose, he'd been smiling, just like this.

Chapter 20

Empress

With no warning, I'm fronting. My teeth chatter from the cold and Ken's surging adrenaline rush.

Now, why am I in it?

I hop from foot to foot, trying to warm up, and also to shake away the weird in-betweeny feeling left over from this surprise switch. It's kinda like when you have to sneeze, and the sneeze gets stuck in your nose, except I am the sneeze and I am the nose.

I'm mostly an insider, hanging out in our castle. I don't complain as much as I could, but yeah, of course I've wished I could front more often—rushing to finish commissions that are late because I was stuck inside for weeks and missing discussions in my chat groups sucks.

But I want comfy-cozy fronting.

Curled-up-with-an-iPad-and-a-five-hundred-episode-shonen-anime-series fronting.

Not meeting-a-group-of-strangers-in-a-wildly-confusing-situation fronting.

I'm standing outside in the frigid cold and several A4 people who look like they're about to ask me to go fetch their bags are filing toward me.

I step behind Celeste, crouching to peek out from beside her shoulder. She turns her head to look back at me, brows bunched cartoonishly. "What are you doing?"

"Just collecting myself, bestie," I say, then wince at the blatantly not-Ken statement.

"Do you need to do it all up on me?" She tries to elbow check me, but I cling harder.

"Give me a minute. Please."

She pauses, and instead of launching me through the air like Miss Trunchbull, turns and folds her arms like Kavanaugh Island is an exclusive club and she's the bouncer.

"*Ken?*" I can feel her, somewhere behind me. She's just dissociating in the void I guess; self-dragging in the abyss. I don't know why she switched out, but I guess it's good that she did because last time she encountered this man we'd ended up in cuffs.

I've ctrl-alt-deleted any memories of our time in the slammer, if I had any to begin with, but I don't think I'll be so lucky the next time around.

"Solomon? Okay, you were right. I shouldn't have judged how others handle things. A little help here?"

He doesn't respond, but I also don't feel like he's ignoring me. He's just not here, possibly from the exhaustion of having been at or close to the front so much.

It's been a couple minutes and I'm already starting to get tired.

(*"I'm here."*) Mesmer, voice shaking like she's strapped to a washing machine during the spin cycle.

Our hands start to tremble and I sigh in frustration.

"Mesmer, if you don't meditate, levitate, or otherwise escort yourself back into the inner world and away from me . . ."

(*"I can't!"*)

Our hands grip and twist Celeste's coat like we're trying to pop a sheet of Bubble Wrap.

"Chill! She will smash us if we rip this!"

I try to let go but can only manage to loosen Mesmer's iron grip. She's stronger than she looks.

"What's wrong?" Celeste glances back, brows raised. "I'm trying to be understanding, but I can't help you if I don't have a damn clue what's going on."

My breath is almost a pant, fast and shallow thanks

to Mesmer hijacking our autonomic nervous system. "I can't. Tell you."

She sighs. "Is this what the gofer was talking about? About you being crazy and having voices in your head?"

"No! I don't know what he was talking about. We're not—I'm not—ugh, this is too hard." I groan. I should feed her one of the many background stories we can call on in a pinch if someone puts us on the spot—Della had drilled us on situations like this! But too much is going on for me to focus on lying and fronting at the same time, and the cat is halfway out of the bag and scratching at her boots. "We have something called dissociative identity disorder. I'm not a 'voice,' I'm not crazy, and I'm also not Ken. I'm not even an adult; please don't be mean to me, I'm baby."

I'm ready for her to call bullshit but instead she asks, "Like, an actual baby?" She gives a small nod, as if impressed. "Your vocabulary is really good."

"Thanks. Wait, no, I'm a teenager, a *figurative* baby. You're just as out of the social-media-slang loop as Ken," I snap, then squeeze my eyes shut as Mesmer's wave of panic permeates me. "Sorry. Kinda stressed right now."

"I'll let it slide this time. What's your name? If you want to tell me. I don't know how this works for you. If you want to keep it secret that's cool, too, and I can just call you Figurative Baby."

I hesitate. I don't think I've ever given anyone my real name in person. I have lots of friends, but they're all people I've met online and like eighty-five percent of them are from other DID systems. In real life, we became so isolated over the last few years that I didn't have anyone to tell.

"My name is Empress."

"That's a nice name. Regal." She nods again, then returns her gaze to the approaching group. She's seemingly unbothered, which is anticlimactic, but I'll take it.

"Don't tell anyone else, okay? I shouldn't have even told you. I kind of effed up."

"Why would I tell anyone? If they think you're crazy for saying it, they'd think I was crazy for saying it too. Besides, if Landon knows, then his father definitely does and the rest of the trust probably does too."

"You don't find this weird? That I was just Ken and now I'm Empress?"

She shakes her head, shifting from foot to foot to keep warm. "I've seen some wild shit in my time, kid. Gonna take more than a few extra personalities to shock me. At least you know you've got them."

Even though she's being cool, I still feel like I need to get in the fetal position for a little bit.

(*"Deep breaths. Just relax,"*) Mesmer chimes in as I draw in a stutter breath.

"How can I relax when you're hyperventilating! You're supposed to be the breathwork master, not me!"

(*"You're right. We need to get our energy into alignment. I'm going to focus on breathing deeply and evenly, and you're going to . . . role-play."*)

"Excuse me? Did you forget I'm a minor?"

I can't see her, but I just know that Mesmer has slapped a hand to her forehead in annoyance.

(*"Get your mind out of the gutter. You told Ken we'd been isekai animed, right? Carried off to another world? Just act like you're you've arrived in Ogrevile—"*)

"St. Ogrine."

(*"St. Ogrine, and encounter the escort party of some weird feudal lord to his castle. What would you do?"*)

This isn't a bad idea. Generally, in an *isekai* scenario I'd be surrounded by a variety of hotties for me to giggle coyly at and not this AARP entourage, but I'll make it work.

I inhale—Mesmer inhales—deeply, hold the breath, and then exhale. A bit of calm seeps into our body, and our hands unclench. I make fun of her a lot, but I feel it, the instant her focus kicks in, and her determination to help. She's doing her part, and I've gotta do mine.

Pearson is a few feet away; he's tall, skinny, with

salt-and-pepper hair and an exaggeratedly correct posture. I've only ever seen his photo; in person he does kind of look like Lord Mantis, the evil feudal lord of St. Ogrine, which helps me get into character.

Behind Lord Mantis is a white woman in a knee-length wool coat. Her dark hair is long and thick, and huge sunglasses cover her face despite the gray skies. She's so close behind Mantis that her arm brushes his.

He turns and looks at her, and she shrinks away from him even though his expression doesn't change. I can barely see her face, but something about the soft curve of her chin and the way she cowers makes me think she's probably his daughter.

(*"I don't remember Landon having a younger sister."*)

A couple of oldish men, in their fifties maybe—both white, salt-and-pepper-haired, and carrying leather duffel bags—march toward the house like they're foot soldiers to Lord Mantis, heading into battle. Two women straggle behind them. They're . . . nondescript, and purposely so. One blonde and one brunette. Dressed in autumn uniforms of infinity scarves, cheap peacoats, and UGGs, looking down at their feet so they don't step into the puddles made by the sloshing river.

I'm not an expert on normal human behavior but I *am* an expert on group dynamics and the vibe is off here.

I step out so I'm standing next to Celeste, who's put a camo-fabric mask on; Della would chide her about it not being N95. I pull on one of the emergency masks, zip the neck of the coat up so it covers the mask, and then shove my shaking hands in my pockets just as the group reaches us.

"Hello," Lord Mantis says, nodding to Celeste. He sounds like . . . a normal guy, not one who spends his time trying to make people like me disappear.

She gives him a lift of her chin in greeting.

"And Ms. Nash." He smiles. "Wasn't expecting to see you here."

"Your son made that clear," I say, hoping the tremor in my voice is lost in the howling wind. "I'm not sure how this mix-up happened, but I'll be going now that my ride is here."

I have no idea where, but the adults can handle that.

He raises his bushy brows. "Going? What do you mean?"

I pluck at my mask. "Landon said I wasn't supposed to be here."

"He's right. You were supposed to be arriving today,

with us, not yesterday. But since you're here now, no harm done. And you don't need that silly mask, by the way. Kavanaugh Island is a place of freedom."

The tremor in my hands spreads up my arms and through my body, and it's not just Mesmer this time.

"But Landon said he didn't—"

"Probably for the best that you arrived yesterday, given the weather." He speaks over me with guileless contempt, like a kid stepping on an ant that he could have walked around. "You might have changed your mind and not come at all. And we both know how important this job is for you; it's not like you have any other option."

He smiles again, then starts to walk past me.

"None of this makes sense. I don't think I can work at a place where the status of my employment changes from moment to moment," I say quickly, before he can talk over me. "I appreciate the job, but I actually do have one option, and that's saying no thank you."

That sounded like a responsible adult human thing to say, I think.

(*"Eloquent,"*) Mesmer says.

"Looks like the trust is having some communication issues," Celeste cuts in smoothly. "Having someone move to an island for a job and then jerking them around doesn't seem like the way to foster a great work environment."

"Oh, it certainly isn't. And I wouldn't want to upset Ms. Nash of all people. She can be quite unpredictable." Lord Mantis chuckles, and tell me why this Geritol Jerry is looking me dead in the face like he wants to get a reaction out of me?

I guess if I were Ken-Kenetria Nash and not Empress-Kenetria Nash, I would be triggered right now, either trying to fight him or thinking about how I did fight him in the past and ruined everything for everyone, blah blah blah—all that stuff that she could have worked out in therapy if she hadn't slunk away into the void instead.

Me? I've survived the triple-T Trenches—Tumblr, Twitter, and TikTok—and the scum of humanity on each app who get their rocks off by trying to push people to the edge. This man is trolling, and that's one of the few things I'm equipped to deal with.

I squint as if I'm smiling widely beneath the mask. "Yeah, about that. Why did you choose me for this job? Hiring someone who rocked your nose into your skull also doesn't seem like the best way to foster a good working environment."

(*"Oh snap! You go, girl."*)

"Mesmer. We talked about this. I know you're excited, but use your own vernacular, please."

(*"Sorry. I mean, jeez, you gave him what-for!"*)

Lord Mantis's smile goes tight. "I'm sure you've seen me speak about cultivating American values—"

"I haven't seen you speak about anything. I have better uses of my time."

"Well, then I'll tell you. We wanted the new Kavanaugh Island to live up to the legacy that was originally planned for it. Helping the disenfranchised dregs of society provide some value to the world. I couldn't think of a better candidate than you."

"If this is your idea of polite conversation, I can see why things played out how they did the first time we met."

"My idea of polite conversation is talking to my friends and making sure you didn't go to jail back then," he says. "You should be thanking me instead of getting sassy."

I hadn't paid too much attention to the outside world back then, right after our doors unlocked, but from what I'd seen having our charges dropped had been some attempt at damage control once his history of harassing women had come out with the wash.

"I'll be taking my disenfranchised behind right off of this island; you do not have to worry about me, *thanks.*"

He's looking at me but doesn't seem to hear a word that I've said. "Don't be silly. You must stay for the meeting."

The girl in the long coat walks up beside him; from this close I can see that she doesn't seem to be that much older than me.

"Babe." She reaches a hand up and caresses his chapped cheek. "I'm starved. Let's get to the house."

(*"That's not his daughter."*) We must have achieved some kind of alignment, because Mesmer's revulsion is at the exact wavelength of my own.

"Today is a fasting day."

"Should I still be fasting? With the—"

"You shouldn't eat anything until I tell you to," he says, patting her hand. "But you're right. We should get a move on."

I remember a disturbing detail of the goblin lore I'd learned from the show: in Episode 11, "The Goblin Bride," when Souta saves Trista from Lord Mantis's mansion and marries her to keep her safe. Someone in the fan forum had brought up an old tidbit of Dutch folklore that stated if a human captured a female goblin in their house, they could force her to do anything they wanted, including becoming his "wife." This girl reminds me of one of the goblin women in the episode who hadn't been saved.

Captain John, the last one off the ferry, is moving toward us in a bowlegged hop-jog and I've never been so elated to see a Boomer in my life. I walk toward him, stumbling a bit with the unfamiliar heft of these freaking boots and because my fronting spoons are already dangerously low. I don't know why Solomon or Ken haven't come back to take over yet, but I can't do this for too much longer.

"Did you get the message?" I call out.

"Message?" he asks, huffing a little.

"That I need to leave the island?" I guess. I wasn't around when Ken called on the CB radio.

John looks at Lord Mantis, then Celeste, then me.

"Now?"

"Five minutes ago would be ideal, but now is fine."

He holds a hand out, palm up to the sky, then frowns. "I didn't get any message, but even if I had, this storm is rolling in ahead of forecast, and stronger. I'm not going back out on the river until it passes."

"But . . . you said you know these waters like the back of your hand." That was what I'd thought I heard while listening in during that first ride.

"I do, and I know when to stay my hand. That isn't the same river I brought you here on yesterday. The ferry was shaking half to pieces on the way here, and that's before we got to navigating the breakwaters."

"But—"

"My wife is mad that I even risked coming here just because the trust waved some cash in my face," he says with a helpless shrug. "I'd rather get chewed out for coming back tomorrow with money for Christmas presents for the grandkids than end up at the bottom of the river with every other sailor who didn't listen to his gut."

A pinprick of icy dread lands on my forehead; then another on my glasses, where it melts and rolls down. Then another. Not dread—heavy drops of precipitation somewhere between rain and snow have started to fall.

The storm is here.

"We're gonna have to ride this out," John says, a deep frown on his face. "Sorry."

Lord Mantis walks past me. "We'd better get up those steps before they ice over. Come on, everyone. The meeting of the Kavanaugh Island Conservation Trust has officially begun."

When I look at Celeste, her glare is directed at me.

"What did I do?" I ask, recoiling.

"You shouldn't have come here. And you should have left when I told you. Be careful with these people."

"I don't know why you're acting like I had any choice in this. I'm baby, remember?"

She opens her mouth to say something, then shakes her head in annoyance and follows after the new additions to the island, leaving me shivering on the dock.

I'd told Ken that we were having an *isekai* adventure, traveling to a strange new world. As the icy rain starts to come down and the banks across the river are blotted out in gray and white, I'm certain that this world isn't full of cute green wives; this is something dark and dangerous, something that's affecting our inner world too.

"Mesmer, do you have any very specific mantras for situations like this?" I ask internally as I start following the group already mounting the stairs. She's usually good with the "We are smart, we are safe, we are powerful"–type affirmations.

She doesn't reply.

"Mesmer?"

Though I feel someone's presence behind me, I realize I'm not shaking anymore—Mesmer is gone.

Chapter 21

Mesmer

I'm back in the inner world. When Empress had been pushed to the front and me alongside her, the castle had been filled with Rapunzel's screams. Now it's quiet except for the wind outside, and that's more disturbing because at least the screaming is a noise I'm familiar with.

I spin around slowly. "Is everyone okay?"

The castle doesn't answer—never answers—but that doesn't mean that it thinks things are fine.

The others joke about my crystals, and tai chi, and deep breathing. Solomon gets annoyed when I move furniture around according to feng shui, and Della would tut when I'd salt our windowsills and doors, even though she didn't really mind. Keke hides when I ethically smudged the house because she hates the smoke, but I have my reasons for everything that I do. When I was struggling with feeling like I had no real purpose, Dr. Reese reminded me that I didn't need to have one because even singlets have the right to purposelessness, but from her perspective I was the headmate dedicated to self-care. She said that even when others don't notice, my actions help to make the inner world a safe and comfortable place.

I know why I'm here: to keep the body, and our home, balanced. I don't always need to know what's happening in the outer world because I feel the castle's energy ebb and flow. Things haven't ever quite been balanced, but we'd reached a kind of normal. I'd been the first to notice Della's odd behaviors, even when she tried to hide them from us, because the house had taken on an astringent energy. And now . . .

I catch sight of footprints in the dust, leading toward the back of the house. "Solomon? Keke?" I call out, though the footprints are too large to belong to either of them.

No response. The hairs on my arms rise.

A noise upstairs.

"Della?" It could be her, back and cleaning her room.

The only response is wind chimes—the ones in my room. Why would someone be in my room?

"Ken?" I whisper. "Ken, is that you?"

Guilt fills me as I realize that I'm glad when she doesn't answer me.

The castle rumbles and shakes again, this time without Rapunzel's screams to give warning ahead of the tremor. There's a tension in the atmosphere and it's coming from within. If it's my job to keep the house's energy balanced, I'm failing. There's something I'm not seeing—not sensing.

Even though I feel rooted to the spot, I make my way up to my room. My knees give out and I let them as I drop into lotus pose and draw in a shaky breath, sniffling as soot rushes up my nose. I can't control the chaos slowly claiming the house, but I can try to counter it.

"We are safe. We are whole. And we survive, together."

I repeat it again, and again, until the words blend into meaningless noise and my mind floats safely on the cushion of sound.

I'm so deep in my meditation that it takes me a moment to realize that a tickle on my shoulder is the salt that had lined my windowsill sprinkling over me. The cool sensation is the breeze from outside.

"We are safe . . ." My affirmation dries up as I look behind me and have a moment of enlightenment, but not in a good way. I'd thought I'd experienced fear before, having lived with it constantly, but this new sensation jolts me with an intense clarity.

"Safe . . ." I repeat. I can't seem to move past this word—maybe because it's become less affirmation and more a plea to the universe. "Safe . . ."

The intruder in my window makes a low, dismissive grunt. "No. Not safe at all."

Chapter 22

Archived Post: Della (4 weeks ago)
(Hidden by Admin)

We got an email today—a follow-up email to be exact, though I never received a first one. Something about a job at a historical home on a place called Kavanaugh Island that one of us applied to.

I should be happy; it seems like exactly what I've been praying for, but it doesn't *feel* right. It doesn't feel like chance. The email gives me the same queasy sensation that I got when Mesmer asked me where I've been going on Sundays and I had no idea what she was talking about.

I googled it and all the links in the search results that should have been blue were purple—the sites had already been accessed. The pages had been visited a month ago. I clicked on an incongruous one about Black women artists of the Harlem renaissance . . . and then what happened?

I don't remember. Ken blamed her amnesia lapses on her ADHD, but I've never had trouble with that.

I'm going to say no. I shouldn't make this kind of decision myself—Empress has already started calling me a dictator and Keke barely speaks to me since I stopped letting her visit the shelter—but if I'm wrong, the others will never know. Keeping us safe is *my* responsibility, and though they haven't agreed with my choices over the last two years, I hope they're never put in the position to learn what they'd do in my shoes.

Chapter 23
Solomon

My head feels like canvas wrapped tight around a throbbing core of pain as I move to the front, and I can't tell if it's from overextending myself or from the forceful jolt of the switch.

Where am I? How long has passed? It's dark out now—has it been hours or days?

I reflexively reach for the cell phone to check the journal app, but then I remember—it's useless now. It has been for months, if I'm honest. Posts about dinners that were cooked but no mention of the fact that they weren't eaten; buoying Bible quotes and reminders that everything was fine even though we could all feel Della's stability crumbling at the foundations.

Our phone isn't in the pocket of the hoodie, but my

fingers close around the pamphlet Ken had stuffed in our pocket.

August 16, 1918

It's been a few weeks since my last entry—I was struck down by the most terrible sickness, and have only just started to regain my strength. I truly thought I was going to die, and though I didn't, I've been left with an unease that creeps up on me at all hours, producing musings more horrible than an opium nightmare.

Simon was already rushing the move from our Gramercy apartment to the castle, as there had been murmurings of a mysterious illness moving through the city, but alas, it was not fast enough for me. Still, I'm glad we're here, even if the tower has lewdly marred my vision—our vision—of the castle. I told Lottie about the tower when last I snuck off to see her, and she said Simon wanted everyone to see his hard-on for vice from miles off.

Once the illness has passed and things are back to normal, I'll get a little apartment on the East Side and Lottie can come live with me. If my brush with the great beyond has taught me anything, it's that I want to live long, and live well. Simon will be busy with his work and his diversions—I doubt he'll miss me.

His friends have come to visit again. He claims none of them are ill, but I've heard coughs echo in halls, so I keep my distance and wear the mask Lottie sewed for me. I'm glad to have reason to steer clear of them. I feel their eyes feast on me when I drop in to say hello; I am Simon's greatest trophy after all.

They gallivant about dressed in their hunting outfits as though the island holds any game but the migratory birds and a few pigeons. They haven't been off to fight in Europe, due to age and wealth, but there is a hunger for violence that peers out from between their teeth as they chomp their cigars. It's something you learn to look out for in a certain kind of man. A violence that believes itself battle ready, but only tests its mettle against those already deemed weaker and less than in our corrupt society.

Have I always thought such terrible, lurid things? The locals say the island is cursed. I wasn't supposed to hear of it, but now that I know I cannot help but wonder at all the things that have gone amiss . . .

I tuck the pamphlet away, unsettled and wishing I hadn't read it when I'm already so confused.

My surroundings slowly start to catch up with my brain as I take a few steps from the corner I'd been huddled in, filling in the clues no one has left behind for me.

The steady brush of rain over the castle, outside, and a low growl of thunder in the distance that raises the hairs on my arms. The storm has arrived.

Something is bubbling on a stove, and the scent of meat permeates the air, with damp stone as a supporting note.

The sound of a knife slicing through something hard and meeting the barrier of a cutting board.

I'm in the kitchen of Grace Castle, and there's enough food in the process of being made to serve several people.

Two unknown-to-me white women, one dark-haired and one bottle-blond, are in the kitchen with me, preparing food. I bring a hand to my nose, making sure I'm masked. Della isn't here, and I'm angry with her, but I keep my promises.

One of the women turns and holds a platter of sandwiches toward me.

"Are you here to read or to work?" she asks half-jokingly. "You can take this in."

"Are you the new caretakers?" I ask without thinking.

She looks at the other woman, their gaze communicative, then turns back to me. "I told you, we're here for a party. This isn't our usual thing, but we're getting paid cash, lots of cash—too much cash, maybe? Making a few sandwiches and playing a game is better than other stuff we've been asked to do."

They're also on the island because they've received an offer they can't refuse. That's an unfortunate common denominator.

"Oh, right. I'll take this then."

"Take it fast, please. That guy acts nice, but he's . . ." She finishes the sentence with a stabbing and twisting motion of her hand, mimicking unscrewing a lightbulb. "Guys like him, it only takes a little thing to set them off."

"Polyester sheets," the other woman says, and they laugh at some shared memory.

"What's going on?" I ask inwardly, walking toward the dining room because I doubt the meal is being held in the bathroom or office. I want to ask where Ken is, but who knows what she got up to in the hours that have passed since this morning.

Empress sighs. (*"Lord Mantis showed up with his escort, then Ken disappeared, then I was fronting with Mesmer, then she ditched me, too, then I got told to help make the food, which was not in our contract, but I didn't want to sit at the table with all of those old people so—")*

"Lord Mantis?"

("Pearson. Landon's dad. He's the head of the trust. And he says we were hired but showed up a day early.")

"Winslow Pearson hired us?"

It's one thing to find myself on a strange island working for persons unknown, but I've been keeping track of Pearson over the years. His brush with accountability after Ken attacked him pushed him from conservative Republican to hard right. This man butters his bread by harassing minorities and the mentally ill, by calling drag queens groomers and in the same breath saying women reach the height of their fertility at sixteen. I'd never begrudged Ken for attacking him because I'd felt her wild confusion when she had, but the man deserved more than a few punches—and he's the one who brought us here.

My head throbs, the ache branching through my skull as if trying to split my brain into pieces.

"Are you okay in there?" I ask Empress.

("I'm in the living room with Keke. Mesmer isn't down here; she's probably in her room trying to re-center. You know how she gets when she has to interact with strangers.")

Her voice is monotone, devoid of her usual teenage petulance. It's the voice she uses when she answers the phone and finds a bill collector on the other end. She's trying to sound like an adult, confident and collected, which is what makes me certain that she's terrified.

"Thank you for handling things. You did a great job navigating this situation," I say. *"I'm sorry about how mean I was earlier. I was out of line."*

(*"Thanks for apologizing."*) Her tone warms a bit. (*"I was embarrassed by what you said, but you weren't entirely wrong. Let's try to communicate better, and I'll try to be less judgmental."*)

"I guess your TikTok psychology obsession does have its benefits."

She laughs, but without much emotion.

I head toward the noise from the dining room.

"Ken." An icy hand grabs me by the shoulder. "You were supposed to leave."

I look down, remember the body's actual height, and then look up to find Landon glaring at me. His lips are pressed into a pale line as he gives my arm a subtle chastising shake. I feel a trickle of "wish a motherfucker would" enter my system and for a moment think that Ken must be moving toward the front.

It's all me.

"Your father says I'm supposed to be here." I tilt my

head and take a step toward him so the toes of our shoes touch. "Why are you two telling me different things?"

His gaze searches mine. "Not Ken."

He lets go of me, angering me in a different way. If I were her, would he have squeezed harder? There's a certain kind of man who thinks he can treat a woman any kind of way once she's angered him enough.

"Does it matter? Answer my question, and Ken will get the message too."

He rolls his eyes. "I don't think this whole multiple personalities thing is even real—my psychiatrist buddy said it's a cry for attention. But if you insist it is, don't feed me some line about passing on messages while acting like you don't even remember the last time we talked. Who did you say you were then? Della?"

I grip the platter so hard I'm surprised I don't bend it in two. "You spoke to Della?"

He makes a sound of frustration. "She—you—snuck up on me while I was on a brunch date, like, two months ago and threatened me. I'm trying to be understanding, but this crazy act of yours is going too far."

Della had spoken to Landon.

Recently.

Now . . . now I think of Landon telling Ken that she'd known about the existence of this island since their third date. Maybe it hadn't been Ken he'd been with, but Della. I think of her cheery journal entry about the job offer, devoid of any relevant information, including the fact that maybe it was her who applied for the job.

I've given her the benefit of the doubt too many times to count over the last year. I understood the un-spoken toll that the pandemic had taken on her and had left things unasked because I assumed she would tell us anything crucial. I thought she'd only been hiding her growing obsessive tendencies, but what else had she kept from us?

Checks and balances, documentation, sharing infor-mation; all of the rules that Della had made for us only work when everyone is mostly truthful, especially her. If she'd lied, even by omission, it feels more insidious than Ken's attempt to harm us.

I can fight a direct attack. What I can't see, don't know to parry, is the real danger.

"What did she say to you?"

He taps a finger hard against my temple. "Ask her."

He strides into the dining room and a moment later Celeste pokes her head out. "There a problem out here?"

Yes.

I take a deep breath, try to wrangle my eyes into

some semblance of neutral even if I'm still frowning under the mask. "No."

(*"She knows about us, too, by the way,"*) Empress says, pulling me back to the problem at hand. (*"I told her when I freaked out but technically Landon had already told her . . ."*)

I inhale deeply, every muscle in my body taut with anxiety. *"That's fine. We should assume that everyone here knows."*

(*"Yeah. Maybe that's why she was so unsurprised. It was pretty anticlimactic."*)

Would they have warned Celeste about us? Is that why she'd watched me so intently earlier, making me think she'd clocked our switch? It shouldn't have been noticeable . . . unless she knew to watch for it.

Her gaze tracks me as I walk by her into the dining room, and I look down at the platter.

The dining table I'd seen earlier has been set with beautiful china and exquisite glassware taken from the display cases. Odd to see the museum-quality pieces in a historical home being used so casually, but I'm guessing no one imagined being stuck here in a storm.

(*"Except they brought all this food with them,"*) Empress points out. (*"They came with provisions. And catering staff. During a storm. That's premeditated meal prep."*)

"Bon appétit." I set the platter down among already-laid-out fruit-and-cheese plates and opened wine bottles as Empress gives me the rundown.

(*"Pearson; his barely legal trophy wife, Lily; the other two are the Edwards brothers, I think. Apparently, they're the other board members. The two in the kitchen are hired for this event. Maria and Diana."*)

"Why are all these people here?"

(*"Bestie, I think the more important question is why are we?"*)

"Have a seat, Kenetria," Pearson says, gesturing at the empty chair next to him.

"I can eat in the caretaker's quarters," I say, backing away.

"Nonsense. This is a welcome lunch. Have a seat."

"Sure. Though, I guess it's more of a goodbye lunch." I slide stiffly into the highbacked chair next to Celeste.

When I glance around the dining room, I notice something in the corner that I hadn't caught in detail earlier—the suit of armor isn't what I imagined it would be. It's posed holding a long Claymore blade and with a battle horn hung over its shoulder. Its mask is a siege helmet designed in the style of a human skull. Metal teeth are carved into the mouthpiece and there are gaping holes where the eyes and nose would be, giving it the unsettling appearance that it's staring at you in bucktoothed malevolence.

"Oh, you've spotted the big man. Do you like him?" I turn to find Pearson watching me with an unsettling interest that sits on my skin like cheap lotion.

"I saw something similar at the Met," I say, then, to strike a balance between Ken and Empress, add, "The sword is badass."

"It's always been my favorite piece in the house. It was stolen by scavengers from the castle years ago, but I was able to recover it."

"Scavengers, huh?" John mutters from across the table and then throws back half his glass of wine.

"Maybe you should have let them keep it," I say.

"The armor caught Kavanaugh's eye at an auction," Pearson continues, "and he thought that the castle was already such a hodgepodge, mongrel place that it couldn't hurt to have this here too."

I nod, though the word "mongrel" rests in the air, noxious.

"I haven't explored every part of the house, but from what I've seen, he certainly did have eclectic tastes."

"In all things," he says with a smile.

A heavier band of rain and sleet passes over the castle, the din of it drowning out the possibility of continuing the conversation. No one touches their food, and the other members of the board sit looking at their empty plates. I reach for a sandwich without waiting, because it's what Ken would do and also because now that I'm settling into our body, I'm starving. All we've had today was coffee.

My hand hovers over the plate—Della hadn't eaten outdoors since February 2020. She hadn't eaten anything from a restaurant since June 2020. She hadn't eaten anything not prepared by her own hand since December 2021. The only time she'd lost her composure with me was when she'd found pizza grease on our coat sleeve and realized I'd snuck a pie from my favorite shop.

I catch myself waiting for her disapproval, followed by relief and worry when I remember she isn't here to stop me. I don't feel guilty. I feel resentful. I'd followed all of Della's rules, and she'd lied to me.

I suddenly remember an incident that had gotten lost in all the instability—a month ago, when Della had been fronting and I'd felt that something was off. I'd tried to go co-con with her and couldn't. When I was finally able to, we were in a crowded sub shop with the taste of an Italian special still fresh in our mouth. She was shaking as she searched for her mask, had knocked over a chair as she ran out. She hadn't even noticed my presence.

Why hadn't I demanded to know what she was doing? How had I forgotten until now? The system is almost back to where we started—everything so dysfunctional that abnormal behavior bleeds into the normal.

Maria and Diana scuttle into the seats beside me, and the two men across the table look at them like they're on the menu.

Their movement breaks whatever had frozen everyone at the table. The sound of napkins being unfolded, cutlery and glasses being pushed around, and plates scraping against one another signal the start of what might be at worst an awkward work lunch, until Pearson stands.

"Everyone join hands."

Celeste's hand slides warm over mine, though I hadn't expected her to follow the strange order. I keep my other hand to myself. Diana and I silently mutually agree that hand-holding isn't necessary.

"We are here," Pearson begins in a suddenly booming voice, sounding more pastor than politician, "to celebrate the legacy of Kavanaugh Island and Grace Castle. Like many things of great value and particular importance in this country—tradition, ethics, morality—it had been eroded by the turmoil and filth of modern times. But we have successfully resurrected it through hard work and sacrifice, a shining beacon in the east, like the rising sun, and today we are almost ready to sit back and admire the glory of what we have brought back into being. Almost. We should be proud of the history we've preserved, and the future we are creating. One that appreciates and uplifts the American dream, the morals and values this country was built on, and not our current nightmare. Amen."

"Amen," everyone echoes loudly, except for me and Celeste. I'm not sure what rendition of the American dream he's referring to, but given his politics it's likely not one that I want any part of.

"It's so good to be back home, isn't it, son?" Pearson reaches out and roughly tousles Landon's hair.

"Home?" I repeat.

He looks around the table in confusion, inviting the others to pay attention, then leans forward and meets my gaze from down the table. "Don't you recall the conversation we had when you were hired?"

Thunder rumbles low in the distance, and I jerk in my seat, trying my best not to react, though I see one of the men across the table grin at my reaction.

"Kavanaugh is our family name," Landon explains, voice rough and awkward before he clears his throat. "Winslow Kavanaugh Pearson. Landon Kavanaugh Pearson. Simon Kavanaugh is my great-grandfather."

"Surely you told her this while you were dating," Pearson says, narrowing his gaze toward his son.

"I told one of them," Landon mutters, looking at his plate, where his sandwich sits untouched.

Pearson breaks into laughter, and the other members of the trust follow.

Celeste is stiff beside me, but beneath the tablecloth, her hand moves to my thigh, giving it a squeeze. It's more fortifying than flirtatious, but the intimacy of it shocks me. For someone so standoffish, she's surprisingly touchy.

"Ken *is* a special case," Pearson says. "Lily did wonder why I chose you for the caretaker position after being a victim of your . . . outburst. Or would you call it an episode?"

He's looking at Landon, even though he's talking to me, but Landon is still staring at his plate.

"I assumed it was because of, like, affirmative action or something?" Lily ventures with a giggle.

"If that happens to be the reason I was hired, I'm fine with it," I say. "It means I'm more than qualified for the job but that you couldn't be trusted not to give it to a lesser-qualified white man."

"I think it was the 'or something,' actually," Celeste says, leaning forward to glare at Lily. "Something like a young woman married to a much older rich man might be assumed to be a gold digger."

"My family is rich. I married Winslow because I can

appreciate an older man," Lily says, gripping her fork. Lightning flashes, highlighting both how young she is compared to Pearson and the affront in her eyes.

Pearson continues his conversation where he'd left off, ignoring Lily and Celeste's bickering. "While the altercation with Ken was shocking, violence is a natural part of human existence. It was certainly among the most memorable introductions I've had. There's nothing like an unexpected adversary to get your blood pumping."

Landon rolls his eyes. "Enough, Dad."

Pearson laughs in a perfunctory way, a sonic semicolon to force a pause between the bizarre things he's saying. "We all know that no matter what happened in the past, Kenetria's presence here is necessary. We couldn't reopen the castle without her."

He gestures toward me as an earsplitting roll of thunder shudders through the house.

I don't process it—in a blink, I'm no longer fronting.

"Necessary?" I say aloud, the question posed to the living room in the inner world, instead of to Pearson.

Keke is next to the window sash, peeking through the curtain, and now I realize that though it's quieter in here, the sound of rain pelting the roof and outer walls has carried over with me. When I push the curtain aside I see a mass of storm clouds roiling above, the flash of lightning glazing tree branches, and the caps of waves in the distance. Like the branch against the window earlier, all of the elements are in motion now. If this were an installation at a museum, it would be the must-see exhibition of the year. But this is my home, and the beauty of the moving landscape doesn't make it less jarring.

"Do you hear that?" Keke asks from beside me, grinning wide enough to show her missing tooth.

"It's thunder," I say, barely able to look away from the scene outside.

"No, not that." Keke sighs, disappointed in me. "Adults do not pay attention."

"She isn't in her room," Empress says from behind us, walking into the room stiffly. "Mesmer. She isn't there. She's . . . her necklace."

I jog to Mesmer's room, though the logical part of me understands that Empress's disjointed explanation can only mean one thing. The scent of patchouli envelops me when I open the door, and a lightning flash from outside the window ripples through the crystals lined up neatly on shelves, refracting around the room. It glints off of something in her meditation nook before the room goes dark, and when I flip the light switch I understand why Empress had barely been able to speak.

Mesmer's amulet, a metal cylinder stamped with

blessings and tied to a leather string, has been crushed and lies draped over something.

"Fuck."

Mortimer the garden gnome sits on Mesmer's bed, and the amulet hangs over the area where its face had once been—it's now a match to the one in the castle. I'd thought it had been left in the apartment by accident, but now I see what it truly is—a threat, and one that's infiltrated our inner world as well.

I rush back downstairs and find Empress sitting on the ornamental carpet with her arms wrapped around her legs and her head on her knees. Only Empress.

"Where's Keke?"

She jumps to her feet, looking around wildly. "She was just right here!"

She grabs a cushion from the couch, as if Keke is a quarter that slipped out of her pocket, and then looks up at me in horror when there isn't a small child there.

Della.

Lurk.

Mesmer.

Keke can't be missing, too, she can't be . . .

"Wait," Empress says, slowly tilting her head as if listening to the storm. Through the storm. "She's fronting."

Chapter 24

Keke

Solomon didn't hear what I heard because he's scared of thunder and because he's worried about adult things and Empress didn't hear because she was sad. I'm sad and worried about adult things, too, but I know there's something that will make everyone feel better. Or maybe it will only make me feel better, and that's also okay. Self-care is important. Mesmer taught me that.

I'm not supposed to front alone, but there's an adult watching me so I won't get in trouble.

I wiggle my fingers because my hands are all big, and it feels funny. After a sneaky look at all the stranger adults at the table, I pull my mask over my mouth, humming the song that I don't know the words to.

Della says we always have to wear a mask so we don't get sick, even though she takes it off sometimes.

Adults don't always follow their own rules, but I'm a good girl.

"Put your mask on," I whisper to the nice-mean lady sitting next to me. She's our friend, so I can say that to her. My elbow knocks over her glass of water and she looks at me real fast with her lips pulling to the side, but then her eyes choose nice over mean and her mouth follows it.

"What are you doing?" she asks in a quiet voice as she cleans the water with a napkin. "And why do you have a lisp now?"

I shake my head. "It's not polite to point out things like that, you know. Put your mask on."

She rolls her eyes as she pulls the mask up, but I see her smile before the fabric covers her mouth.

"Kenetria, are you listening?" an old man asks, but I'm not supposed to talk to strangers and then a softness brushes against my leg under the table, and I have to go under the table to chase it. My head hits the edge of the wood hard. I don't make a noise, even though it hurts real bad—I can be quiet when I have to. And careful.

When I go under the tablecloth, there are two eyes shining at me.

254 · ALYSSA COLE

"Puppy!"

Puppypuppypuppypuppy.

In front of me is a hot dog with a wig on—ha-ha, no it's a long-haired dachshund. I've only seen one in a picture book before, and it's very pretty in real life. It's shaking so hard that it's dusting the floor, and when thunder rumbles again it barks again, and spins in a circle.

"It's okay. I'm your friend," I whisper, reaching slowly for it. It scurries away from me, so I wait a little. I cross my legs and try to look interested in everyone's shoes under the table. The shoes are not fancy dress-up shoes—boring hiking boots and sneakers, though someone has something fancy tied to his ankle.

"Lily, I told you to leave that creature at home," a man says. The one we are scared of.

(*"Be careful,"*) a voice whispers.

Then I feel another adult right behind me in my mind, someone with a lot of big feelings that press into me. I don't say anything to her, either, because, like with a strange puppy, letting her come to me is better.

(*"Get out of the way so I can front,"*) Ken says.

"Ask nicely."

(*"Get out of the way, please, you little brat."*) I feel the pressure of her all against me, and I want to move, but even I know things don't work like that.

"We don't have control over that. You and me don't."

("Why didn't you say that to begin with?")

She backs away a little bit, but I feel like my body is suddenly harder to move. Co-fronting is when two people can control the body at the same time.

"You have to ask nicely when you want something, even if you can't have it." The puppy starts to creep toward me and I feel Ken watching it too. She's not shoving anymore.

("Why are we under a table?")

"There's a puppy here."

("I see that. I mean what happened while I was gone?")

"The scary grandpa showed up with a bunch of people and Empress had to make lunch like The Help and Solomon got scared by thunder—real thunder, not painted thunder—and Mesmer wasn't in her room, and I heard a bark!!"

("I thought John was getting us off this goddamned island.")

"He said the storm is too strong."

("I've seen videos of ships cruising through hurricanes and he can't get us twenty minutes down the river? What a crock of shit.")

Della says that cursing is undignified, but I like that Ken talks to me the same way she talks to the adults. Everyone else treats me like a baby.

I reach my hand toward the puppy as it sniffs by my knee, and it takes a step back.

(*"Just grab the damn dog already! You're stressing me out. Grab it, cop a furry feel, and then let me have control of the body so I can get us out of here."*)

"You have to be patient with scared creatures."

(*"I remember when you could barely hold a conversation without crying, and now you're trying to give me life lessons? Damn, I feel old."*)

"You aren't old. Della is old, if she's still alive."

(*"What?"*)

"Yay!" I shout as the puppy jumps into my lap, sniffing and snuffling. I pet it slowly, letting its long ears slip between my fingers as I whisper, "You're safe, puppy. Ken is here to protect you."

(*"Ken doesn't give a good goddamn about this mutt. Tell me why you think Della isn't alive."*)

An arm reaches past me, pushing me to the side, hard. I start to fall over and—

Chapter 25

Ken

My knees press hard into the floor and my thighs strain as I keep our body upright when Keke would have tumbled over.

I have a puppy in one hand and, in the other, a forearm draped in some kind of silky fabric. While the puppy is in a soft hold, I'm gripping the shit out of that arm, squeezing it like a tube of expensive oil paint with a few strokes' worth left inside.

"Ow! Let me go! You're hurting the baby!" A girl's voice, and I turn to look into the face of a young brunette who doesn't seem pained in the slightest.

"The dog is fine," I say.

"I mean the baby growing inside of me, duh," she sneers, starting to lean back on her heels.

I let her go and she scrambles out from under the table and places her hands protectively over her stomach.

"Ken?" Landon yells angrily, rushing over so I once again get a view of his pants and loafers, this time beside the woman's long skirt and Chanel flats. "Did you hit her?"

"Why would I hit her?" I crawl out from under the table, the dog under my arm like a football. "I was catching this thing."

"You don't really need a reason, do you?" Landon asks as the girl calls out, "Chalamet!"

The weird-looking fur pellet snuggles into the crook of my arm, and when the girl reaches for it, it barks at her. She seems like a regular human—dedicated to bothering me when I'm trying to mind my business—but might be straight-up evil if a dog prefers me when given the choice.

Keke giggles as the dog stretches up to lick my chin.

(*"Puppies can tell when you're good. And this one likes you."*)

"Dogs like anybody. Even people who kick them," I say. *"Go back inside, where it's safe."*

(*"Inner world is scary right now. Since you can't come in with me, I'll stay here. You told me you would protect me from the monsters."*)

I'm pretty sure she's just finding an excuse to stay

out for longer, like any kid worth their salt, but she's a distraction I don't need right now.

"If something happens in there, holler and I'll come to you, okay?"

A long pause. (*"Do you promise?"*)

Her voice is so abruptly grave and adultlike that it startles me. She's dead serious, and even someone as oblivious as me can sense that talking down to her would be a misstep.

"I promise."

With Keke gone, a more distant headmate becomes apparent, but too far for me to pinpoint who. Probably Solomon, not coming closer because he knows I'll cuss him out for letting Keke front alone. Or maybe Della, laughing her ass off while we deal with this shit.

"Chalamet, come here, sweetie," the girl whose arm I'd held croons.

Lily. Pearson's wife. Landon's stepmom.

The knowledge comes to me in an impulse, not a headmate's stray thought or direct conversation, and that's enough to almost make me drop the damn dog.

"Give it back to her, Ken," Landon says. "Or call out one of your buddies who knows how to behave."

That's enough to make me consider shoving the dog into my hoodie. Then I remember what Celeste had told me: the wife of the board's director was the last person to die here. Landon's mom. She'd fallen down the stairs. Pearson had remarried, quickly, and to someone who could be his granddaughter. I guess I can understand why Landon is being such a dick.

"You should put a leash on it," I say as I hand it over. "I thought it was a rat. Almost stomped on it. It might not be so lucky next time."

"Are you threatening my dog?" Lily asks.

I ignore her, trying to situate myself now that I'm out from under the table and have to act like I've been here the whole time.

The first thing my gaze jumps to is a big-ass sword being held by a suit of armor that, despite this being a castle, seems out of place. I'm tempted to ignore everyone and go check it out, because it's cool as hell, but John and the people from the trust I'd seen filing off the boat are seated at a table in what must be the castle's dining room, staring at me.

Pearson looks the most intent, and the sight of him makes my scalp crawl. I'd worried about our organs being harvested but now I wonder if this isn't some kind of test, or worse, a plot for revenge. I force myself to stare back, even though I'm worried that I'll have a repeat of our first and last meeting, but I don't feel the urge to bash his face in. I guess I should feel apologetic, but I mostly feel regret—this is what I'd ruined my life over. Some man who can now sit and look down at me because he's seen me at my worst.

There's no reason for him to be so damn smug. Maybe he wants to get punched again.

(*"Careful,"*) someone whispers.

I pick up a cup to casually take a sip, but when I notice the red lipstick I realize I've grabbed someone else's—a dark-haired white woman seated next to me. I smile at her, but she gives me side eye and whispers to the woman next to her. Who was fronting before Keke? How had they interacted with everyone?

Celeste is seated beside me. Her gaze meets mine, and she raises her brows just as thunder cracks loud and hard, shaking the house and inducing another round of barks from the dog. The noise must explain why Solomon left Keke to fend for herself. And they call me irresponsible.

"I told you not to bring that thing," Pearson says, coming to stand behind Lily, who's hugging the squirming dog against its will. His hand brushes over her hair like she's the dog at heel and not Shalimar or whatever the mutt's name is. "I thought we agreed it was best to find a new home for it. Before the baby arrives."

"I will," Lily murmurs, then whips her head up at him and says more decisively, "I mean, I did. I did! But they couldn't pick him up as planned because of the storm, and there was no time to find a sitter so I just put him in my purse. I thought one more night wouldn't hurt."

She smiles, but she's blinking fast, like some weird version of *Speed* where her face will give way to her real emotions if she stops fluttering her lashes. Lightning flashes and for an instant they're frozen like a photograph—one that would fit right in at the prayer-grotto shrine below the house.

"One night won't hurt, Dad," Landon chimes in.

The air is heavy with tension, and then Pearson releases her shoulder. He holds his hand out to her and when she takes it, he tugs her to her feet and against him, hard and fast.

"One night won't hurt!" he cries out jovially, then adds, "We'll see if he survives the night."

"What's up with them?" I ask Celeste as I take my seat. I throw an arm over the top rail of her chair and lean back on the rear legs of my own to watch as Lily placates Pearson. Even though I feel on edge and confused, I can't let Pearson or Landon know that I'm freaked the fuck out. I feel like they would enjoy that too much, and I won't give them the pleasure.

"Ken?" she asks in a low voice, and I remember with not a little chagrin that Landon had spilled the beans about our condition.

"The one and only," I say with a wink.

"You weren't here for her little affirmative-action joke. Don't feel too bad for her." Celeste shoots a nasty look down the table, where Lily is holding a sandwich in front of Shalimar, then looks back at me. "Was that a kid who dove under the table to play with the dog? I don't think it was Empress or Solomon."

I drop my chair back onto all four legs. The DID beans have not only been spilled but served with a side of Way Too Much Personal Info. I'd never really spoken with anyone about the DID, never talked about it with anyone except shrinks and public defenders and the judge.

"It was Keke," I say instead of telling her to mind her damn business. "She loves dogs."

"Do you?" she asks.

"No. I mean . . ." I honestly don't know what I like. I'd thought that painting, partying, and punk were the width and breadth of my personality, and once those things lost their availability and appeal, it was reasonable to assume that I hated everything. But I haven't been asked in so long, or even asked myself, that now I'm caught up short. "I don't dislike animals. Shalimar had some pretty soft ears, so he's cool."

When I lean back in my seat, I find John watching us. He gives me a repentant dip of his head. "Sorry I couldn't bring you back."

He gestures toward the sleet peppering the glass windows.

"Not your fault," I say. "I should have taken you up on the offer yesterday and never stepped off of the ferry."

"Can't disagree with you there," he says. "Feels a bit sinister in here with this weather. Maybe I'll finally get to meet Grace."

"Why did you arrive a day early?" One of the other men at the table leans forward to get my attention, face screwed up. "You were told to come to the meeting point today."

Was I, now?

"I get dates mixed up all the time. That's probably what happened."

Celeste clears her throat. "She didn't swim here. John showed up to pick her up, meaning she was expected. Guess you all weren't as clear as you thought."

The man looks at John. "Yes. How do you explain that, Captain John?"

John looks around the table, and a hint of the sneer that'd been in his tone every time he'd mentioned the trust tugs at his mouth. "Sure, Gary. I got a text message from Pearson saying to pick up the new caretaker a day early. I can show it to you. Didn't quite make sense, but wouldn't be the first time you all had made a rude request of me."

Everyone looks at Pearson, who still wears the same smug grin, though the crow's feet around his eyes deepen. "I didn't send a text."

Lightning crashes and Shalimar barks in terror, shimmies out of Lily's grip, and runs out of the room. When she stands to chase after him, Pearson raises his hand, staying her without even a touch. She doesn't flinch, but she does sit back down, her eyes on the door and her hands limp in her lap.

"You didn't happen to use my phone to text John yesterday, did you darling?"

"Of course not." She laughs as if it's the silliest thing she's ever heard. "I don't concern myself with what the trust does. That's not my business. You made it clear that it isn't."

Pearson transfers his calmly disquieting gaze to Landon, who scoffs.

"Come on, Dad. Why the hell would I invite my weird, violent ex? She's the last person I wanted to run into here, or anywhere for that matter." He shoots me a dirty look. "I don't know how much clearer I can make this—I don't want her in this house or on this island. You decided that."

Celeste tugs me closer to her side, chair and all, the screech of wood on stone punctuating his statement. The flush on his cheeks deepens, but he doesn't look our way.

I shrug. "No need to solve this mystery. Once the storm dies down, I'll be out of everyone's way."

I think of what I'll do then. Check into a hostel? Sign up for that couch-surfing website if it still exists?

I should have thought of these things when I first woke up on the dock, fuzzy brain or not, but this job had been presented as our only option. It's not though. We don't have to end up on the street. I'm a resourceful bitch, even if I lack other talents.

Pearson lifts a hand magnanimously. "None of us are leaving until tomorrow. If we make it, that is. After all, this is Daybreak Island and the Goblin King—the Storm King—is hurling everything he's got at us. How fortuitous."

I smirk at him. "I already survived my first night, and the goblins spared me. Godspeed to the rest of you suckers."

Pearson chuckles. "Well, the goblins are the ones who need to worry when the Kavanaughs are in residence. That said, we have no evidence that you actually stayed here due to the mix-up. Your official first night will be tonight."

His tone raises my inner alarm bells. It's laced with the kind of smug sadism that men lapse into when they think they have you cornered. And he does. I can't leave this place of my own accord, which makes me effectively trapped.

An impulse blooms in me: Fight. Run.

(*"Careful."*) That whisper in my mind again.

I press my heels into my boots, forcing myself not to bolt out of my seat. Heat rushes to my face. My heart is pounding in my ears and my fists clench at my sides. "Fine. I'll stay, but don't forget that you have to survive the night too."

A hacking, ugly cough cuts through my rage. The woman next to me is hacking up a lung with no attempt to cover her mouth, making it rain on the food sitting on the table. I make sure my mask is on correctly, bending the metal nosepiece more firmly. Everyone else except Celeste just sits there like they're the ones who just woke up during a pandemic.

Her friend leans closer to her, patting her on the back.

"Sorry, I have that weird cold that's going around," she says once she collects herself. "Sorry for interrupting. It won't happen again."

Another boom of thunder, one so loud and rattling that it feels like it's coming from within the castle itself, crashes around us. The lights flare and then dim as the noise moves away from us; they don't blink out so much as fade, leaving the impromptu lunch party in a pitch-black dining room.

My heart starts to race but before I can panic, Celeste's hand slides around mine, and then a bright light illuminates her face from below her cell phone.

"We'll go check on the generator, and the dog," she says, dragging me up from my chair.

"My last duty as caretaker," I say with a salute, but no one laughs. Their silence follows us out into the hallway.

Chapter 26
Solomon

Co-consciousness drags me from the castle, where Keke and Empress are barricaded in their room. The door's locked from the inside, and an armoire is pressed against the window, an illusion of security when I have no idea what they're being protected from.

In the outer world, Ken is walking with Celeste, who is holding our hand again, and shining a camera flashlight with the other as we enter into Grace's studio.

"I don't know what Pearson wants from me, but it can't be good," Ken says, then her inward attention snaps to me.

(*"Where have you been? Why was Keke fronting alone?"*)

"She's supposed to be unable to front without supervision. I couldn't go co-con, so I assumed she was with you, and I was right."

("She almost got hurt and—")

"Since when do you care about Keke? Or any of us? You seem to be perfectly content on your little lover's jaunt while I'm dealing with real issues on the inside."

("What issues could you have in your safe little world? I didn't ask to be here, and now I'm stuck with Pearson, Landon, and their friends who all treated me like a freakshow. I'm the one who has to figure out how to get us out of here. Spare me about how hard things are in your cushy castle.")

"You are so . . . selfish, Ken." The words slip out before I can swallow them. "It's always about how you feel and what's unfair to you. You don't care about Keke. You don't care about anyone but yourself."

She flinches, and I should feel good that I've finally given her a taste of her own medicine, but instead I feel hollow. I've never talked to her like this, and it wasn't worth it. Nothing is resolved, I'm still angry, and now I can't even ask her the things I need to, like "Have you by chance gained entry to the inner world and been picking off headmates?"

"I apologize," I say. "I shouldn't have snapped at you."

When she replies, her tone is petulant but shaky,

like it always is when she's at the summit of the self-pity slip-n-slide and about to hurl herself down it.

(*"No need to apologize. I prefer knowing where I stand with you."*)

"You arguing in there?" Celeste asks her, releasing our hand to tap at her own head. "Cause I didn't say anything and you look pissed."

"Solomon," Ken says, startling me. "He's just . . ."

She makes a growling sound and I feel how angry she is, how close to the edge. I'm so tired that I had jumped to defense instead of realizing Ken is barely keeping it together herself.

"I thought you two were close. Special friends or whatever," Celeste probes. She drops on her hands and knees to look under a desk, making her lack of interest a bit too overt. How does she know anything about me, and how close Ken and I are? Had Empress told her about us?

Ken is surprised, too, but her anger overrides everything else now that she's found someplace to vent it.

"Special, my ass. He acts like he supports me, but all he does is judge. Like everyone else." She scuffs her boot on the carpet protecting the hardwood floor. "He knows everything about me and . . . I wish he didn't. You know how much it sucks for someone to know you inside out and confirm that you suck?"

Celeste makes a thoughtful noise. "Sounds like you're talking about an ex."

"It's not like that," Ken says, too quickly for my liking.

"A brother, then?"

"Fuck no. You probably can't understand this, but I used to think he was part of me and not a part of me, even if that doesn't make sense. This aspect of myself that I could trust. But he's not. He's his own pedantic person, but that's not even what bothers me. It's that he pretends to care about me when his actual concern is keeping me in line so our headmates can be comfortable. Fuck how I feel, you know?"

I don't say anything, even though I want to protest this misinterpretation of things. If she spoke to the others, she'd know that they feel the opposite, that I always take her side. But I stay quiet. She knows I'm listening, but this is something she'd never say directly to me without Celeste as a buffer.

"That's tough," Celeste replies with surprising warmth in her tone. "But maybe he was just doing what he knows how to do to stay safe, how you're doing what you know how to do to stay safe. That's how most of us end up hurting people we care about without ever meaning to."

Ken laughs ruefully. "I've meant harm and I've acted on it. That's the problem."

Celeste continues her search around the room but glances at us to let Ken know she's listening.

"I guess some people see their headmates—that's what we call each other—as family," Ken says, filling the silence. She isn't looking for anything, because she's deep in thought. "With our system it's more like a group of people who know how to work together, and then me, the asshole shitting the place up."

Celeste laughs. "Did it come natural, their working together? I'm guessing it wasn't always easy, because it isn't for anyone. Divorce rate wouldn't be so high if it were easy to communicate."

Ken sighs, the exhalation soft with embarrassment. "They did therapy to figure it out. I rip van winkled myself because that was better for everyone."

"Interesting," Celeste says, looking behind a bookshelf.

Ken swings our head toward her, searching for sign of judgment. "Are you gonna say I'm just a punk who ran away because I was scared or something? Because that's not what happened. They wanted me gone."

Celeste looks into our eyes, her gaze still flinty but imbued with a softening earnestness. "I was just thinking . . . assholes are made for shitting, aren't they?"

"That's what you were thinking?" Ken asks, her words riding on a gasp of incredulous laughter. It cascades over me—it's been so long since I've felt this kind of unguarded pleasure from her.

"It's true though," Celeste continues. "What's so bad about an asshole, Nash? It's part of the digestive system and plays its part. Keeps things going smoothly. You know what happens to a person when their asshole malfunctions, when the shit just gets stuck all up in there? It's not good. Now, it's not good when the shit is flying everywhere either. Think about it: well-functioning assholes are what make the world go round."

Ken presses her lips together trying to hide her grin of pleasure—the one that lifts up more on the right side of our face that means she's happy. "If I'd known all I had to do was bring up butt stuff to get you talking, I would have done it earlier."

"Sorry to interrupt your flirting, but where are we going?" I ask. While I appreciate her good mood, I'd spent most of my existence supporting her, and I can only take so much of her little crush when I'm right here.

(*"If you hadn't ditched me, you'd know."*)

There's just enough sulkiness in this response to please me. She's talking to me again, and she wasn't happy that I'd left her.

"I didn't ditch you. I told you I wasn't able to go co-con."

(*"Pearson's wife's dog got loose, so we came to find it. Good excuse to get away from the weirdo fest at the table,"*) she says, talking around my question.

There's another sound from down the hall, and Ken takes off running after it like a child excitedly playing hide-and-seek who's just found her quarry. She gets to the tower door and pulls it open, releasing a blast of cold, humid air.

"Shalimar! There you are," she says, stepping in to scoop up the shivering dog from the stairs. I expect Keke to come bounding forward, but she doesn't. For the first time in years, she's completely silent even though we're this close to a dog.

Ken holds the dog awkwardly. (*"Are you scared of dogs?"*) she asks, feeling my unease.

"No."

(*"Did you know I like them?"*) The question is so free of hostility, so open and casual like our connection had been before, that it startles my drifting attention back to her.

"Yes. You used to walk Miss Pamela's shih tzu for extra money in high school since our parents wouldn't let you have one."

(*"Oh, right. I'd forgotten that. I got it a little spike collar and everything."*)

The wind stops suddenly, but the air around us is icy, colder than it had been a moment before.

Ken pauses, her gaze drifting to the stairs, where she'd spaced out earlier. I can feel her trying to contain a reaction. Not exactly fear, but a mix of concern, deep curiosity, and frustration.

"What is it?" I ask. *"The same thing happened earlier. What are you afraid of?"*

(*"You won't believe me,"*) she scoffs. (*"I barely believe this shit."*)

"I've disagreed with you, and scolded you, but I've never called you a liar. Despite what you told Celeste, I've always been right here by your side. Even when you didn't want me there."

(*"That doesn't mean you'll stay there. If you were smart, you wouldn't."*)

The urge to snap at her again rises; instead, I pay her the courtesy of doing what I'm asking of her. I tell her the truth. *"I've waited six years for you, Ken. I'm not going anywhere."*

Warmth suffuses me, riding on a sensation I'd once

taken for granted: Ken's acceptance of what I've offered her, with no argument and no resistance.

(*"There's a lady in white. I saw her before, the first time we went into the tower. She seemed pissed off at me, and she kept yelling about a promise."*)

"A lady in white, like a ghost?"

(*"Yup."*)

Our body tenses as if she's bracing for something—my disbelief.

"*I can't see anything, but I felt the wind last night. I think it would be more unbelievable if this place wasn't haunted.*"

I feel our mouth curve up.

"*You asked me about promises before we went into the tower though. On the ferry.*"

She perks up, but then groans a little. (*"Right. About that. I have to tell you something else. Don't get mad about it."*)

"*What did you do?*"

(*"I didn't do anything!"*) She sighs, and then answers like I'm forcibly tugging the truth from her. (*"When we were pulling up to the island, someone screamed in my head that we'd made a promise. But I don't know who it was, and they wouldn't explain further."*)

Now this is a little harder for me to believe. I'd been there, and I hadn't heard a thing.

278 . ALYSSA COLE

"Could you not tell who it was or you didn't know them at all?"

("I don't think I knew them. Whoever it was felt chaotic and angry. They made me want to jump off the ferry and into the river.")

It could have been one of the headmates trying to disguise themselves, but that's less likely than a more disturbing possibility: a new headmate, who just so happened to emerge when Ken awoke from dormancy and others have started disappearing. When we'd shown up to this cursed island. I would know if a head-mate had unlocked their door—I've always known in the past, even when I wasn't quite aware of what I was knowing.

"Why didn't you tell me when I asked what was wrong?"

("Because I'd just woken up and didn't want every-one to immediately think I was more of a mess than when I'd gone to sleep,") she snaps.

This makes no sense, which is why I believe her. Ken isn't logical. Holding important information close to her chest and straight-up pretending something hadn't happened until it showed up to screw us over were both trademarks of the system's Ken Era.

I'm sure she knows this, which is why she continues on the defensive.

(*"And you're one to talk. You've been acting shady since I woke up—before you jump up my ass, what are you keeping from me?"*)

I'm not sure how to tell her the truth—that members of our system have been disappearing one by one, and that she's the number-one suspect. My fear of her reaction aside, whether she's guilty or not, there's another possibility. Could she be making this up to throw me off of her trail? To get me to reveal what I know?

How could she see things I hadn't seen or hear things I hadn't heard?

(*"Well?"*)

I offer her up something other than my suspicion of her; unfortunately, there are a few things to choose from. *"There have been changes in the inner world. Usually there's nothing outside the window but the void, but now a landscape is . . . painting itself into existence. It's being built up in layers and it looks like Kavanaugh Island on the outside too."*

(*"What in the hell? I meant were you hiding something about Della, but this is a hundred times more concerning. Is there carbon monoxide in the inner world and can it leak? Because what do you mean 'painting itself'?"*)

I sigh and share my memory of what I'd seen with her; sharing with her is too easy, from force of habit, and I have to try hard to make sure nothing else bleeds into the mental snapshots.

(*"Doesn't this style look familiar?"*) she asks.

Before I can answer, I sense distress from the inner world and turn toward it.

"I'll be right back."

She calls after me, but I'm in our kitchen; drawers have fallen out, spilling utensils, and glasses and plates have been shaken from cabinets onto the floor. A low rumble of thunder rattles the glass shards and metal against each other.

I catch a blur of motion; a figure running through the hallway ahead of me.

"Wait!" I call out, pounding after what is possibly a newly conscious headmate, one either freed from a locked room or created due to our recent stress. One who might harm us, either accidentally or on purpose. "Who are you?"

It's when the figure turns to head up the stairs that I'm able to take in more details: a woman in a white gown and red scarf.

A memory that isn't mine comes to me: a woman standing in the candlelit tower, a writhing mass of angry brushstrokes where her face should be, yelling, "You promised!"

Another memory, an older one, given the faded

nature of it, of a woman in white holding our hand and leading us up a set of spiral stairs. "Quiet and careful," she says, her voice kind and her hand cold.

By the time I start up the stairs, the woman has reached the second-floor landing, turning left toward Keke and Empress's room.

"Stop!" Fear blots out everything but my need to get to the girls.

The landing is empty when I reach it, and the few seconds it takes me to get to their room and unlock the door are harrowing, my heart pounding and my gut convinced that this stranger has taken them too.

I find both of them sleeping soundly on the bottom bunk as I burst into the room, and a quick scan of the room doesn't doesn't reveal any intruder. I lock the door with shaky hands and then collapse on the floor next to the bed. My panic slowly dissipates but not the sickness twisting my belly. The girls were safe, but not because of anything I'd done.

A hand brushes my neck and I jump, turning to see Keke's gap-toothed smile as she rests her head on the edge of the bed.

"Adult problems?" she asks sleepily.

I tilt my head to the side so that my cheek touches her warm, grubby little hand.

"Adult problems," I say on a sigh.

She pats my cheek. "It will be okay. Or maybe not."

Not exactly reassuring, but accurate.

"Keke, you haven't seen anyone in here, have you? Someone you haven't met before?" I think of that slight possibility that Ken had gotten in. "Or anyone who shouldn't be in the castle?"

"No," she says, already slipping back into sleep. A moment later her soft snores fill the air.

Ken had encountered a woman in white who yelled at her, and I'd just seen the same in here, though she'd been silent.

She'd been in the tower both times Ken had seen her in the outer world, and the last I'd seen her she'd been running in the direction of the tower in here. Could she be what's tormenting Rapunzel and making them scream the castle down? Could she *be* Rapunzel?

I stand, swaying on my feet, my body heavy from dread and fatigue. I need to rest, but sleep isn't an option. Ken needs me, and more than that, I'm terrified of what changes will reshape our inner world if I close my eyes for too long.

Chapter 27

Ken

I always get accused of running away from my problems, but Solomon sure does love to make a convenient exit, stage the inner world, when it's time to talk about something important.

I smile a little as I think about the strain in his voice when he'd said, "I've waited six years for you." The words have been replaying in my head, drowning out ugly thoughts that try to surface.

Shalimar is resting on one hand, so I tuck the index finger of the other into my pocket and let the sharp corner of the folded note I found in my boot poke me. "You've been missed" it says, which hadn't made sense until I heard his anguish. It's fucked up how good this makes me feel, but it's kinda like when I pinch myself;

sometimes pain is necessary for clarity. And sometimes the ugly sting of it—even if it belongs to someone else—is its own kind of deep pleasure, one that can't be attained through anything positive or beautiful.

I think of the painting downstairs, of the autumn landscape being ravaged by the storm outside. If an autumnal tree doesn't know that it will awaken in spring, it needs to know that its death has brought despair as well as delight. Solomon's words make me feel like a vermillion leaf in winter, clinging to a branch with the knowledge that one person is inspired by my beauty.

I'll never tell him this of course, but maybe if we figure out what the fuck is going on, I'll give him a hint one day.

When Celeste and I get back to the first floor, we follow the dim glow coming from the parlor, where everyone has drifted from the dining room. Candles have appeared from some storage place I hadn't had time to find, but the light they give off doesn't feel comforting or even very illuminating. Dark shadows are thrown every which way, exerting their dominance over the flames that flicker in the wind that slips in through cracks in the windows and doors.

It takes me a moment to realize that the other women have changed clothing as well as location while we were gone. They've thrown on sack-like white linen dresses, though it's well after Labor Day. Paired with the setting and lack of electricity, it's as if we've stepped back in time, to a period I definitely *don't* want to be in.

"What in the sister wives? I don't care what I might have said in the past, there's no way in hell I'm wearing one of those, even if it's a job requirement."

"Chalamet!" Lily snatches the dog roughly from my arms, snuggling him against her stomach. "These dresses are from Target. Modesty is in right now."

She looks over my outfit and doesn't hurl the barb I know is sitting on the tip of her tongue. I guess that's as close to a thank-you as I'll get for finding her pooch.

Pearson steps away from a huddle with his two buddies and turns his attention toward me and Celeste, his gaze sharpening on the dog even as he fakes a smile of relief. "Oh, you found it. Good. Great! Maybe he can participate in the festivities too. He's a bit small, but even small dogs like this were once used for hunting."

"Hunting?" I ask.

"Festivities?" Celeste's question lands at the same time as mine, and it's the one that gets answered.

The older guy with more gray at his temples looks at her. "Landon is becoming a full member of the Kavanaugh trust."

"There are traditions to be upheld," the other

man, Gary, says. "The kind that made this country what it was."

"Traditions are cool," I say. Contrary to what everyone thinks, I don't always say what I'm thinking—not in situations like this, where there's a weird charge in the air that I'm not sure I can contain if I accidentally set it off. "I like turkey on Thanksgiving."

"This tradition includes you, Ken," Pearson adds.

(*"Ken."*) Solomon is back, and I nod as Pearson continues, though I'm not listening to him.

"Miss me?" I ask him, allowing myself the comfort of his familiar presence.

(*"Always. More pressing issue—I saw the ghost."*)

"Nice. Let's start a club."

(*"I saw her in our inner world."*)

I lean against a wall and cross my arms, giving Pearson my best "paying attention" face while my brain tries to wrap itself around what Solomon's telling me. I don't need any other weird-ass complications to this situation, and this one is pushing credulity even though I'm the one who told him about the ghost to begin with.

"You saw her . . . in there?"

(*"I felt distress and thought Keke and Empress were in danger, but when I went back inside I saw someone running. It was a woman in a white dress."*)

My gaze jumps from Lily to Diana to Maria, all three bustling around in dresses that look like fast-fashion versions of the one the ghost had been sporting.

"*Jesus.*"

Solomon is speaking haltingly, as if his thoughts keep getting tangled up in the multiple layers of fuckery we're currently picking our way through. (*"I wonder . . . it sounds absurd, but do you think that the ghost could have somehow . . . crossed over, into the inner world? The castles are the same."*)

"Fair warning, this is the point where I fucking lose it. I'm already dealing with all kinds of shit and now there's a ghost in our brain? Give me a second." I take a couple of deep breaths, like Mesmer had done this morning. *"I mean, everything is possible, but ghosts being able to stroll into the system's home is too close to the idea that you guys are demons and I need an exorcist instead of a shrink."*

(*"I feel the same way, but I don't know how else to explain it. If the ghost you saw is Grace Kavanaugh and she's been haunting her castle for a hundred years, what would stop her from being as confused as we are?"*)

"And then there's the painting," I say. "You said that someone started painting Kavanaugh Island onto the void and Grace's paintings of the island are all over *this house. She's an artist. But then that would mean a goddamned ghost is having a paint and sip party in our brain, and I'm not willing to accept that."*

My heart is beating fast and even though this situation is ridiculous as hell, it's scarier than the more tangible threats of homelessness and whatever Pearson and Co. are up to. One of the reasons I'd reacted so badly when I realized I had DID is that any illusion I'd had of control over even my own mind was stripped away. If this job has accidentally led to spirit possession, I'm really gonna have to figure out a way to beat Della's ass when next I see her.

"The ceremony doesn't officially start until tonight, but it's already dark out. We can start with the story." Pearson's voice interrupts. He's using his politician voice now, talking like he expects everyone to shut up and listen, and they do.

(*"I'll go check on Keke and Empress again."*)

"Why aren't Mesmer and Lurk with them?"

Solomon recedes without answering.

Pearson moves solemnly through the room, stroking the grooves in the wainscoting and the curve of a high-backed chair before turning his gaze toward his captive audience. "Simon Kavanaugh, my ancestor, comes from a background which has many a tradition of its own. Once he bought this island, he became interested in, or obsessed with, the Dutch goblin mythos that pervaded the region. In the Celtic traditions the fae are often beautiful and invulnerable, and humans are at their mercy. But goblin stories are different. They're nasty, greedy, ugly things, always trying to sneak into human society through cracks and crevices to steal and sully." He glances at me, his pupils dilated so that, for a second, his eyes seem completely black. "And that struck him as a wonderful parallel of what he was seeing around him in the world. Men obsessed with sex and degradation, and women who through their own moral weaknesses allowed those men to debase them. And a good bit of the old folklore was about how you should deal with goblins and their vice. You could seal up the cracks to prevent them from getting in, but that's an almost impossible task. Or you could deal with them harshly to make an example of them. They could be broken and domesticated—even made into wives if they were females—or they could be rounded up and killed."

He laughs as if he's told a joke, and I understand that he has. I remember how Landon had grabbed me earlier, how he'd called me old and thought it was an insult even though I'm lucky to still be alive. I see now where that disturbing smirk he'd worn had come from. It's inherited.

"And Simon, well, he devoted his life to ridding American society of its goblins. He took the moral of the story and transposed it onto the modern filth his society was dealing with. And now I do the same, and hopefully my Landon will also follow in our footsteps."

"Are you serious?" I'd wanted to keep a low profile, but the ridiculous, monotonous mix of family history and fairy tale feels charged, like a spell that only works if everyone sits silently like good little minions. "I can't believe you brought me here for this shit. You can run your goblin LARP without tricking people into jobs. If you wanted to fuck with me for what I did to you, okay, you've succeeded. Now I'm going to go back to the apartment until morning, like Landon suggested."

"No, you should stay. You're the perfect participant for the ceremony." Landon stands and strides over to me, glaring at me with bloodshot eyes. "You're exactly the kind of mouthy whore who—"

My hands are on his tie, my fingers carefully adjusting the knot so that it brushes his Adam's apple.

"Watch what you say," I grit out in a tone starched crisp enough to cut.

Solomon. Co-fronting. His presence is suddenly all around mine, his fury vivid and barely contained, flashing like sirens in my mind's eye.

He's left the rest unspoken.

To her.

Watch what you say to her.

Landon grins, trying to egg me on.

"Let's go, Solomon. Leave them to their games and we'll wait it out until morning." The fact that I'm the voice of reason here might be more worrisome than everything else combined.

Our hands grip Landon's tie for a long moment, and then drop loosely to our sides. Landon hesitates, leaning forward like he'll grab me, but his father cuts in.

"Yes, you should go to the apartment. Take your special friend with you."

When I look his way, Pearson gives me a dismissive flick of the head, meaning I've finally crossed the invisible line in the sand to make him stop trying to include me in this shit. Great.

I nod, feeling everyone's eyes on me as I walk out, my footsteps shadowed by Celeste's.

"Should we go too?" Diana asks.

"No. Our celebration will continue as planned."

"But the storm—"

"The storm changes nothing," Pearson says, his tone sulky.

Then the door closes behind me.

"**I don't** get what kind of tradition requires this weirdness." The apartment that had seemed like a nice enough place to crash, minus the ghost, now feels tainted by Landon and his father's presence.

"Rich people worship all kinds of things," Celeste says. "'Tradition' is just the word they use to make it sound good."

I'm trembling slightly, my nerves shot and my thoughts an overwhelming cacophony despite the lack of input from my headmates. I busy myself with checking that the windows and doors are locked and moving the dresser back in front of the interior door. I need a distraction, any kind of distraction, and there's no booze, tobacco, or drugs to be had. I turn to Celeste, whose hand had been wrapped around mine for a good portion of the night. "So are we just going to sleep now? It's still the afternoon."

She stands by the couch, rubbing at the spot between her brows with her eyes squeezed shut. "I need a nap. Didn't get much sleep last night."

I stand next to the bed, nervous energy that needs to be alleviated coursing through me. I need something to throw myself into and blot out all the troubling questions that coming to this island has raised, questions that I won't be able to ignore and surely won't like the answers to.

"That couch will jack your back up, trust me. You can sleep in my bed. With me," I say. I smooth my hair down with the palm of my hand, wondering if my game was always this bad, then lift a shoulder. "Or we don't have to sleep at all."

Solomon sighs.

Celeste looks at me for a long moment, gaze warm as it runs over my body like a fleece glove. Then she shakes her head.

"I'm good with the couch," she says, turning and dropping onto the seat. "Softer than a lot of places I've slept, and won't lead to any confusion."

"Sure. Right," I say as I pull off my hoodie, then put it back on, and then slide onto the top sheet fully clothed.

(*This is somehow more offensive than you trying to get laid while I'm standing right here,*") Solomon says. (*"At least take off your boots!"*)

My cheeks are flaming from her rejection, but the urge to say something else overrides my plan to perhaps turn into dust before I have to speak to her again.

"Sorry, Celeste," I say, looking at the top of her cap peeking over the couch. "Everything is just kind of jumbled. In my head and outside of it. Sex with a stranger is an easy distraction. I shouldn't have propositioned you."

Solomon makes a "humph" kind of noise, but I can feel his approval.

"It's all good," she says in her gruff but affable tone. "I wasn't offended. And my saying no was a compliment."

I snort-scoff, but the smile on my lips as I drift into sleep is real. I have no idea what the fuck she means by that, but I understand it on some level, and for some reason that distance between us is more comforting than having her in my bed. The way Solomon stays close behind me is a different kind of comfort, like I'm sandwiched between something new that might just be friendship and an old friendship that's definitely something more.

Long minutes go by where I try to ignore the thoughts swirling in my head about Landon and Pearson and what we're doing on this damn island, but I'm too keyed up. I make a grunt of frustration and roll onto my stomach, digging into my pocket as I tug out the pamphlet I'd found and flip on my phone's flashlight.

"Ken?" Celeste calls out.

"Yeah?"

"Never mind. Try to get some rest. It might be a long night."

Chapter 28

October 25, 1918

*I've been told by Father in his latest letter that
the tower room is a perfectly fine place to recover,
with beautiful views and a bracing breeze. The
door is locked for my safety, and the nurses have
been informed not to indulge my paranoia so that
I might better recover.*

*As to Simon's behavior: I'm being hysterical.
Apparently, once you've married a man, you must
accept every aspect of him while shoving down all
the parts of yourself that cause him the slightest
discomfort. I am full to bursting, with all of my
vices and all of his. Now I understand how he's*

been so successful at rooting it out in others—his own wickedness acts as a dowsing rod.

The money that built this castle came from harassing and jailing women who've done no worse than me. Why didn't I think I'd be made to pay for my pleasure too?

Sometimes he brings them here. Women. He says it isn't true, and that the illness has left me mad, but I've heard . . . I can't even bear to describe it.

I must write to Lottie again. Warn her. In my last letter I begged her for help. I need to tell her all is well, and to stop thinking of me. No, that won't work. I will curse her and rebuke her—whatever it takes to make her never think fondly of me, or this wicked castle, again.

Simon and his friends are laughing, and singing, and the violence pants hungrily in the lulls of their amusement.

I wish I were mad but I am not.

They are up at all hours of the night, moving through the trees, and sometimes their rustling is interrupted by a scream.

Chapter 29

Ken

S leet scours over brick and stone, like someone's dropped us into a Slushee machine. The strange song that's been tugging at my frontal lobe since I woke up fades as if someone had just hummed it into my ear. Neither of those sounds are what woke me; it's the screaming. A wail that's not inside my head this time and is coming from outside the door of the apartme— Oh shit.

Shit, shit, shit.

I sit up in the freezing darkness, goose bumps crawling along the bare flesh of my arms and my hands pressing into dusty, gritty ground instead of the firm give of the mattress.

This isn't the apartment.

Where am I?

Somewhere pitch-black and musty.

I can't see.

Fuckery is my sweet spot, but only when I can see it coming. In the dark, I'm just a punk who wants a grown-up to turn on the light.

A whimper crawls up my throat and I swallow it. The smell of decay and soot and something else fills my nose and mouth, caught in my chattering teeth like gamey meat. There's a taste to the scent that bats a memory precariously close to the edge of some inner shelf, like a cat threatening to break something fragile and irreparable.

(*"Where are we?"*) Solomon interrupts, his terse voice driving away the taunting cat of recall. (*"How did we get here?"*)

"You're the sleepwalker, you tell me," I snap, moving slowly so that I don't start flailing and scrabbling around trying to figure out the answer to his question. All it takes is one false move to descend into real panic, especially with the adrenaline already pumping in my system, like I'd been in a nightmare and then woken up into one. I need to stay calm.

I dust off my hands and they stick together instead of sliding apart. Gummy, like when I'd come out of a painting fugue state with only the art, flashes of working memory, and the mess I'd made as evidence that I'd had anything to do with the finished product at all.

(*"I walk at night, and I know where I'm going when I do. You were taking an afternoon nap, and so was I."*) His pause is a Looney Tunes anvil waiting to drop, and I really hope that I'm the Road Runner and not the coyote.

The darkness contracts somehow, and my heart thuds heavily against my rib cage. Sweat pops up at my brow, but I don't want to touch my face with an unknown substance on my hands.

"You didn't bring us here?" I move around cautiously, restraining myself from launching into a blind run when my hand slips along a crumbling ledge. Edge. It could be a cliff in this total darkness, but is more likely a step.

I try not to scream. Darkness can't hurt me, I remind myself.

(*"Darkness keeps you safe, darling,"*) a voice whispers in my mind.

The commotion nearby is getting louder.

Bat, bat goes the cat of memory.

Whispers in the cold, penny-dank darkness, hiding from the ugly laughter. But this noise is different. Someone is crying, not laughing.

(*"Quiet and careful,"*) the voice whispers.

Solomon's presence pushes up on me, his worry chafing me. (*"Ken, if you've done something, either in the inner world or the outer, you need to tell me. We can figure it out, but we can't keep secrets anymore.")*

I'm already scared, and the unspoken sentiment behind his tone is jarring—he isn't just talking about whatever is happening right this moment.

"I'm not keeping any secrets. I already came clean about what I was hiding, unlike you. You told me you would always be by my side; now here you are insinuating . . . I don't even know what you think I've done." My focus is on him, but the stench in the room is filling my nose, affecting even my usually cast-iron stomach.

His frustration butts up against me, but I have nothing to tell him. If this motherfucker wants to accuse me of something, he should just come out with it instead of acting like he's trying to help me.

("This smell. Please tell me you didn't—")

A door swings open and I jerk my gaze down, away from the sudden intrusion of light. Now I see what the stickiness is, know why the smell is familiar.

Blood.

I'm in the tower instead of the apartment, and I'm covered in blood. The white tank top I'd been wearing under my Henley is covered in red gore, and so are my hands.

This isn't the first time I've come to covered in blood, but it's the first time that I don't remember why.

Chapter 30

Ken

I sit on the floor of the tower entrance, shivering like a rat whose niche has just been exposed, as the people lining the hallway outside the door look down at me. The two women—Diana? Maria?—stare in confusion and horror. The two men I don't know watch me with open contempt. John looks at me sadly, while Landon glares with hatred burning in his eyes. Lily is kneeling down keening over something on the floor—someone.

Pearson.

Pearson, a bloody mess, but not from a punch in the nose. No. He's been beaten, severely, and what I can see of his head is a caved in mess, the gore so hyper-real I can't take it in. This is more than a simple act of violence; it took strength, stamina, and determination.

And the weapon used to do it?

A candlestick that's rolled against the baseboard, leaving fine red lines on the beige carpet that mark its path.

Solomon's voice is brittle when he says, (*"That candlestick surely has your fingerprints all over it."*)

Everything falls into place after that brief sweep of the hallway. Someone invited me here. A big scene was made about how Pearson had forgiven me for my past attack. And now he's dead and I'm covered in blood.

I would remember if I did this; I remember all my mistakes in vivid detail. It's the good things I forget.

I push myself to my feet—my body aches and my clothes are damp from sweat and blood. I'm an icicle except for my feet, because despite forgetting my hoodie and coat, I'm wearing my boots. I refrain from checking the soles to see if there's brain matter in the treads.

"I didn't do it."

That's all I can manage. If I have to ask him to believe me—if I have to plead my case . . .

Why did I ever wake up? The unfairness of it all weighs me down, adding to the burden of their accusatory stares.

(*"I believe you,"*) he says, and though it's what I wanted to hear, I scoff.

"Sure, that's why you asked what I'd done."

("I asked and you answered. I have a choice, and I choose to believe you. We have other issues right now; stop trying to argue with me because you're scared.")

"If I go to jail again, you do, too, and we won't get a slap on the wrist this time." I try to snark, but it comes out sounding hopeless.

("We aren't going to jail.")

Solomon doesn't lie—I'm not sure he always tells the whole truth, but this motherfucker doesn't lie. His reassurance puts a little steel in my spine because, like he said, all evidence is pointing at me right now, and whatever happens next isn't going to be easy.

"What happened to him?" I ask aloud through chattering teeth.

"What do you mean 'what happened?'!" Landon yells, lunging toward me. If he'd wanted to scare me earlier, now he's ready to beat my ass for real. John holds him back—I was right about the Greatest Generation spunk, because he holds Landon firm until he stops trying to extricate himself. "You killed my father! He tried to help you, and this is what you fucking do?"

His mottled face is contorted by anger and grief—snot, tears, and saliva trickling along the lines bracketing his mouth. His mother died here, and now his father has, too, but this time it wasn't an accident.

"I didn't," I say, my mouth twitching. "I wouldn't."

"Wouldn't you?" Lily asks, her cheeks glistening with tears but not swarming with them like Landon's. "You threatened him when he said you had to stay."

I roll my eyes, not at her but at the fact that I'd taken Pearson's bait when I should've kept my mouth shut. "I didn't threaten him. Besides, I would be crazy to think I could get away with something like this."

I gesture toward Pearson, and this time when I look at him I take in every detail. This is a human being, one I'd interacted with, whose life had affected mine for the worse. Now that life has been ended in sickening violence. Vomit surges thick up my throat, and I turn toward the corner of the hallway, retching up whatever the others had eaten earlier. A hand comes to rest on my back, but I can't move from this helpless hunch until my stomach is empty, and then some. I turn expecting to see Celeste, but it's John, eyes red-rimmed and concerned.

"You are though," Landon says. "You are crazy."

"I think we should cover him up and go downstairs," John says, putting a bit of the tourist-herding bass in his voice. "We can call the police on the CB."

Landon's sobs echo through the hall, and I understand why. Calling the police makes it real. I feel for him, but that makes it real for me, too, because I'm definitely the prime suspect.

Shit.

"Solomon?"

(*"I'm here."*)

"Tell the others I didn't do it." My inner voice sounds small and pathetic, but I need them to understand. They've been so quiet since earlier, like I'd scared them off again. *"Make sure Keke knows I didn't."*

(*"I will."*)

Puking has cleared my head, and my thoughts start to sharpen as the gravity of the situation sets in. I'd fallen asleep in the apartment. Celeste had been on the couch. I don't sleepwalk—I switch out. If the body moved, one of us had to move it. *"And ask who walked us to the tower."*

Could one of my other headmates have done this? Solomon had immediately put me on the spot, asking if I had anything to confess, then flipped the script to be all supportive again. I hadn't known him to be violent, but I'd had to make him release Landon earlier. People had changed while I was gone; I can't really say what he's capable of anymore, even if I refuse to believe it's possible that he had a hand in this.

I don't think Empress, Mesmer, or Keke could have done it, and Lurk definitely wouldn't, but Della had set this whole job up—I'd imagined it was some kind of extreme therapy, but maybe it was revenge for leaving her in charge of everything. From all I've gathered, she'd lost her grip on things to some extent. Enough to plot against me to her own detriment?

None of the headmates I know hate me more than they love their own freedom—I doubt any amount of time could change that.

But there's the mystery headmate. I'd assumed they weren't capable of fronting, because if they had been, they would have ferry-jacked John and had us back on the dock, preventing any of this mess from happening. But they had voiced the only and strongest dissent to us coming to the island, and I had been the only one to hear it. If the others hadn't known they existed, could it mean they don't know that they front?

And the ghost—if she really is in our inner world, could she function like a headmate and get a turn at the wheel?

I'm really regretting not having paid more attention to Dr. Reese when she tried to talk to me about system dynamics, and encouraged mapping out ours. Back then, all I'd known was that I'd lost what I felt was rightfully mine—my talent and my voice of reason and the daydreams that had been my refuge from the world. I hadn't cared enough to help create a user's manual, and now I'm here with more questions that I should have the answers to, staring down the possibility of a murder rap.

As we shuffle down to the living room, I try to get a sense of what Solomon is feeling, but he's sealed up his emotions Ziploc tight.

"*Where were you before we woke up in the tower?*" I ask.

(*"In Empress and Keke's room, asleep. I was watching over them, so it wasn't them either. The door was locked."*)

"*Are you certain one of them couldn't have slipped away like Keke did earlier? Where were Mesmer and Lurk? Even if none of us did this, maybe they were out walking and stumbled on the body.*"

(*"Mesmer and Lurk didn't move us from the apartment,"*) he says.

"*Let me ask them that,*" I say. "*Or speak to any of them. Why is it that you're the only one I can talk to?*"

He sighs, deep and ragged. (*"Something is happening in here too."*)

"*Yeah, the void filling in. You told me.*"

(*"Not just that. Della didn't just disappear; her bedroom window was smashed. Then Lurk went missing. And then Mesmer; we found her amulet. It had been crushed."*)

The ice from outside may as well have been injected into my veins as a chill sweeps through my body. I have a vague memory of Mesmer's tremulous voice calling my name, and trying to walk to her . . . where had I been? When had that happened?

"That makes no sense."

(*"I know. That's why I had to ask—if you have anything to tell me, anything you've done that you want to explain."*)

Oh. This is why he's been walking on goddamn eggshells. He thinks I have something to do with my missing headmates when I can't even enter the inner world. It was one thing for me to think myself a monster; it hurts like hell for Solomon to confirm that he thinks so too.

(*"Let me help you, Ken,"*) he pleads.

"I don't need your help, because I haven't done anything." Panic and anger drive my words, lashing them around me like a whip to drive him away. *"You talked all that shit about staying by my side while thinking I was hurting our headmates? Fuck off. Never talk to me again."*

(*"I don't see what that will accomplish but—"*)

A sudden silence in my mind, quickly filled in by my own frantic thoughts. I know what this means, but I call for him anyway.

"Solomon? Solomon!"

I'm alone.

Chapter 31

Groupthnk: Collaborative Journal

Archived Post: Della (4 weeks ago)
(Hidden by Admin)
Edited by: Della (2 weeks ago)

The others think I'm okay.

Maybe they don't. Only one of them would be rude enough to ask me what the fuck is wrong with me and she isn't here.

I understand now what she must have felt. To have people in your mind, demanding you do things that go against your very nature. The others want me to go back to how I was before 2020, but I'm not that person anymore.

I'm not eating or sleeping. I'm losing time, and wonder who has found it.

Someone replied yes. To the job. I am the only one who knew about it, but someone replied yes.

I tried to make an appointment with a new therapist, but everyone I can afford is booked out until 2024. I called a helpline because my thoughts were frightening me, and the volunteer told me that I heard voices in my head because the FBI was controlling my mind through nanoagents in the vaccine. I shouted at him about his silly conspiracy theories and hung up.

I know what the real conspiracy is, and it's much worse: they made us abandon one another. It's so easy for humans to do that, and so hard to see until it's too late.

I'm sorry, Ken.

I'm not okay. I have to tell the others. I need help. Before I

Edit: Della

Before you what, darling?

Chapter 32

Ken

I step into the parlor, the desire to run arcing through my muscles and sinews like the lightning in the storm raging outside. Although everyone crosses over to the other side of the large room and huddles around the fireplace, I post up on a wall next to the door. I'm no longer shivering, just jerking in fits and starts, as if every few moments my body remembers that we're—I'm—in the deep end of the cesspool.

Landon has gone to the office with Celeste to call the police using the CB radio, and I've chosen a spot where no one can sneak up behind me and where they can't box me in.

The silence feels unnatural, inside of my head and in the room. Headmates are missing. One of the people who'd been sitting with us earlier is lying dead on the floor upstairs.

Why is everyone so quiet?

Because they've all already decided that I'm responsible for this shit.

I feel a presence behind me, but far enough away that I can't tell if it's Solomon or one of the others who hasn't been and-then-there-were-none'd.

"You should know that if I was going to do something in the inner world—if it was possible for me to— that I would be the same as I am out here," I shout into the void. *"There wouldn't be any guessing game, because I'm not a fucking punk who creeps around messing with people. If I was going to hurt someone, even if I didn't know why, they'd know that it was me."*

Whoever it is turns away.

Not unexpected, but fuck it hurts more than I'd imagined. I was just starting to get used to those fuckers, and now . . .

Solomon hadn't even put up a fight, just been there and then gone—I push off of the wall, standing bolt upright.

Could something have happened to him? If he wants to ignore me, he's more than capable of doing so while still breathing over my shoulder. Why would he completely pull away like that?

Pinpricks tickle down my neck, and my mouth pulls into a grimace that I can't control. I try to take deep breaths, but that choking feeling that I'd had on the ferry starts to squeeze the air from me. Mesmer should be here to help with this but she's missing too.

"Look at her, Klaus," the man who might be named Gary says, tapping his buddy. "I told Pearson that there were limits to this. Bringing in a deranged person was bound to upset things, but he wanted unpredictability and now he's paid for it."

No. Hell no. I can't let them talk like this is over and settled.

"I don't know why you 'brought me' here but I didn't kill anyone."

"That's what every criminal says," Klaus sneers. "'I'm innocent,' or 'I was abused,' or 'my mommy didn't hug me enough.' And yet someone had to commit the crime."

"Someone who had a motive, which I didn't." I look around at the others, who are watching uneasily. "I just started a job that was going to be the easiest money I'd ever made and without which I'll be homeless and broke. But all of you showed up here on some shady vibes for some weird ceremony and suddenly Pearson is dead. The number-one suspect in murders is usually a spouse or partner, isn't it?"

Lily's eyes go wide and Shalimar slips out of her grip again and runs in circles in front of her.

"Are you saying I did this?"

Footsteps approach from the hallway, and I side-shuffle away from the door so I'm not in grabbing distance of anyone walking into the room.

"I'm saying you're just as likely a suspect as I am. A very young woman who married a much older man; a wealthy, controlling older man. His death means you'll inherit his money and spend it any way you please without sucking on dangly balls for the next twenty-five years. You'll get to keep your dog too."

Lily folds in on herself, tears spiking her lashes. "You're disgusting."

"But she's so small," the dark-haired woman says. "She couldn't fight him."

"She's the same size as me," I say. "And strong enough to swing a candlestick. I haven't forgotten how you pushed me over under the table."

"I didn't do it," she says, voice firm and gaze on me hard even as tears spill from her eyes. "We all know you're the only criminal here."

John rests a heavy hand on my arm. "Now, Ken, just calm down—"

"And you, John! Talking about the trust like they'd taken something from you. I've barely spoken to you and I know you hold a grudge deeper than anything I've got against Pearson."

"You saying it was me?" Betrayal chases anger across his face, and I growl in frustration.

"No. I'm saying that I'm not the only suspect or even the prime suspect."

"I had some issues with the trust, but I thought they were just yuppies sticking their money where it didn't belong. I didn't know they were descendants of Kavanaugh. That changes everything."

Landon and Celeste step into the room, and though I hate to do it, I have to point out the obvious.

"And even Landon—yes, he's his son, and because of that he probably has the biggest grievance of them all. I won't rub salt on the wound, but we all see how Pearson talked to him. I'm far from the only suspect, and when the police get here, they'll think the same."

"Do you see yourself?" Landon asks in a dull voice. "Trying to solve a crime while covered in the blood of the victim. You really can't accept responsibility for anything, can you?"

"If I did it, I'll accept responsibility, but the evidence we have is circumstantial at best." I have no idea what the fuck circumstantial even means in a legal sense, but I'm pulling out my degree from *Law & Order* University.

"The fact that you can't say you *didn't* do it is evidence enough," Landon says. "Maybe one of your personalities did it, but either way you're going to jail with them."

"No."

"No, none of them did it or no you're not going to jail if they did?"

"Is she really crazy?" the blond-haired woman asks, stepping toward her friend. "We're not getting paid enough for this. This was supposed to be a party and then the hunt. Not people dying."

I lean against the wall for support, because even I can't ignore how fucked I am right now. "I don't have to prove anything to you people. I'll talk to the cops when they get here."

"About that." Celeste's voice is gravelly and rough, like she's still tired from our nap—or exhausted because she hadn't taken it. I don't air my accusations, but she's clearly not a fan of Pearson either. "Someone got to the CB radio too. There's no calling the cops." She looks at me. "Even if there was, there'd be no getting on or off the island until morning."

"A CB radio? Why don't our phones work here? It's almost twenty-fucking-twenty-three! Who only has a CB radio?" Lily starts to melt down, making it clear that she's not much older than Empress. "I told him he needed to get an antenna or something, but he never listened to me, ever, and he said he would and now he's dead and maybe all of us will be soon!"

She presses her hands to her mouth and screams into her palms. The dog jogs around her feet, but she ignores it, completely zoned out now that she understands no one is coming.

"That's very convenient for someone," John says. "Ken, didn't you tell me you used the radio to send me a message? One that I never got? If it was working then, as you say it was, was it still working when you *left* the office?"

I have no idea. When I look to Celeste for assistance, she's staring resolutely into the corner. What had she told Landon when they found it? What if what I say contradicts that?

"I think so. What do you mean by broken, Celeste?"

"It was smashed," she says, then glances at my boots. "Or maybe stomped, since it was all over the floor."

Does she suspect me too? Why is she being so icy and distant after the warmth that had been between us earlier? Or worse, is she part of whatever this setup is? She works for the trust.

"No one knows what's happened here but us, and the police can't be contacted until morning, if we're lucky and the storm passes quickly," Landon says, sitting at the head of the table where Pearson had been seated before.

He stares at gouges in the wood, tracing them with his finger. "I think . . . I think my father would want us to continue the ceremony."

Lily sniffles. "Are you fucking serious? Do you know how morbid that is?! Your father is in a puddle of blood up there. His brains—" She covers her mouth again and dry heaves.

"If we don't, it would mean that all the work my father put into this island, this castle, and preserving our heritage would be for nothing. It would mean he came here for nothing and was killed for nothing."

"The boy is right," Gary says. "We should continue. Relight the candles."

"Lily, take this." Landon hands her an old-fashioned key similar to the one I'd been given for the door between the apartment and the main house. "You go into the master bedroom and lock yourself in. Maria and Diana, please go get the drinks from the kitchen." The two women scurry off, though I seem to be the only one who notices they were already halfway out the door. "You two will need to stay here."

Celeste scoffs. "Me? What do I have to do with this?"

"You also have a criminal record," Landon says. "And you're dating her, aren't you? Maybe you decided to help your girlfriend finish what she'd started with my dad."

"That's some bullshit, and you know it."

"I know that Ken can be very convincing. After all, I once thought she was a loving partner who wanted nothing more than to please me. It was an act. She doesn't even know herself, does she?"

I'm used to this—people talking about me like I'm not even in the room. His words still hit like rock salt, spraying over that internal wound that won't heal. I say nothing, because at this point I'm not yet defeated but I might as well be. Celeste had tried to help, and now she's caught up in my shit too.

The thoughts slash down on me like the sleet outside the tower, chilling me from the inside.

Stupid. Worthless. Fuck-up.

One of the thoughts differentiates itself, loud though it's a whisper. A woman's whisper.

(*"All right so you're a fuck-up. What are you going to do about it, darling?"*)

It's a voice that seems like a stranger's at first, but now that I've homed in on it, it seems obvious and familiar, like the birthmark on my ass that I only remember if I catch myself in the mirror from the right angle and immediately forget about afterward.

"Who are you?"

The presence that had been near me recedes, and again there's something familiar about the sensation, a withdrawal that isn't the same as when the others go back to the inner world.

I won't get any reply, but the question she'd asked needs an answer. What am I going to do about it?

I look around the room.

"So all of you are dead set on believing I did it—I didn't. And Celeste definitely wouldn't put her ass on the line to help me with a murder—she barely knows me. Everything will come clean in the wash. Landon? You're grieving and everything, but you've been over-stepping since I ran into you. If you really believe I'm capable of murder, keep my name out your mouth until morning."

I walk over to the table, pull out a chair, and plop into it, legs spread wide.

"We've got all night. I'll find out which one of you motherfuckers did it and save the police the trouble."

Landon is unmoved by my bluff.

"I already know who did it," he says confidently, then leans toward me. "It was Della."

I'm glad I'd taken a seat, because my knees would have given out even though I manage to keep my ex-pression impartial. How the *fuck* does he know about Della?

"Who is Della?" Klaus asks. "I thought the other one was Celeste."

"One of Ken's other personalities."

Ice creeps into my veins at how he shares this. Not as if he's just found out, but as if he's recalling some important detail.

"Why would Della want to harm your father?" I ask. "She's not like that."

"She came up to me and told me flat-out that she was going to make my father pay for what he'd done. Since you and the other one don't even know she spoke to me, you wouldn't know if she killed him, either, would you?" He looks at Celeste. "I tried to warn you so you didn't find out how I did. Ken is cracked in the head, which is why my father brought her here. I told him not to, but he went against my wishes. I told her to leave. Neither of them listened. Now he's dead. Hopefully you'll be smarter than both of them."

"You're right, Landon," Klaus says, chuckling gruffly and looking my way. "I think the bastard would want the ceremony to continue."

Landon nods. "Let's get started."

Chapter 33
Ken

I'm still trying to wrap my mind around the possibility that one of my headmates had murdered Pearson. I don't think Della is capable of that, but she was the one who had set up this whole job, leaving no trace of our employment here. Had she expected to slip in, do a little murder, and slip out? If that was the case, why was I awake?

Landon keeps glancing at me with a sick smirk on his face, like my confusion brings him joy. "Oh, here they are!" he calls out when Maria and Diana come back into the room. They're rolling a dessert cart, one pushing and one pulling. A huge wooden box sits on the top level, and John's eyes go wide when he sees it.

ONE OF US KNOWS • 323

"Ours weren't this fancy," he says. "We made them ourselves from scrap wood."

He runs his hand over the smooth wood gleaming with varnish. The hinges and edging are in a dark aged metal, with hatched markings carved into it.

"My dad used to make them himself, but there are more options online these days," Landon says. "A lot more people interested in tradition. Go ahead and open it."

"Me?" John's eyes sparkle, and just like that I see exactly what his price to tell the police I killed Pearson is. Landon nods indulgently and John flips back the lid, revealing four small glass bottles nestled into perfectly arranged moss.

"That's Rekksblod. Authentic Viking warrior potion. To be taken before the hunt."

"Well, would you look at that?" John says, as if he's talking about a pair of sneakers and not some weird wannabe Viking shit. "I thought people just drank Red Bull now."

I glance at Maria and Diana, and they watch apprehensively but are not as freaked-out as they should be.

"Are we doing the hunt as well as the ceremony?" Maria asks. "I don't think it's really possible with this storm."

"We paid you," Gary says. "You'll do what you were paid to do."

"I think we should stop," Diana says, eyes going flinty. "We didn't expect a big storm and we didn't know a man would die. That changes things. And we're allowed to say no, no matter how much you pay us."

"We'll pay you triple," Landon says easily.

"That's nine thousand dollars. Each?" Maria says, confirming the price.

Landon smiles at her. "Hazard pay."

The women look at each other and then nod, reluctant but unable to resist a windfall.

I should be quiet, but the way everyone is speaking makes me feel like this is some other aspect of life that became normalized while I was sleeping. "Can anyone explain what's getting hunted when there's nothing out there but trees and rocks?"

Maria looks at me uneasily. "We are. Some men like that kind of thing. The chasing, and the catching."

Diana winks at me. "If you can get paid for it, why not?"

A pursuit kink. I instantly think of the pictures in the grotto, and the men in their hunting attire despite there being no game on the island. They'd brought it in themselves. Kavanaugh, whose job it was to stop vice, had built his own little vice wonderland.

"So you two are the goblins," I say.

Maria lifts a shoulder. "Yeah."

Gary starts handing out the vials of the Viking fruit juice. "We're the hunters. Goblins could be anyone."

Landon hands John a vial. "We have an extra, since my father . . . is gone. You can have it. These things cost, like, five hundred dollars each; he wouldn't want it to go to waste."

I stand up, for once feeling like the sane person in the room. "A man is dead and you're all getting ready to play triple-x hide-and-seek? This is a terrible idea— I'm not going to comment on desecrating the dead, but this castle is a crime scene. You shouldn't be running all over the place for sex games before the forensics team shows up."

Klaus laughs at me. "This isn't a police procedural. We can do whatever we want. We already know who killed him."

One by one the men drink their weird little drinks, grimacing and gagging to get it down.

"This is what my father would have wanted." Landon removes the moss-lined top layer of the box and then pulls out a wood-handled knife with a jagged blade. "The goblin hunt is a symbolic cleansing. It's a removing of impurities. If anything, my father's death means we've gone too long without the tradition."

A headache branches through my skull, painful and

disorienting. Although my eyes have mostly adjusted to the glasses, my vision blurs as I watch him.

"Last time we tried this I was just a boy, and my father made the mistake of going too big: too many hunters, too many goblins. The castle almost burned to the ground. We'd already decided that tonight would follow the basic rules: One night. You run, we hunt."

"It sounds worse than it is," Maria says, looking at me. "Don't worry. We've done this kind of thing before; it's become popular. There are even summer camps! The knives are just for show."

My headache builds and I truly wonder if I've lost my grip on reality. I don't understand how everyone is acting so calm, but then I realize that I am too.

I nudge Celeste. "I think we should go to the apartment."

"You go," she says, cold as when I'd first seen her on the dock. "We're not friends. I'm not going to jail again just because I felt sorry for you."

Her words barely register. So much is going on that I've reached capacity for the ability to have my feelings hurt.

Gary laughs, examining his glinting knife in the firelight. "Oh, how quickly they turn on one another! All of you ladies run along, now. We'll do our private portion of the ceremony and give you plenty of time to hide."

Even though I'd been planning to leave, the excitement in his voice welds me to my seat. Right now they consider themselves hunters; anyone who isn't with them is prey.

"I'm going to stay here," I say. "I never agreed to be part of this and if you really think I'm a killer why would you want me to participate?"

Gary reaches down to his ankle, and when his hand comes up there's a small pistol in it. He aims it at me, then fires two rounds that hit the chair next to me with a quiet pop.

Celeste jumps to her feet, but Diana and Maria are already halfway out the door.

"I'm not going to do any back-and-forth bantering with you," he says, waving me away with the gun. "Get."

"The bullet isn't real, but you do not want to be hit by that," Klaus says. "We take this very seriously."

I stand slowly and back away to the door. I don't buy for a second that the gun isn't real. I don't check where Celeste has scattered to. I've been abandoned by everyone, including my headmates. When I get to the threshold, I run alone.

Chapter 34

Keke

Solomon and Empress keep ignoring me, whispering and looking worried. When they act like that, it makes me feel like I'm not real—a dream, a ghost, a fig mint of imagination. I go sit in front of the tower door and talk to Rapunzel. I can feel them on the other side; heavy, like a big rock pushed against the door to keep me out.

"I know I'm real," I say quietly. "You wanna know how? Because I do remember one thing from when I was little. I had an imaginary friend once."

Rapunzel doesn't answer but I don't mind.

"It was a lady, in a white dress. She talked to me when I was somewhere cold and scary. I wanted to scream, but she said if I was quiet and careful, she could keep me safe. So I kept my scream on the inside and locked it up tight."

Their voice comes from the other side of the door, squeaky like an old door opening. "Quiet and careful."

"You can talk!" I shout, then cover my mouth, speaking through my fingers. "Say something else!"

I wait for a few minutes but they stay quiet.

"Rapunzel?" I press my ear to the door, then try to peek through the keyhole. It's dark in there but I see the shadow of someone big moving. "Do you want to know a secret about my imaginary friend that no one else knows?"

The movement stops, as if they're listening, and I whisper through the hole to make sure no one else hears me.

"She still talks to me."

Chapter 35

**Journal of Grace Fontaine Kavanaugh,
1918–1919**

December 5, 1918

*I hear them down there. Scrabbling, scrab-
bling. Laughing. Clawing.*

Beasts.

*Simon doesn't tell me I'm crazy anymore—he
says it's necessary, to cleanse the world of filth.
It's tradition. He says if I were a good woman, I'd
understand.*

*I think the truth is that he does it for the thrill
of it.*

*This morning, when a ferry arrived with three
new women, one face stood out even from this*

distance: golden brown skin beneath a halo of dark hair.

Lottie.

I don't know if Simon tricked her here or if she came to find me on her own, but I can't let them harm her. I will kill him, and the pack of drooling dogs that call themselves his friends.

He always says that a woman must know her place. Mine is with my knee to his chest and his head on a platter. Holofernes, vanquished, by flame and not steel.

He should have taken my turpentine and not just my brushes.

I will save us.

I know already what people will say if I don't succeed, and how they will sigh over Simon Kavanaugh's well-loved wife. His fourth wife. He loves them so well, you see.

I will create my own legacy.

Chapter 36

Ken

I pound down the hall toward the door leading into the apartment—it's locked. I'd made sure of it myself that morning, screwing myself over as usual.

"Fuck!"

I pat my pockets but they're empty. I even bend over and check my boots, and sigh in relief when my knife is still there. But my phone, keys, and the rest of my belongings are behind that door.

I give it a kick, pissed at myself for being my own worst enemy, but . . . the door is locked and I don't have the keys.

How had I gotten into the tower while still dry if I'd gone around the house? The rain is blowing sideways against the castle—I'd be as drenched if I'd even opened the outer door.

I shelve the thought; once I find a good hiding place I'll have plenty of time to think it through. I run through the kitchen and grab a large knife that rests on the counter, and then head for the back door.

"You don't want to go that way," Celeste says in a low voice from behind me.

I ignore her.

"Come on," she says, and I whirl toward her.

"What the fuck? Why would I go with you?"

She draws her brows together. "What kind of question is that? Because we're being hunted."

"You betrayed me," I say, unable to hide the hurt in my voice, and she closes her eyes and exhales deeply.

"We already discussed what would happen if shit went down and we don't have the time to rehash it. You and your headmates need to get it together. I'm not trying to have the same conversation eight times a day."

"That's easy for you to say. You have no idea—"

"Just shut the fuck up and come with me," she snaps, eyes beady with frustration. "You can tell me how mean I am later, if we're still alive."

I want to grab one of the decorative jars on the

counter and smash it into her face, but she's the one who knows the island and the house, not me.

"If you double-cross me, I'll kill you."

"If you get me killed while I'm helping you of my own volition, I'll haunt you," she says. "That door leads to a slope that would have you slip-and-sliding right off a cliff in this weather. Come with me."

We jog quietly down the hall and head into the library, where she struggles with a window that's bloated in the jamb. With my help she gets it up, then slaps my leg down as I prepare to climb out.

"It's called a decoy, Nash. I thought you were supposed to be street-smart or something."

She knocks over some books on the shelf next to the sill to make it look like we've scrambled through, then takes off. I follow again, hating that I have to trail behind her like a dog.

Puppy.

Box full of cuddly canines.

My thoughts of dogs get no reaction from Keke. Solomon had said headmates were going missing, and I haven't heard from any of them. If they all really disappear—

(*"Then you'll have gotten what you wanted,"*) the whispering voice says, not hiding its mocking tone.

(*"Play stupid games, win stupid prizes, isn't that your motto?"*)

I focus on Celeste's back, swallowing against the sudden thickening of my throat.

I'd wanted my headmates gone. I'd wanted my life back. But how would I be able to live knowing that all of them had disappeared and only me, the worst of us, was left? Keke's sweetness, Solomon's goodness, Della's faith, Empress's snark, Mesmer's kindness, and Lurk's . . . whatever he contributes, all gone, with only a few other people even knowing that they'd existed?

I don't want to deal with this. The weight of this responsibility is too much. Goddammit, this is why I should be—

No. I shouldn't be asleep. This isn't an opportune time for epiphanies, but it all makes sense precisely because we're running for our lives.

Fucked as it is, I see why I'm awake. If someone is scooping up the inner-world headmates, I'm the one person in the system they can't reach. If fucked-up shit is popping off out here, I'm the one person in the system who actually stands a fighting chance.

I don't know how we ended up in this mess, but I'm good for one thing in this world and it isn't art—it's being a menace who makes people regret they ever crossed my path.

I'm an asshole and I'm going to shit all over Landon's little game.

Celeste circles us back around toward the kitchen as we hear some kind of chanting coming from the parlor where Landon and the other men are. They're singing something, and unfortunately for me, I finally have the words to the earworm that's been bothering me since I woke up.

"The goblin king who never sleeps,
awaits us at the stormy keep."

We head into the office, where Celeste closes and locks the door.

"When all is dark, in dead of night,
The hunt begins, as is our right."

We pass the desk, where the CB radio lies in pieces on the floor, and I hop over them, wondering if I had smashed it.

"Nowhere to run, nowhere to hide,
Which leaves one choice: to die."

She pushes aside a section of the long wall of curtains, revealing a half door—this room had to have once been part of the kitchen to have this kind of exit. She pushes, bracing against the wind and rain, then looks back at me, brows raised.

Maybe I did kill Pearson. Maybe I'll have more blood on my hands by the time this night is over. But one thing for damn sure: I'm getting us out of here. If I achieve one thing in this life, it'll be making sure we don't go out sad at the hands of some losers pretending to be Vikings.

I nod, and then we push out into stinging sleet and freezing rain.

Chapter 37
Solomon

K eke is acting weird. Super, super weird."
Empress watches her across the room like she might lash out, even though Keke is playing quietly with a doll.

"Rapunzel talked to her," I say. "They said 'Quiet and careful.'"

"That's what Keke used to say when we first met her. When she used to cry," Empress whispers, throwing a frightened look across the room.

"If Rapunzel holds our trauma, they might have memories that Keke couldn't deal with." I sigh. "I think that we were here, in this castle, when we were a child. When Keke was a child. She came in, and I don't know how long she stayed, but it wasn't Keke who left.

Or she didn't leave alone, if she was still fronting at that point."

"Holy crap. Ken. This is—yes, it makes sense."

"We know what Ken does anytime she's fronting."

"Makes a mess of things?" Empress guesses.

"Think harder," I press. I search in the upholstery toolbox that I've brought from my room and finally find what I want—my mallet.

"Gets trashed. Argues with total randos even if they're triple her size if they rub her the wrong way." Empress unfurls a finger as she counts off each of Ken's sins. "She chased a truck down Broadway because some dudes catcalled a teenager. Kicked a chick in the shin for making fun of a—oh my God. How did I miss it? All of this studying how we function in systems and I was so focused on her being a jerk that I never even considered it."

I exhale, glad that she sees it too. "Ken isn't a persecutor, or not just a persecutor—"

Rapunzel shrieks in the tower, shaking the house, and when we head to the end of the hall to peer out the window, we see that the painting has almost been completed. Kavanaugh Island at night, oil-paint raindrops slipping down the living canvas and lightning streaking across the landscape like stop-motion.

"She's a protector. Who went dormant. And she came back right as we arrived here."

Empress hugs herself. "At the place where she—our system—was born."

I squeeze her shoulder. "Stay here with Keke. If this is where we were born, it means nothing good has brought us back here. We can't wait any longer to figure this out."

Rapunzel yells again and again, the violence of the noise making my head feel like a church cloche, but I head toward it anyway.

I stand in front of the door to the tower in the aftermath of the bellow, and then knock three times because I don't know what else to do to get Rapunzel's attention.

"Rapunzel, I need you to talk to me," I say.

Silence.

"I know that you talked to Keke, and now I need you to talk to me."

A scraping sound, like metal being dragged over stone.

"I don't know how to unlock your door. If I could, I would. But if you know what's going on, please tell me so I can get us out of this situation."

I expect no response, but then I hear it. Laughter, low and not joyful at all. It sends a shiver down my spine but inspires me to push harder because it means they understand me.

"Do you know who's doing this? Is it . . . is it the ghost? Grace Kavanaugh? Is she why you've been screaming since we arrived?"

They ignore me, and I try again with something easier to answer. "Do you remember what happened to us here when we were young?"

The house shudders and ash falls all around me.

"All right. I know you can't come out and tell me. So I'm going to come to you."

I heft the mallet in my hand, take a deep breath, and swing.

We were warned to never force the sharing of memories because it could lead to system destabilization, but if Rapunzel knows what happened here in the past, then they have the key to why we're here in the present.

My headmates are missing. Ken surely thinks I abandoned her. I've let everyone down despite trying my hardest—I'm going to get the truth for us, no matter the cost.

Chapter 38
Ken

I've walked through storms before, in an effort to feel something in my worst depression spirals, but not while running from a pack of crazy white men. The lashing wind and cutting sleet don't feel like a refreshing slap in the face; they're an obstacle to freedom, and something that might get me killed.

I'd wanted off this garbage heap plane of existence for so long that my visceral anger at the prospect of death surprises me.

How dare these fuckers put us in this situation? How dare they think they could get away with it?

Celeste reaches an arm back as the wind drives at us, and I clamp onto it. Together, we hustle down the slick stone stairs of the grotto. She pulls out her key ring and tugs at a metal door embedded in the wall, and we slide inside, hunkering down in the walled portion of the niche beneath the photo of Kavanaugh. Now I understand why it had unsettled me so much, and what it is that the Trust worshipped here.

Tradition. Power. Death.

Celeste locks the gate after us, then slides to the ground beside me.

"We can't stay here all night," she says. "But this will give us a place to regroup."

"Okay, why don't we start with what in the entire fuck is going on. Did you know about this hunting stuff? Have you participated in it before?"

"I only found out about it recently," she says. "I was helping a friend research the castle and she came across something about the goblin hunts. She asked if I knew anything about them, since I worked here. I asked why and she had a real crazy story. I didn't want to believe it, and I definitely didn't want to help her, but I decided to listen to her."

"Why?"

"People have joked about goblin hunts for a while around here, and usually when they're talking about people they consider 'undesirable.' I started poking around in the paperwork and I noticed that in the recorded accidental deaths on the island, the victims almost all fit a certain description, and they weren't the kind of people who usually kayak out to deserted islands."

"They weren't white men," I say. "Statistically, most accidental deaths are men."

"Ah, the trivia," she says. "But yeah. Almost all women. Undocumented immigrants. Black. Queer. Most of them from situations where they wouldn't be missed—or that would make an offer of cash irresistible."

I scoff, remembering what John had told me about the island's mission statement. "I guess that's one way of helping the underprivileged. Bringing them to an island and killing them."

"I wanted to think it was just a coincidence, or even a curse, but then they messed with someone I care about. I sent an anonymous tip to the police and they never responded or acted on it."

"But what about Landon's mom? Was she an accident?"

"She got Covid in the first wave, and it left her disabled from chronic illness. From what I know she'd been a doting wife and suddenly the tables turned and her husband had to take care of her. I think he thought it'd be easier to get rid of her and trade her in for a younger model."

I remember Landon's weird remarks about my age.

If his father shared the same sentiments, he def could have given his wife a helping hand down a set of stairs.

"This is insane! I know rich people get bored, but they could be using this island to make even more money, and they're just having hunting parties instead?"

"I'm sure they'll figure out how to monetize it."

A flashlight beam bobs down the steps, and we duck before hearing the patter of bare feet. "I'm turning into a block of ice! I can't do this all night."

"I can for nine thousand dollars. That's enough for a year of my kid's school plus a summer vacation."

"Listen. One of them is coming. I'm just going to stay in here and get this over with where it's kinda dry. I didn't sign up for this ice storm."

The patter of feet through puddles, and then the chattering of teeth.

"Should we bring her in here?" I whisper.

Celeste nods and starts to stand, then drops back down. She tilts her head toward the stairs, then places a finger to her lips. I grip the kitchen knife in my hand.

There's silence, and then, "Oh! You scared me. Looks like you found me, big man."

A giggle.

"Do you want to play out here or should we go inside to one of the bedro—"

Her words are cut off by a gurgle, followed by the sound of slapping and grunting. Lightning flashes, and the shadow of her struggle falls over us—someone is choking her.

Maybe this is foreplay, I tell myself. I've enjoyed a choke-out or two myself, but it doesn't stop, and the sound of her gags and useless gasps echoes in the grotto. The slaps are what make it clear this isn't a sex game—it has to be her hitting him, trying to pull his hands off her neck.

I stand to peek at what's going on when her face slams into the bars, eyes bulging and bloodshot. Her gaze pleads with me, her mouth opening and closing like a fish.

She bucks back against her attacker with a burst of strength, maybe her last, and he laughs, spinning so his back is to me. She whimpers—screams robbed of their oxygen.

It's Klaus, and he's so invested in his kill that he's not paying attention to his surroundings.

"I know you like that, whore. Right? You're gonna die, bitch. You won't see a cent of that money we offered, and that's what you get. How does it feel, knowing you're gonna die because you're a slut with no principles? Huh?"

He's speaking low and lewd in her ear, thrusting up

to knock her knees from under her as she tries to get a footing on the slippery stone. He leans back against the bars to keep her from wriggling away from him, and I spring forward, slipping my arm through the bars and around his neck, then press my palm behind another bar to prevent him from running. Now he's the one choking and gagging, and she drops to the ground, gasping raw, ragged breaths.

Anger and fear explode in me as I struggle to hold him still, to give Diana a chance to escape. He was going to kill her. He was going to enjoy it.

"Seems like you *don't* like that, whore," I growl into his ear. "Maybe you shouldn't go around trying to kill people, you little bitch."

His nails dig into my arm, ripping at my skin. I press harder—I'm not trying to kill him, just get him to pass out. My grip starts to slip, but then arms wrap around mine and warmth presses up against me—Celeste, adding her weight to mine so we can hold him more firmly in place.

Diana rises to her feet and staggers toward him. She reaches forward, toward his tactical vest, and from the pocket she pulls out one of the fancy blades from Landon's artisanal psycho kit.

He kicks at her, but she catches his leg under her arm and starts slicing viciously at his thigh, ripping at

348 · ALYSSA COLE

it with left and right swipes as he convulses in my grip. Blood sprays from his femoral artery, spreading pink across her soaking dress, and she screams hoarsely—in fury, not in fear. I release him, but she keeps stabbing, only stopping when the blade slips and digs into her palm. She kicks him and stumbles off toward the woods, throwing a terrified glance our way as she turns the corner of the house.

"You're welcome," I mutter, but I wouldn't be stopping for chitchat in this situation either.

Celeste is already at the lock, getting us the hell out of our short-lived sanctuary. My shoulders are screaming from the resistance the guy put up, but I don't think anything is torn or dislocated.

"Grab his feet," she says as I move to run past him. I expect him to kick, but he's motionless as we take either end of him and then heft him over the low grotto wall into the trees below.

"They don't need to know if the blood is from one of ours or one of theirs," I say, wiping my hands on my jeans.

She shakes her head. "You make it hard not to like you when you say things like that."

I laugh without humor, but we're already in motion, searching for a new place to hide. I think about what the man's pulse had felt like under the crook of my elbow, and what his body had looked like tumbling into darkness.

I should feel sick, but maybe that will come later. For now I can think only of what Empress had said about goblins turning into stone at dawn. These motherfuckers had underestimated all of us. If even one of us survives, they're going to be surprised that the game doesn't end when they want it to.

"Come on," Celeste says. "There's a toolshed but they'll probably check there first. I know a place."

Chapter 39

Ken

I have no idea how long we've been shivering in the dark huddled together against the abutment of the bridge Celeste had shown me earlier. Water passes beneath us, growing louder and higher the longer we sit, and every crack of a twig and groan of a tree in the darkness makes us jump.

I almost yell when something grabs my leg until I realize it's a branch floating past us.

"I can't do this. Just sitting and waiting for something to happen. Let's just get in your boat and try to make it to shore. It's not that far."

"It's not, but the currents around here are rough even on a good night. I'm not going to choose drowning over getting away from these guys." Celeste is calmer now, maybe because hypothermia is setting in.

"Do you have any weapons stashed around here?" I ask. "A gun? Something that doesn't require getting so close?"

She shoots me a look that's still withering even at a quarter of its menacing power. "Why would I have a gun? Because I went to prison? I was in there for shoplifting."

I roll my eyes. "Because you're a woman who works alone on a cursed island. I'd have weapons in every knothole and tree stump. Besides, I thought everyone in this part of New York had guns."

"I hate guns," she says. "I hate violence."

I scoff and rib her with my elbow. "You and me just tossed a body over a cliff. I didn't think you were squeamish."

She squeezes her eyes shut, and something about the oddness of the movement catches my attention. "Sometimes I am."

"I'm not thrilled about what happened either," I say, though I don't feel particularly bad about it. I'm far from emotionless, but my pity is reserved for people who don't choke out women while groaning bad porn lines in their ear.

"We won't be able to stay under here much longer," she says abruptly.

The stream under the bridge starts to lap at our shoes. More debris could be heading our way, too, and we wouldn't see it coming.

Turning on a flashlight would be like sending up a flare to every wannabe hunter on the island.

"Do you think they're really out here in this weather?" I ask in a low voice. "What was in that potion? For five hundred dollars it might make them see in the dark. What do Vikings have to do with anything?"

"A surprisingly high number of people see one percent Scandinavian heritage in their 23andMe and decide they are descendants of Vikings, and also that Vikings are super racist killers."

"I guess it's kind of the same as this goblin stuff," I say. "Taking something that's tradition or myth but when you peel back the thinnest layer there's just a wet sack of racist, misogynist shit underneath."

We sit shivering in silence again, and I'm about to ask where we should go next when the wooden board above us slowly creaks. A high-powered beam of light cuts through the dark to the right of us and I reach into my jacket and wrap my fingers around the knife handle.

"I don't see anything. You really think they'd come this far?" someone says. It's John. Probably the most dangerous of the group because he knows the island well and he has something to prove, the fucker. "They have to be closer to the house. It's not like they're dressed for the elements."

"There was blood leading out of the grotto. Someone was injured, and if it was Klaus he would have come back into the house. We need to run her down."

Hearing them talk about one of us like we're a deer they clipped makes my stomach churn in a way that handling a dead body hadn't.

The light passes over the other side, sliding under the bridge a few inches away from Celeste's boot. I feel her tense up, ready to scramble back, and I prepare to move with her. Then the beam jerks away.

"Did you see that? Something white passing between the trees."

It dawns on me then that the white doesn't represent purity or some religious shit. It just makes the women wearing it easier to hunt in the dark.

Their boots rattle the boards over our heads as the water splashes against the sole of my Docs.

"The water is rising," I whisper. "We need to get out before we get trapped under here."

"They're too close," Celeste hisses. "We could step out right into an ambush. We don't know that they really saw someone."

My thighs burn from crouching to keep my ass off the wet ground.

There's a thrashing in the distance that isn't thunder—it might be a tree falling, or it might be one of the other women being attacked.

I'm debating whether it's time to go when the water laps at my ankle, making my decision for me. I begin to slowly duck-walk out, trying not to snap any twigs or make a sound.

"Where are you going?" Celeste whispers. "You don't know this island in the daylight, let alone the dark."

"I can't swim, and I'm not waiting for a giant branch to knock me into this creek," I say.

I'm almost out from under the bridge when something snags around my feet.

A brief flash of lightning illuminates what at first looks like garbage. Then it hits me. The red isn't the words "Thank You" printed on white plastic. It's a white dress, stamped with blood. I tug at it, but it clings to my feet and ankles.

A shout startles me, and I turn to Celeste before

realizing that it wasn't from out here. Someone in my head is yelling.

"Solomon! Solomon, what's happening?"

This is the first I've heard from anyone for hours, and something is going wrong. I have to get in there, I have to—

Chapter 40

Solomon

I've been hammering at the door for I don't know how long. The only marker of time for me is the pain in my shoulders, the cramps in my hands, and the intervals between Rapunzel's screams.

"You sure you want to do that?" a voice whispers from behind me, but when I spin around there's no one there.

I turn back and see how little damage I've done. The door isn't just for show—it's constructed to repel an attack and my little mallet has barely made a dent.

"Just open the door, Rapunzel! Come on!"

I lean over and place a hand and my throbbing head on the door. I pant and watch my sweat pool on the floor beneath me. I'm so angry that I wonder if I should just try ripping the door off the hinges.

Why won't they just talk to me? This is a matter of life and death. They scream as if they're trapped and in pain, and yet they refuse to do the one thing that could free them of it.

My thoughts crash into a fissure of awareness in the corroded shell of self-righteousness I've been carrying like a weight. I lift my head and stare at the door, a sound between a chuckle and a sob escaping me. I'm furious at the headmate who has suffered more than any of us over the years. I expect them to open the door willingly and share the secret they've protected for decades, when I keep all my own far-less-substantial feelings trapped tightly inside so that even my headmates usually have no idea what I'm thinking.

I've grown so accustomed to living in the background that I told myself that the best way to help my headmates was with a quiet diligence, anticipating their needs without asking. I've hovered over and chastised Ken, and been frustrated when she doesn't listen to me. I said nothing to Della and tiptoed around the issue as it spun out of control. I call it self-sacrifice, but I act like a martyr when my assistance is neither successful nor appreciated.

I ball my hand into a fist and knock once.

"Please. Rapunzel. You've held this for us for so long. We need to know what happened—but more than that you deserve to be free of it. It's not fair that you're stuck in there, in pain, carrying this burden by yourself."

Something scrapes against the other side of the door; they're there, and listening.

"I don't know how to help you, but I want to. Do you know how I can? Do you even want me to try?"

There are no screams, but no answer either. Not for long minutes.

I sigh, dropping my mallet to the ground.

"Yes." Their voice comes from the other side of the door, low and hoarse, but understandable. "Help."

Then the door moves under my palm—the inexorably slow turn of a rusted locking mechanism being activated, followed by a jolt and the scrape of wood. It stops short.

They push at the door again, hard—once, twice—and then it swings forward with a creak of stiff hinges. I jump back, my heart pounding, as it opens fully.

They step out from the darkness behind the door, and it takes a minute for me to realize that they aren't made of shadow themself. Matte-black metal dully reflects the warm lighting of the hallway lamps, and when their foot touches the floor, there's a clanking sound.

I look up into their face, which towers over me, and

see the eyeless sockets of the skull-faced helm. The suit of armor that stands in the dining room of the castle is walking toward me.

I stare, unable to believe my eyes.

"Rapunzel?"

"That is not my name," they say, their voice still echoing even though they've left the tower.

They reach for the helmet and pull it off, revealing that there's nothing inside.

Our headmate isn't in the armor—they *are* the armor.

"Help," they say gruffly, and then in one smooth motion they reach forward and drop the helm over my head, blotting out everything but the sound of my heartbeat and an eerie song that comes at me from all directions, overwhelming my senses.

"The goblin king who never sleeps . . ."

I shout and try to resist, but it's too late; there is no escaping the past.

Chapter 41
Ken

I open my eyes to see the island rearing up in the distance, the castle at its peak lit up from within. It takes me a second to adjust to the sudden change in perspective, and to realize where I'd have to be standing to take in the island from this angle: the half-sunken turret in the river.

The drowned fairy tale. The sky is a swirling gray mass of clouds above me, and the stormy swells below surge against the turret as they course by, but there's a deeper uncanniness to the landscape.

It's painted, like Solomon had been babbling about.

I'm in the inner world.

A wail reaches me over the muted roar of the river, too human to be mistaken for the howling wind. Unlike the last time I heard someone screaming, I know exactly who it is.

"Solomon!" I yell as I stand up. "Solomon!"

The turret sways in the water and I crouch again, grabbing hold of a brick parapet for stability. It breaks off, plummeting into the water below, and I teeter on the precipice, about to follow it.

Water laps at my feet—I'm back in the outer world. I slam my eyes shut and like so many times before try to will myself into the inner world.

"Let me in! Dammit, let me in!"

For a moment I'm back on the half-sunken turret, but I can't stay long—I'm fronting.

The shout I'd heard is a ball of lead in my belly, and I blink back tears of frustration and cold.

"Hey! Snap out of it. Branches are piling up—we need to go now!" Celeste pushes me to run, and I move because I have no choice. Whatever is happening in our inner world, I have to keep us safe out here.

I sniffle, the rain driving into me like BB pellets as soon as we step out from under the bridge. My glasses are almost impossible to see through. I end up holding on to Celeste's arm but as she moves away from the house, I tug her back.

"We have to go inside," I say through chattering teeth.

"Are you out of your mind?"

"They're out here, hunting. We can't hear, and we can't see. They might have night-vision goggles or other tech." A bout of shivering forces me to stop speaking for a second. "We need to go back now, get to the t-tower. It's a position we can defend. Out here we're sitting ducks. They'll find us eventually or we'll freeze."

She stares at me for a minute, exhales a long plume of breath, and then turns and starts heading toward the house.

Every chorus of sleet or crash of raindrops on the way back to the house makes us jump out of our skin— two of them had passed over us on the bridge but we don't know where they'd gone, when they'd be back, or where the third one was.

"Should we c-climb in the window you left open?" I ask, deferring to her.

She pauses, then says, "The house isn't that big. One guy in the main entryway would cut off any path to the stairs and there's no other way up."

"The l-ladder," I say, and when she raises her brow I tug her around the side of the house. I run my hand through the freezing leaves, wondering if I had imagined it, when finally my hand hits a branch-entwined ladder rung.

"Do you know how long this has been here?" she asks. "It could break apart as we climb."

"I'll go first then," I say, and search for a foothold. The branches have so completely engulfed it that there is only the suggestion of a ladder. Maybe the actual ladder has rotted, but the tough, interlaced branches that have grown around it hold strong as I begin my climb. Sturdy as they are, the leaves and branches are slick with sleet, and a gust of wind nearly rips me from the wall. I cling, waiting for the sustained wind to calm.

I think of Solomon's shout and the stretch of water between the tower and the house as I cling there, then shake my head. I have to focus. Besides, Solomon is way fucking smarter than me. He said he was handling things on the inside, and though the thought of something happening to him makes me want to puke, I have to believe he'll be okay.

I start climbing again and feel the bounce of Celeste starting up after me. The window overhead is dark, and I have no idea what room it opens up into, but if it can get us within dashing distance to the tower, it'll be worth it.

When I reach the window, I don't allow myself even a moment of relief. The wind is trying its damnedest to push me off the side of the castle, and one look below will probably give me vertigo. I start trying to push it open, and it doesn't budge. I consider just breaking out the glass, but that would be announcing our entrance to anyone in hearing distance.

Fuck.

I reach my mostly frozen fingers into my pocket and pull out the kitchen knife, forcing my fingers to close around it, and then try slipping the blade between window and sill. It budges. I move the knife along the window, levering up and down to loosen it, cutting through old paint, and then push it all the way under, levering it to lift the window about an inch—enough to fit my fingers under.

I don't trust myself to get the knife back into my pocket without dropping it onto Celeste's head, so I shove the dull end of the blade between my lips and teeth, trying to push the window up with one arm.

Despite the progress I'd made, I'm not strong enough to lift it one-handed.

I have to loosen the death grip my other hand has on the ivy branches and hope that I'm able to do it with two. If we make it out of here, I'm taking up powerlifting. Della can drink protein shakes if she still has a fear of eating, because being this weak is annoying as hell.

I strain against the window, then reposition my hands and push one more time.

It moves, sliding up with enough resistance to make

the branched rung I'm on crack as I push against it, but the window finally gives and slides up completely.

I scramble up, pulling myself over the sill, and as I start to slip into the room something launches at me. My choices are fall to my death or keep going, so I don't startle back, lifting myself into the room headfirst and then throwing my arms out to catch my weight.

The knife slides out of my chattering teeth but lands soundlessly on the carpet. A warm, solid mass slides against my face, followed by a rough tongue and dog breath.

"Shalimar. Quit it!" I whisper as I slide my entire body onto the floor.

The dog doesn't bark but continues trying to kiss me on the mouth, as if it can tell that my defenses are down. I quickly stand and reach out the window, grabbing Celeste by the slick arms of her coat to help her in.

I rear back, using my weight to haul her in and ignoring the burn in my shoulder and the strain in my lower back. She throws her leg over the sill and steadies herself, but I don't get to savor the brief victory of my ridiculous plan's success.

A flashlight's beam cuts through the darkness, pinning us in a bright spotlight before widening and illuminating the rest of the room.

"Don't move. Either of you."

Lily, who of course has brought a gun to a knife fight, stands pressed against the wall on the other side of the room, chest heaving and eyes wild. Her fancy flashlight sits on the ground, carving ghoulish shadows into her pinched features.

Shalimar sits on my foot, getting comfy.

"We're just passing through," I say. "We're not here to hurt you, didn't even know you were in here."

"You're supposed to be outside," she says. "Landon said I didn't have to participate. That I could come down when it's over."

"That's still true," Celeste says, slowly sliding her other leg over the sill. "You don't have to do anything. We're just going to walk through to the hallway. You can pretend we were never here."

She doesn't lower the gun, but does slide away from the door, edging down the wall toward her bed.

"I don't have anything to do with this stuff. That's man business. I'm a lady. A w-widow. Because you killed my husband."

"I didn't kill your husband, and I definitely don't want to hurt you. I can't say the same for the men out there. They might change their mind and decide you need to go too. Like Landon's mom."

"She fell down the stairs because she was old and disabled," Lily says. Her cheeks are flushed red and her eyes are teary. "Landon was so upset, but she was dying anyway. And Pearson needed someone to take care of him. They both needed me."

Celeste glances at me quickly.

"Well that's not any of my business. Lock the door and window after we leave and you'll be fine," I say.

A burst of static grates the air in the room.

"You good, babe?" A walkie-talkie on the nightstand, and Landon's voice coming through it. "Babe? Answer me so I don't worry."

Things suddenly get much clearer. Pearson dead. Lily and Landon, who had waxed poetic to me about the kind of woman he deserved—namely, young—left to carry on the family name. Lily pregnant, by a Pearson but possibly not the one who will be on the birth certificate.

I try to keep my expression neutral, but Lily is smart enough not to trust me.

"You know, I could just shoot you," she says, hands shaking as they both grip the gun. "Two criminals who came into my room with a weapon. You might mean to hurt me. Even if the cops were to find you, which they won't if I kill you, it would be deemed justified."

"We didn't hear anything, and we don't care what you get up to," Celeste says in a tremulous voice. I whip my head around to check that it's really her. "No one would believe us anyway."

She starts edging toward the nightstand.

"Yeah," I say. "Come on, if you kill us, you'll get blood everywhere. It'll be a mess."

The walkie gives another burst of static and Landon's pleading voice comes through. "Lily? Don't be mad. I told you I'm only hunting. Not anything else. You're the only one I want, okay?"

I start to bend down.

"Don't move!" she yells. "Don't. The knife is too far away. I'll have a bullet in your brain before you reach it."

"I'm not going for the knife. I told you we won't hurt you." I reach down and snatch Shalimar up, then wrap my hands around his neck. "But this little guy? I will fucking end him if you don't drop that gun."

"No! Let him go! If you hurt a hair on his head—"

"That's your decision," I say. I don't plan on hurting the dog, who is maybe the only creature in the house that actually seems to like me, but she doesn't need to know that.

"I guess you don't care, you can buy another dog."

I press my knuckle into the dog's neck; it cracks loudly just as he yips from the pressure.

Lily's face contorts and she drops her arms in shock. The instant the gun's muzzle moves away from us we both launch at her. Celeste smashes a hand against her mouth and we both tackle her to the floor. I already know she's stronger than she looks, so it doesn't surprise me when she fights back hard. She thrashes and kicks, bucks and rolls; she gets a few licks in but only succeeds in smashing her flashlight before we overpower her.

"Tie her up," Celeste says.

I use the kitchen knife to strip a bedsheet more expensive than anything I've ever owned, and we make a gag and bind her wrists and ankles, then toss her on the bed. Shalimar runs back and forth over her, thinking we're playing some fun new game.

The walkie bursts with static again, and Celeste strides over to it. "Whatever, Landon! I'm fine!" She doesn't sound exactly like Lily, but a passable-enough imitation that Landon will think she's sulking and ignoring him.

I grab the gun. "Thanks for this! Women helping women."

"I know that's right," Celeste adds.

We pull the door open slowly, listen for a long moment before moving into the hallway.

It's pitch-black but I'm not afraid--I have a purpose that blots out my fear. I could walk into a black hole right now with all the adrenaline pumping through my system.

We jog down the hall, past Pearson's body, and step into the tower, closing the door behind us. I take a strip of the bedsheet that I'd carried with me and tie one end to the doorknob and another to a metal spike in the wall that had once held a stair rail.

"We have to go up for this to work," Celeste says. "We're gonna have to get over that part where the stairs caved in."

"We'll figure it out."

We start up the stairs hand in hand for stability just as a flash of lightning illuminates the way before us. As it fades, a section of light remains—a woman.

"Ah fuck. Look, I'm sorry but I really don't have time for this right now," I say as the woman in white materializes, the paint strokes covering her face trembling.

She doesn't yell this time.

"There are monsters out there, little girl," she says quietly before slowly fading away. Her quiet words shake me more than when she'd lunged at me; something about the resignation in her tone reverberates against a deep sadness within me.

"Who are you talking to?" Celeste asks.

"No one."

We continue to climb.

Chapter 42
Ken

When we finally make it to the tower door, sweaty and sore, we're greeted with laughter.

"Fuck!" I bite out.

Landon and his gray-haired minion Gary stand in the dusty tower chamber when we arrive. I'd found him scoping out the area earlier, when our paths first crossed. Now I know why.

"Hi Ken," he says. "Knew I'd find you here eventually."

Gary flips on his flashlight, blinding me, and I cover my eyes with one arm. "Would shooting them take the fun out of it?" he asks with a laugh. "I think it'd be too quick."

There's a pop, followed by another, and the blinding

light drops onto the ground, spinning to illuminate Gary, who's lying on the floor bleeding out.

Celeste crumples to the floor too. At first I think she's hurt, but when I drop beside her I realize she's shaking from fear not pain. I want to help her, but Landon is making his way to us.

"What are you doing?" I grab at her arm. "Shoot him, too, and then this is over!"

"No!" She throws the gun across the room. I watch it slide across the stone in disbelief.

"Celeste!" I hiss. "What the fuck are you doing?"

She curls up into the fetal position, her body racked with sobs.

"You're not supposed to touch that," she says in a voice unlike any I've heard from her. It's high-pitched, like a child's. "Look what you made me do! Why did you touch it?"

Oh *fuck*.

I think about something Solomon said once—that even "normal" people act differently all the time. Since I arrived here, Celeste has been rude and grumpy, measured but flirty, capable of meting out violence and also terrified of it.

It all fell within the range of normal to me—until now.

"Sorry, sorry, sorry," she repeats over and over

again in her little-girl voice, the same way Keke used to chant "Quiet and careful."

I want to stay with her, but there's still a problem to deal with in the room, and she just threw the solution about as far away from us as it can get.

"Just let us go, Landon," I say, standing and rolling my aching shoulders. He's searching next to Gary's body, likely going for the flashlight so he can figure out where the gun went. I don't look at his face anymore— I'm watching his hands, his feet, his hips, the places that will give me a millisecond's advance warning if he makes a move.

"I'm not going to do that. You're going to die here. Both of you. Don't you get it? Do you really think I didn't know you'd be here? I'm the one who made sure you got hired."

I pull my face into an expression of deep confusion. "Why would I take this job if I knew about Kavanaugh Island and its connection to you?"

He laughs, picking up the flashlight. "Oh, the third-date thing? I never told you about the island. That was a lie. And I don't know why you wandered up to find my father, but great job. Made things a lot easier for me. I thought I'd have to work to pin it on you, but you have a real knack for screwing yourself over."

I shout, the absolute fuckedness of the situation

pissing me off. "You wanted me gone. You kept telling me to leave! How did that fit into your little murder plot?"

"My father thought he was so damned smart. 'You have to finish what you started, son.'" The disgust when he mimics his father is palpable. "I told him not to bring you here because I knew the controlling fuck would double down on it. Giving me the perfect setup to finally get rid of him."

I move closer to him, but despite his shit-talking, he's paying as much attention to my moves as I am to his.

"And you? Putting every single bit of information about your system on the internet was the perfect present to me. I can't even feel bad for you. You had drawings of the castle, descriptions of all your little friends. I know more about your system than you do. You can thank Empress for that." He pretends to jump forward and then laughs when I brace in response. "Watching you all scramble every time I lied and said one of you had done or said something was more entertaining than I thought it'd be."

"You've been stalking me like the loser ex that you are, and I'm supposed to be the one who feels dumb?"

"You don't have to feel anything. You just have to know that I let you get away once and it's not going to happen again. You can fight it, and I guess it'll be more fun for me that way, but that's the only outcome here. You and your little girlfriend are gonna die."

Celeste makes a horrible, high-pitched squeal of fear.

I crouch like I'm moving to comfort her, then push off the foot nearest to her and dash across the tower, zeroing in on the gun, which I've had my eye on since it skidded to a stop after Celeste threw it. Six years ago, I would have made it across the room. Six years ago, I'd had muscle mass and glutes and stamina. Now I'm weaker, stiff from cold and fighting and climbing. I push myself as hard as I can, but Landon is the one who's been working out and maybe taking steroids for half a decade. He's read my moves, and his hand comes into view when I'm still a few steps away. His fingers are closing around the barrel when I decide to slide. I have no fucking idea how to do it, since I'm not the sporty type, but my leg reaches out, propelled by dust and rain, and I kick the gun just out of his grasp while also fucking up my shin.

"Ouch!" I scream, and he looks at me, gauging weakness. His hesitation wins me a couple of seconds of forward motion before he registers that I've never stopped moving. I roll to the side and shimmy back to bring my boot down on his face. Not nearly hard enough, given my awkward positioning, but enough to throw him off balance and hurt him a little. I scramble forward, laboring to my hands and knees and driving my head into his diaphragm as he rears back, knocking the wind out of him.

I have no idea what I'm doing—I'm not a trained fighter, I'm a dirty one. I throw clawed hands and swipe at his face and neck as I try to figure out an opening, but he swings an arm out and knocks me onto my ass.

"You were always talking about how tough you were," he says. "You said you could probably take me in a fight. It took all my willpower not to laugh. Now we get to see, little miss feminist. I'm going to knock that smirk off your face."

I hear Celeste's whimpers in the background, but I'm focused on going hard at Landon. I need to get the gun or get him away from it.

I swing wildly, and as my cracked nails dig into his face and he screams, I'm thankful to Della for growing them out.

I scrabble across the stone floor and grab the gun with my right hand, but he reaches around my waist from behind and lifts me up, slamming me into the wall. I try to figure out how to turn the gun toward him, but between the cold and it not being my dominant hand, I'd more likely end up shooting myself or Celeste.

He moves to slam me against the wall again and just

before I hit, I shoot out the glass of the window, tossing the gun through it as I hit the wall full-force.

Blood fills my mouth. My entire body feels like a tender bruise, and I try to stand but stumble back to the ground.

"You stupid bitch." Landon laughs, circling me. "That was your only hope and you threw it away. You really have no sense of self-preservation."

He kicks me, and I curl into a ball, bringing one hand over my head and the other to my ankles. Pain screams through my scalp as he grabs me by the hair and pulls my head back so that I'm facing him. Blood wells out of the scratches on his forehead and cheeks, framing his dilated pupils and wild eyes.

"You didn't recognize this place and you didn't recognize me," he says, then laughs. "You still haven't realized why I even paid you any attention when we met? Why you even got into that program? You were a hot piece of ass, but not someone I would bring home to Dad—if you hadn't met him already."

I chuckle, because I can appreciate that I should have figured this shit out a long time ago. I bet the others already have. "I was here. As a kid."

"That's right, genius. Look at you, picking up all the hints I laid out, eight years later." He scoffs, shakes his head derisively. "The funny thing is, you're just as stubborn as my father. I knew telling you to leave would make you more inclined to stay until it was too late."

I scream in his face and swing to punch him, but he catches it. "My dad isn't around anymore to be on my ass about letting you get away. But I'm going to finish the job for myself, and when I run for office, I'll have this great sob story about how the underprivileged bitches he tried to help repaid him by killing him. I can ride that to the presidency in this climate."

He brings his mouth to my cheek, his breath hot and funky.

"Thanks, babe."

Then his hand is at my throat, lifting me up toward the window. "Bye."

I grin at him as his hand squeezes—this motherfucker had supposedly been too squeamish to slap my ass during sex—but don't claw at him. Instead, I bring my knee up to rest on his stomach, finally bringing the tongue of my Docs that I was fiddling with while curled up on the ground closer to my hand. My fingers have been slipping off of the button tab that I'd sewn on, but finally it pops open.

Landon stares at me, teeth bared and eyes bright as he squeezes then releases—edging me toward my own death.

My middle finger slips into the cool metal loop

and I tug—my boot blade slides out easily. I know it's sharp—Solomon wouldn't have neglected this when he maintained my boots for me. I'd scoffed when I read his little note, but he'd done that as a testament of care and a hope for my return.

I'm back and I'm not dying today. None of us are.

Landon releases and I sip in a breath, swing my arm back as far as I can, and then drive the triangular blade deep into his side, hoping I've hit a major organ or at least dissected some necessary vesicles.

He yells and throws me away from him, and I land on my back, lifting my head to prevent a concussion as best I can, though my neck pays the price for it, wrenching painfully. Landon is bent over, holding his wound.

"Did I get a kidney?" I ask, pushing to my feet with a grin, the blade still on my knuckle.

"Fuck you," he says, but doesn't move toward me. His face is contorted in pain and I run over and give him a hard kick in the exact spot where I'd stabbed him. He rolls onto his side and vomits, then goes slack.

He's not dead, but I don't need him to be for a few minutes. Incapacitated is enough.

I shuffle over to Celeste, who's rocking with her head in her hands.

"Celeste!"

She doesn't look at me.

"I need your help," I say gently. "And then we can leave here."

I feel the presence behind me a millisecond too late. This is what happens when you get soft. Danger can walk right up behind you and bash you in the head.

I'm still awake as I go down, just long enough to hear John say, "I know what to do with you."

Chapter 43

Solomon

Rapunzel's helmet drops me into darkness, and memories flash by like snippets of film projected against a dark wall.

Being dragged screaming from my mother's arms as my parents try to grab me and are held back by police.

Strange older white people yelling at me and shoving me into a dark closet.

A middle-aged Black man removing his belt; the whistle in the air as he brings it down toward me.

A white woman with crimped hair and blue eye shadow smoking something from a pipe as I sit in a room filled with smoke, alcohol, and adults strewn everywhere.

Being on a boat to the island, with the same woman, so happy that I get to do something fun for once. I get to go to a castle! "It's a party, Keke. You have to be good so I can make some money for us."

Being kicked from behind and turning to see a boy with blond hair and cruel eyes standing over me with a baseball bat. He brings it down onto my stomach and it hurts so bad. What did I do to deserve this? Miss Barbara said we were going to a party. This isn't fun.

I see the familiar ivy pattern on the wall behind him. "You little crack baby! My dad says kids like you should be rounded up and dropped in the river."

Someone yells at him, "Just kill it and be done, Landon. Wasn't supposed to be here anyway. The women are more fun!"

He looks over his shoulder and nods, then raises the bat high over his head and stares down at me. His chest is moving in and out so fast, and then he brings the bat down hard. I close my eyes and scream—when it hits the floor next to my head it's so loud. When I open my eyes, the boy's face is red and he looks mad at me.

"Die!" he screams, and then runs away.

I crawl under the table in the hall. Maybe I can hide here. I tried to hide behind the armor, but that's where he found me downstairs.

I blink and the image turns more three-dimensional. I'm back in the castle next to the tower door. But then I realize that it's not the same—it's shabbier, dirtier, and closer to what it looked like when our doors first opened in the inner world.

There are no light fixtures, and weak flashlight beams bob down the hallway from me. Everything is slightly cloudy, like when I'm wearing the wrong prescription lenses. It feels like I'm here, but I'm not.

This isn't the present—I'm still in memory, but more as third-party viewer than experiencing it myself. I know that I've only felt a fraction of our lived experience and my heart is full of confusion and betrayal and pain. I can't imagine how a child must have processed these things.

A whimper sounds from behind me, and when I turn my heart drops.

Keke.

She's still under the table in the hallway. Instead of her usual cute floral dress, she's wearing what at first seems to be some kind of gunnysack, a simple white sheath. Her knees are pulled to her chest, her arms wrapped tightly around them, but that doesn't stop the violent tremors that quake through her. Her eyes are wide and vacant, and the tears that streak paths down her grubby cheeks fall unnoticed.

From the end of the hall, there's a piercing scream, like something from a horror movie, followed by the sound of laughter.

"Got one! Got one!"

The white woman with crimped hair and heavy blue eye shadow rounds the corner as the laughter continues. She is also dressed in white, though her dress is ragged and she's barefoot and bloody. Her eyes go wide as she spots Keke and she runs toward her.

"Miss Barbara! The boy hit me with the bat and before they hurt the lady and—"

The lady slams into Keke, her eyes darting about wildly like a prey animal.

"Shh, honey," she whispers. "I'm sorry I brought you here. I didn't know this was gonna happen."

She drags Keke from under the table and starts to pull her.

"I'm scared, Miss Barbara! This isn't fun!"

The woman tugs at the tower door, but it doesn't open. She tries again, then looks down at Keke and releases her hand.

"I'm sorry. This is my fault, but they don't pay enough for this. You understand, right?"

She opens the window at the end of the hall and starts to climb out. Keke runs and grabs her leg, holding it, working herself up into a wail.

"No! Don't leave me. Don't leave me!"

The woman looks behind her and frowns. She kicks Keke off of her, hard. Keke's chin splits open as she hits the ground, and she lets out a high-pitched squeal.

The woman glares at her, eyes watering. "If you don't shut up, you'll never see your mommy and daddy again! Do you understand? Do you want to see your mommy and daddy?"

Keke hiccups and nods.

"Good. Just stay here."

The woman slips out the window and Keke sits shivering on the ground beside the door.

"Come back," she whispers. "Don't leave me."

Tears stream down my face as her confusion and heartbreak flood me; for a brief moment, her pain is mine, fresh as when she'd felt it, and I realize that Keke may be the strongest of all of us.

The door next to her creaks open—it might have been blown by the wind, but it's wide enough for Keke to climb to her feet and squeeze through.

She pulls the door shut as a burst of noise erupts in the hallway. Outside the door are the sounds of screams,

386 · ALYSSA COLE

laughter, and horror, and Keke toddles to her feet and reaches for the doorknob as if to go back out.

"Where you going, darling?" a soft voice asks from behind her. She turns, and I do, too, to see a Black woman standing on the debris-covered steps. She wears a white dress that's blackened along the edges, and a red headwrap, and her medium-brown face is ashen and gaunt. Dark circles cup her baleful eyes, and a dimple at her chin offsets her small red-painted mouth.

"I have to find foster mommy. She's in danger," Keke says with a familiar stubborn determination.

"There are monsters out there, little girl," the woman says, amused and sad, and it's only as she takes a step down that I realize she's not walking—she's floating an inch or so above the stairs. There's an ethereal quality to her that isn't a quality of her personality or a trick of the light or of memory.

"Are you another imaginary friend?" Keke asks.

She reaches for Keke and the wan light from the lancet window shines through her arm and hand.

Ghost.

She's a ghost.

She's *the* ghost.

The woman in white, in the tower and in the inner world, isn't Grace.

A loud scream erupts just outside the door, and the

ghost's hand slips over Keke's mouth. I see the goose bumps rise on Keke's skin and feel them rise on my own.

"I'll be your friend, but you have to be quiet. And careful."

Quiet and careful.

Keke nods.

I blink and the memory changes, a jump in time.

Outside the door, horrible sounds of laughing, ripping, and screaming—the screams stop, dying down to whimpers, and something dark and viscous slides under the door. The puddle surrounds Keke's Mary Janes and she stands shaking, too terrified to move.

"Close your eyes," the ghost woman says. "Cover your ears. Quiet and careful, darling."

Another time jump.

Keke is sitting on the bottom step as smoke curls under the door, her eyes beady and blank. Traumatized. Daylight filters in from the windows above.

The ghost woman speaks from behind her. "Promise me you won't come back here, Kenetria."

Keke nods.

"Promise me!"

"I promise, Lottie."

The door swings open and the frazzled woman she'd called Miss Barbara reaches in and grabs Keke, dragging her out.

"There you are. Everything is fine. Everything is fine. We're leaving now. Nothing happened."

"You left me," Keke says, dry-eyed and stone-faced.

"No. You imagined it, didn't you, hon? Nothing happened. It was a fun party."

"You left me with the monsters." Keke swings a blood-and-dirt-caked fist at her, catching the woman on the cheek. "Fuck you! I'm gonna tell Miss Charlie! Fuck you!"

The woman stares at Keke as if she's never seen her before, then her expression is pinched by fear and anger.

"After I took you in, this is what you do? You can't tell the social worker because she won't believe you. If you tell her, or anyone, what happened, you'll never see your mommy and daddy again. Do you hear me? You can never tell anyone or you'll never see them again!"

She shakes Keke, hard, and then the helmet is pulled off of my head.

"Keke. Where is she? Keke!" I try to take a step forward and drop to my knees. I wipe tears from my eyes, swallowing the sobs rising in my throat.

"Those are not all of the memories," Not-Rapunzel says slowly. "I will not burden you with them all."

My hands are shaking and I feel sick, but I manage to push myself up to my feet as they arrange their head back onto their body.

"Thank you," I say. "Thank you for holding them for us. And for protecting us."

I reach for their hand, unsure of how to comfort a creature made of armor and pain.

"It was not my choice," they say, then point with their other hand. "It was hers."

I already know who I'll see when I turn, but it's no less shocking.

Lottie—not Grace—walks slowly toward me, but I can see now that she isn't a ghost. Here in this world, she's as real as me.

"Where are they?" I ask. "Tell me where my friends are."

"Solomon, be a dear," she says. "Bring Ken in here."

"Ken can't come inside even if I could tell her what to do."

"We'll see about that."

She moves so quickly that I barely see her hand move, and then something sharp jabs into my side. I let out a guttural yell as my vision blurs. The last thing I see is Lottie smiling sweetly and Empress running down the hall toward me.

"Keke is gone!" She stops short when she catches sight of Lottie.

"Keke." I'm not even sure the words leave my mouth as I fall. "Where is—"

Chapter 44

Ken

Sleet slaps me in the face and I come to, head throbbing, and this time not from a switch-induced headache. John had knocked me the fuck out, and now I'm being carried over someone's shoulder.

I start thrashing immediately and receive a humiliating swat on the ass. I cry out in pain—at this point my whole body is a collection of welts and bruises—then press my teeth into my lip and start struggling again.

"Your choices are my shoulder or getting tossed over the side," John says, voice as jovial as ever. "Behave."

"Where's Celeste, asshole?" I say—even my tongue feels bruised.

"Don't worry about her. She's my special treat. I

always did think she had a thing for me. The way she glares at me sometimes . . ."

Somehow—somehow—I'm still able to be shocked. I hadn't trusted John, but I'd thought he was at least moderately not horrible, and now he's the one who's going to take me out.

I bounce on his shoulder as we head down the stairs into the grotto.

Strained, ugly laughter from up ahead, and a shuffling step.

Landon. He's still alive.

"Why don't you just kill me now?" I ask. "Come on. Throw me over the cliff."

There's a chance I can take him with me.

"That'd be no fun," he says. "That's what people like you don't understand. It's not just about killing. This is tradition. Goblins bring chaos to communities; you take them out in the same way."

I grab onto the bars of the niche as we pass by, struggling to hang on with fingers that are stiff with cold. Landon punches my fingers, hard, the pain somehow magnified by the cold, and my grip loosens.

"I think we should just off her. I'm bleeding out here and can't get to a hospital till morning."

"You'll be fine," John says. "Injury is a risk you take."

He speaks so confidently, all the aw-shucks coating gone from his words.

"Were you part of this all along?" I ask.

"Oh, no. I've been on many hunts over the years, though they'd mostly died off with all the cell phones and cameras. I didn't think I'd get to participate in one again before I passed. But I guess my good luck is your bad day."

I remember that this motherfucker loves talking.

"But why do this? What's the point? Killing people you think are below you doesn't change anything, even if you're right. It makes you a murderer. Isn't that worse?"

"It's a service to the community," he says. "But honestly? It's just fun."

He pauses and I notice the wind sounds different here. Like it's blowing over a mason jar.

"We opened up the pond," he says. "It already needed to be drained and the rain has been filling it up. It's not quite there, but it'll be over your head soon. This generation wants to kill the women quick, but I'm an old-fashioned guy. This is a judgment, a punishment. You should suffer. Adios, Ken."

Then I'm flying through the darkness. I land in water so frigid that it knocks the breath out of me. I hit the water hard, and I thrash in panic as it goes up my nose and into my mouth, tasting of dirt and algae.

I splash helplessly, trying to figure out up from down as my head goes under again and again, and finally my boot touches something solid and I push myself to a standing position.

The beam of John's headlamp lands on me like a spotlight; he and Landon are two shadowy figures through the streaked and cracked lenses of my glasses. The water is at my waist, swirling around me as the driving rain slips down the sides; at the rate the water is rising there has to be a gutter or something collecting the water and dumping it here. The walls are slick with ice and moss. It has to be nine feet deep, at least, despite its small circumference, and the short ladder is a few feet higher than my arms will be able to reach before the water is over my head.

"Enjoy your swim," Landon says, then before I can give him a final "fuck you," John reaches for him. Landon makes a gurgling sound and brings his hands to his neck and then tumbles face-first into the pond—I dive to the side to avoid him landing on me.

"What the fuck?" Landon gurgles and thrashes in the water as he bleeds out from his slit throat.

John crouches down. "Goblins are nuisances, degenerates, and outsiders. You're Kavanaugh's descendant, but you don't respect tradition. You could have bumped off your old man any other time, but

394 · ALYSSA COLE

you did it tonight so I took you out, like I would any goblin." Then to me: "I'll pass along your goodbyes to Celeste. I have a few hours of fun ahead of me with her and Lily. Like I said, I'm old-fashioned. I'm not in a rush."

He stands and leaves, taking the light with him. In the darkness, everything seems louder, more frightening. My heart is beating too fast and I am frozen, both from cold and fear. Something bumps into me and I push it away, my hand sliding through Landon's hair, slick with the scum that fills this water.

Fuck. Fuck. Fuck.

I failed. I fucking failed. Of course I did.

I'm going to die. We're going to die. Because I didn't follow my instinct and stay on the fucking pier when John's ferry first pulled up.

(*"Ken! You have to—"*)

Solomon's words cut through my thoughts, a serrated blade tipped with pain and confusion.

I squeeze my eyes shut. Whatever is happening in the inner world, I can't fix that either.

I hate this.

Hate everything.

Hate myself.

Why is this happening?

"Ken!"

When I open my eyes, I'm still in water up to my knees, but I'm in the inner world. I'm in the turret.

Solomon had called me, but in the inner world, it's Keke I hear. Screaming with a fear that threatens to overwhelm me.

"Keke!"

I slosh toward the edge of the turret and look out into the storm, where the churning water separates me from the island. Keke screams again and I prepare to jump—except I can drown in here as much as I can out there. I might not die, but I sure as hell wouldn't make it to the castle. Debris bumps into my shin and for a moment, I think it's Landon again. When I look down, I see a palette with a paintbrush. It's the first one I'd ever owned, a gift from one of my teachers who thought art might help quell my bursts of rage.

I almost stomp it into the water, but instinct tells me to pick it up. Two globs of paint rest on the plastic oval: black and white. A fine-tipped paintbrush like the ones I'd splurged on back in the day rests beside them.

I look out toward the castle, at the path in the foam-topped waves where the breakwater should be. Then I pick up the brush and dip it into the velvety black oil paint.

I have no idea if this will work, but I imagine the space between me and the castle as a canvas, stretched taut. I reach out a shaking hand and make a bold slash where the path should be, and suddenly it's there: the waves break against it.

It's been so long since I've even touched a brush, but I made this one line and it's changed this world. Now I just have to make another one. I lay down stroke after stroke, the flat black support structure of the pathway. Then I mix black into the edge of white, using quick flicks of my wrist to dab the stone-lined path. One after the other, not worrying how it will look but only that it can take me to those who need me. White to accent the gleam of stone and chipped rock.

I have no idea how much time passes, but when I'm done, I've painted a fucking hideous pathway that any art teacher would have given a D minus to, at most. But water surges on either side of it, and when I take a tentative step onto it, it holds up my weight. After one step, my boot suctioning in the tacky, still-wet paint, I start running. Rain pelts down on me and I scream my anger and my joy and my pain as I ignore the water slapping over the edges of my creation.

When I step onto the island, I don't stop running until I'm at the front door.

I've waited so many years for this moment, but there's no time to lose to triumph.

I'm winded and sweaty by the time I reach the

second-floor landing, and when I turn Keke is nowhere in sight but the woman in the white dress stands over Solomon. Her face is brown-skinned and beautiful without the paint squiggles marring it.

Lottie, I think as I fly at her, everything wiped from my mind but stopping her. "What did you do to him!"

"You did this, darling," she says calmly, dodging my charge. "Did you really think you could just leave and everything would be fine?"

I skid on the wooden floors and turn to charge her again. "What the fuck are you talking about?"

"Everything that's happening now is your fault," she says, her expression darkening. "You were so busy feeling sorry for yourself that you never thought about what would happen while you were gone. The system was a mess before this. Della fell apart! Solomon overwhelmed himself! Our trauma began knocking again, and then it began to scream. And me—me?" She laughs. "I had to manage all of it. I had to start fronting to make sure we ate. I had to deal with Keke's outbursts and Empress's resentment. And you dare to feel sorry for yourself!"

"You did this?" I ask. "You led us to the island?"

"I can't take the credit, but I seized the opportunity when it arose. Landon invited us here, and I accepted." She laughs. "I was the only one who knew that his family owned this island. Della had no idea what was going on, the poor dear. Pearson thought we were his plaything and Landon wanted to play the player. But I knew. I knew who I was—who I had been—and once I saw the castle, I knew what they wanted when they emailed us. I don't have the real Lottie's memories, but I had her name, and she made it clear what had happened to her when she made me promise not to return."

"Why did you accept?" I'm so pissed I feel like I could knock her head clear off her shoulders. "Do you know what I've been through tonight? We're probably going to die, and you think this is funny!"

"Oh, now you care about dying. You know, I think you're jealous. You couldn't even cut your own wrists right. I'm going to kill us in a much more dramatic fashion, and it wasn't even what I wanted to do."

She bursts out laughing and I leap for her, tackling her to the ground, grabbing her by the collar of her dress.

I land one, two punches in her face and then she reaches a hand up as if to slap me, but caresses my cheek gently.

"You thought you were the worst thing that could happen to this system? You're an amateur, darling. It's quite adorable, in a way."

"Why are you doing this?"

"Because you left me!" she screams, her face contorting with pain and anger. "You left! Fuck you!"

I blink and suddenly it's not the woman I have yoked up by the collar. It's Keke. Tears stream down her round cheeks, and her expression is filled with anguish that shouldn't be possible for a child.

"Why do people leave and then scary things happen? You're supposed to protect me!"

She beats her fists against my chest and I stare at her, unable to move.

"How—"

She wails—the same cry of pain I'd heard that had made me find a way into our inner-world home. I'd thought someone was hurting her, and I'd been right.

Me.

I'd hurt her.

I let go of her collar and sit back, pulling her into my lap.

"I'm sorry. I'm a jerk and I'm selfish and—"

"Stop it!" She covers her ears.

Shit. I don't know how to comfort a kid. I don't even know how to comfort myself. I have no idea if anyone is fronting and we're about to drown anyway, but I don't want us to go out like this.

"Keke, look at me."

She refuses, and I take her chin gently and turn her face toward me.

"Please look at me."

She glares up at me, but her mouth wobbles.

"I'm sorry, and I won't leave you again."

"Do you promise?" she asks in a voice rough with tears.

"I think we need something stronger than that. Do you want to pinkie swear?"

She holds out her hand to me, pinkie raised, and I wrap her little finger in my own.

Strong arms close around both of us and I turn to see Solomon's face beside me.

"You scared me, you asshole."

He wipes a tear from my cheek. "You have to front."

"Where are the others?"

The door to the tower slowly opens, and Della steps out, eyes wide with fear and confusion. "Ken?"

A shadow falls over her and the evil-looking suit of armor from the castle's dining room steps out.

"Shit, do I have to fight this thing too?" I groan, starting to heave Keke aside.

"No. That's Rapunzel."

"Not-Rapunzel," the armor says in the same voice that had yelled at me when we pulled up to the island.

"They tried to protect us in their own way when they realized we were coming back to the island," Solomon says.

"The tower is safe," they say solemnly.

My throat goes rough. "Right. Okay. I have to go figure out how to get us out of this mess."

I pull Solomon in for a kiss, short and sweet, and everything I remembered from my fantasies. "In case I fuck things up."

"You won't," Keke says in her own voice, and then in the voice of the woman I'd fought, "You'd better not."

I sigh and close my eyes.

When I open them, I'm foggy, my numb body pressed against the freezing stone wall and icy water lapping at my lower lip. Lightning flashes, reflecting off of the ladder above.

I try to scramble along the wall, but it's useless. The icy rain is coming down harder, and I now have to keep pushing off of the floor to keep my mouth and nose above water.

"If any of you know how to swim, speak now or forever hold your peace."

I start to sink down again and my feet don't touch the bottom, and panic overwhelms me—I instinctively open my mouth to suck in a breath and suddenly calm wraps around me from behind.

"*Calm down. I can hold my breath for a long time, but you have to let me help you. Can I help?*" Mesmer asks.

"*Please.*"

The tightness around my lungs releases, just a bit. I no longer feel like I'm tensed around a ball of air, but like I'm consciously not releasing the air in my lungs. My body slackens and then my boots touch the ground and I kick off toward the surface.

I gasp in a huge bellyful of air, and when I go under again I'm still anxious as fuck, but more in control.

"*We survive together,*" Mesmer says, and I let her optimism buoy us toward the surface.

We can do this. I just have to keep jumping for as long as it takes, no matter how tired I am.

After a couple of minutes, I realize that optimism won't be enough.

"*Guys, I'm tired,*" I say, and when my legs hit the bottom, my kick up is so sluggish that we barely reach the surface. Just as my face is about to breach, Landon's body floats by, blocking my exit.

We can't take in another breath.

"*It's okay,*" Mesmer says urgently. "*Don't panic.*"

I don't suck in air, but I do start to thrash in the water. I can't feel the floor—I don't know where the walls are. We're going to drown.

I gasp out a bubble of precious air.

Fuck!

I feel another headmate's presence glide over mine. They are absolutely unbothered, despite the fact that we're in the process of dying.

Slowly, my spastically flailing arms and legs start to gain control. Our arms pull in closer to our body, and our legs kick effortlessly to the surface. When we breach the surface I gasp, preparing to sink again, but instead our arms move back and forth and our legs kick lazily in circular motions.

We're doggy paddling.

"Who the fuck—?"

"I like swimming," Lurk says. *"But only when it's not cold. The pool at the YMCA was heated."*

I should be furious, but I shudder out a laugh.

"We can go swimming more if you'd stop stealing my swimming lessons," I say. *"If we don't die, the next lesson is mine."*

"Okay," he says, then flips me onto my back to do a lazy backstroke.

Finally, the water is high enough that I can stretch my arm out and reach the lowest rung.

I hang there for a moment, too tired to pull myself up. Then my right arm reaches for the next rung.

"We can do this," Solomon says. *"Let's get out of here."*

"*Sorry I made you doggy paddle through my garbage patch,*" I say. "*Thanks for staying with me.*"

He laughs wearily. "*I prefer your garbage patch over smooth seas. Because it means I'm with you.*"

"*I'll try to throw some good stuff in the water too,*" I say. "*If we survive.*"

That's probably the closest either of us will get to saying I love you for the moment. But since we understand each other better than anyone, it's enough for now.

I reach for the next rung and he reaches for the next, and a few minutes later we lie on the cold stone floor, battered and breathing heavily, but alive.

Chapter 45

Groupthnk: Collaborative Journal

Archived Post: Empress (2 years ago)

I was reading about subsystems and stumbled across the wildest DID factoid yet: Headmates in a system can have DID themselves! Headmate inception! Wild! It makes sense when you think that we're all susceptible to the same mental-health issues singlets are, but things get kind of amazing when DID happens in an inner world: don't forget, anything goes in here. The DID can manifest like in the outer world, with headmates sharing a single body with others, and changes only visible through behavior or if they tell their other headmates.

But inner-world headmates can also have totally different appearances when they switch, and appear to their other headmates as different people! Now I'm trying to think of which headmates I've never seen in the same place at the same time . . .

Chapter 46
Solomon

I drag us up to our feet, though my hold on the front seems tenuous at best. We're all exhausted and barely hanging on.

"Celeste," Ken says. "She's still inside, with John."

"I don't know if we have the strength to save her and ourselves."

"We have to," Lottie says, and I realize now that I've heard her voice many times before. "Celeste is my . . . friend. My special friend."

"Hold up," Ken says. "You're Celeste's girlfriend? You're the friend she helped to research the goblin hunts? You mean technically I've already smashed? Noice."

"Ken," I chide, though I know she's mostly trying to bait Lottie to keep the mood light.

"Was it you, having those meetings when Della would act unlike herself?" Mesmer asks. "Why did you do that instead of talking to us?"

I remember the sub shop I'd gone co-con in, and Della's confusion. She isn't close to the front right now, and I'm sure she'll have nothing pleasant to say about being tricked for months and then kidnapped.

"As gatekeeper I have to decide what you all needed to know—and what to remember. I stayed hidden to prevent any number of issues that we're going to have to deal with now. But I'm also vulnerable to the chaos in the system, especially when Keke experiences it. I haven't been myself either."

It's still odd to think that this woman has been watching our every move, perhaps for the entirety of our existence. Adjusting to the new knowledge, and new headmates, will be difficult, but I hope we're lucky enough to get the opportunity.

"I know I haven't ingratiated myself to you all, but please. Celeste was against me even coming here. She's only here today because of me."

"All right, all right," Ken says. "We like her, too, and we're not going to leave her behind."

So it's decided.

We head back toward the house, the quiet chatter of headmates soothing me as thunder rumbles loudly, but not as loud as before. The rain and sleet still drive down, but the storm is moving away from us.

Ken leads us into the office through a half door hidden behind a curtain, and we shed our soaking-wet clothes. A quick search of the office reveals no weapons, but Ken, ever resourceful, climbs a bookshelf and pulls down a heavy pointed curtain rod.

After wrapping ourselves in a gauzy undercurtain that will be light enough for us to maneuver in, we separate the rod into its two halves, one for each hand, and head into the hallway.

"*Guess I ended up in the white dress after all,*" Ken says. "*I would prefer a buck-naked berserker attack, but I guess this adds some drama.*"

"*Bestie, I've had more than enough drama for a lifetime,*" Empress says.

We stalk quietly through the halls, toward the sound of the crackling fireplace in the parlor and the scent of smoke, and tobacco. The dining room.

When we peek in, we see John standing by the hearth, highball glass in his hand, puffing a cigar as he stares at the ground in front of him. One of the tables from the hall burns behind a grate, throwing light onto Celeste and Lily, who are both tied up on the floor in front of the fire.

"Well, we only have a few hours left, ladies, but now

that I've got my strength back, and the Viagra's kicking in, we're going to have us some fun."

He crouches down and runs a hand up Lily's leg, then takes the cigar from his mouth and presses it into her thigh.

She screams, and he smiles, the fire's reflection in his eyes making him look like some kind of demon. From somewhere upstairs, the dog barks fruitlessly.

I grip the curtain rods and crouch so he doesn't catch sight of us, thighs burning as I duck-walk closer.

"Just rush him!" Ken shouts.

"We're not strong enough."

I glance around the room, but the only weapons are in the wooden box Landon had brought, and it sits directly next to John.

Lily screams again, more loudly, and I grit my teeth.

If it comes down to a one-on-one test of strength, we'll lose. But he could kill either one of them at any moment if we wait too long.

I loosen the cord tying the curtain around us, just slightly, and then take a deep breath.

"I'm going now."

I run quietly, one rod pointed and one raised just over my head. For a second I think it will be over quickly, but then he turns as if sensing my approach, batting away the rod just as it begins to press into his neck. It slices him, but not deeply. Still, he reaches for his neck, smiling at me, and I bring down the other rod over his head. It breaks and he barely seems to feel any pain, not flinching as he swings his heavy fist toward my face.

I dodge it, and then land a quick, fluid blow to his kidney. He inhales sharply and I land a flat-palmed punch to his chin.

Not me. Mesmer.

The blows she's landed are sped-up versions of the moves we do every morning.

"Tai chi," she says shakily, "is a martial art, even if it's a meditative one."

"Looks like I should have just thrown you over the side," he says, cupping his chin. "I'm not going to be nice this time."

"You call leaving us to drown nice?" I ask.

"Hell of a lot nicer than what's going to happen to you now," he says, chuckling.

He swings and Mesmer dodges, then lands an open-handed punch to his diaphragm that makes him keel over. With his face unprotected she lands a flurry of hits before he staggers away.

"I can't front anymore," Mesmer says, her voice distant. *"Sor . . ."*

We each have our limits, and Mesmer has gone above

and beyond hers. John catches the sudden change in our demeanor and lunges forward, hugging us around our waist.

"Got you now," he says.

"Candlestick time," I say. *"Thanks for the idea, Ken."*

I fully undo the cord on our makeshift dress, and as John pulls at the gauzy material it slides off us. He's still grabbing at fabric when I land a knuckles-out punch directly to his eyeball, and he shouts in pain. He brings one hand to his eye and stalks toward us as we back up into solid cold metal—the armor.

I turn and grab it, and though the suit is bolted down, the sword isn't. I feel Not-Rapunzel's presence overlap mine and reposition my hands on the sword. I had been planning to lift it and stab, but instead I turn at my hips, swinging it like a golf club.

I catch John in his side just as he reaches for us.

The blade goes in deep, pushed in by momentum and the weight we had planted behind the swing. Blood spills out of his mouth as he stares in disbelief, and he crashes back onto the dessert cart, crushing the wooden box.

We stand panting heavily, waiting for him to spring up like a monster in a film.

"Nah. We're not waiting for shit." Ken takes control of the body and places a foot on his chest and tugs the

sword out of him, leaving a spray of gore in its wake. She struggles with the heavy weapon, then uses that weight to her advantage, driving it into his belly. He buckles, emitting a wheeze, then collapses back to the ground.

The fire crackles loudly and light rain pebbles the window.

Our legs go weak, but we manage to make it over to Celeste before we collapse, undoing her bindings with shaking hands.

"Are you okay, darling?" Lottie asks out loud.

"No bitch, we're not okay!" Celeste says, slapping us away. Then her sullen expression morphs into a worried smile and she pulls us into a hug.

We loosen Lily's bindings but don't untie her completely. Even though we're exhausted, Ken drags us up to make sure the dog is all right before we're able to collapse.

"Puppy!" Keke squeals as the dog nestles into our lap.

We lay on the floor by the fire, our hands entwined with Celeste's, watching out the window. The sunrise is a muted one, a hazy glow beneath a bank of gray clouds.

"Remember this," Ken says. *"We're going to paint it when all this mess is over."*

"Yes," Lottie says before I can. *"We are."*

Chapter 47

Groupthnk: Collaborative Journal

**Collaborative Group: Bad Day System
(aka Kenetria Nash)**
Pinned Post: Members of Bad Day System
(known/verified headmates)
by: Empress
Edited by: Della

Lottie (role: gatekeeper – 27 years old – she/her – active)

Ken (role: protector, host – 37 years old – she/her – active)

Solomon (role: manager – 30 years old – he/him – active)

Della (role: caretaker [tasks], host – 65 years old – admin – she/her – active)

Empress (role: teenager – 16 years old – she/they – active)

Mesmer (role: [self-]caretaker [emotions] – 20 years old – she/her – active)

Keke (role: little – 4 years old – she/her – active)

Lurk (role: chill dude – age unknown – he/him – active)

Rapunzel (role: protector – immortal? – they – active)

Epilogue

Ken

One week later

Celeste's loner vibe wasn't a front. We sit in front of a crackling fire in her cabin on a small parcel of land she'd inherited from a distant relative who'd lived in the region since the post–Revolutionary War days. There's no interior design to speak of, or maybe it could be called recluse chic: Old tools and piles of wood. Faded furniture and aged copper pots and pans. There are two newer items in the cabin: a huge IKEA bed, and a shiny easel with a blank canvas.

We've been here for the last three days, after being released from police custody. Of course things hadn't gone smoothly when they rolled up on two bloody Black women with criminal records, a heap of dead white men, and one pregnant white damsel in distress screaming we were killers. But once the story had made the news, Diana had come forward to back up our version of events, after striking a deal with the prosecutor not to be charged since their johns had tried to kill them.

I still haven't processed what happened, really. Not yet. Too much is going on and I'd rather wait for the therapist's appointment that Celeste hooked us up with before delving too deep into my psyche, or anyone else's. For now, I'm adjusting to being part of my inner world while navigating the outer world, and juggling the overlap of the two now that I can't just block out one or the other.

I've just switched to the front after Celeste and Lottie had spent some quality time together. We're both freshly showered and I'm in a robe, so I assume a fun time was had by all. Lottie lingers in the background, her presence no longer hidden—at least not when she wants us to know she's around, like when I'm sitting in front of a roaring fire with her boo.

"How does your system handle this? The whole dating and sharing a body thing?" I ask. "I only dated when I wasn't aware I was sharing. This shit is difficult. Like, polyamory on expert level."

I assume I'm asking Celeste, but it's RayAnne—gruff, to the point, and the person I get along with most in Starlight System—who replies in her smoky voice: "We have to talk it out a lot. All the time. Had a fight or five when someone crossed another person's boundary or tried to sneak in and make a twosome a threesome without asking. But me, Celeste, and Carlos date Lottie, and she gets along with pretty much all of us in the system. All of us that she knows."

I nod, still taking everything in. The unlikely matchmaker in all of this had been Empress. Her posts had given Landon a scapegoat but had also connected us to Starlight System, aka Celeste Wilson. RayAnne had seen a drawing of the castle, and when she reached out about Kavanaugh Island, Lottie had intercepted. When RayAnne and Celeste brought Lottie to see the island on their boat, a secret romance had been born that inadvertently set this entire situation in motion.

"This is still so wild. Lottie kept herself hidden from us for years and your relationship hidden too. In addition to managing the system and making sure shit wasn't running off the rails. I'm still kinda pissed about that, but also: Lottie for president. She gets shit done."

"I won't apologize, but I do hope you can forgive me," she says from just behind me. *"If you could be a darling and talk to Solomon and tell him I'd like to be friends."*

"You could have talked to Solomon," he cuts in stiffly, his voice somewhere closer to the inner world. *"Instead of setting up this situation that could have killed us."*

"I didn't set it up," Lottie counters. *"I accepted Landon's invitation as a means to an end. And it worked. What would you have done?"*

I sigh and stand, heading to the mulled wine simmering on the stove. "They're fighting again. I never would have thought that I'd be the peacemaker of the system, but here we are."

A sly expression slides across Celeste's face as Carlos, their fun-loving mediator, switches in. "Go talk to your man. Make him feel better."

I take a sip of the delicious cinnamon-spiced wine and then close my eyes. When I open them, I'm in my room in the inner world. The sunken guard tower has risen above the waterline now. Solomon has carried over his bed and a few pieces of furniture that he knows I like: The cherry-red vinyl ottoman, for example. Black lacy curtains that give the room a fun goth feel when paired with the rough stone.

He's already there, stretched out on my bed with a sketchbook propped up on his bent knee. He doesn't take his eyes from the page but holds his arm out to me.

I wait a minute, still unsure about all of this. How easy it is. How good it makes me feel. That was all fine when it was fantasy, but I didn't think my life was supposed to be like this.

Then he looks at me, his dark eyes sparkling with amusement.

"Ken. Please join me on the bed. I want to feel you in my arms and have you close to me. You know why."

"Because you're pissed at Lottie and want to angry bang?" I guess as I slide onto the bed next to him.

He drops the sketchbook to the other side of him—I see a new sketch of our system is underway—and then brings his hand, gritty with charcoal, to my cheek.

"Because I love you," he says.

The one thing about Solomon is that although he lied by omission to suss out whether I was a serial headmate killer, he pretty much always tells the truth.

"Thank you," I say, then shift uncomfortably. "You're not so bad either."

He drops a kiss on my lips, the swipe of his tongue a deliciously lewd counterpoint to his usually composed behavior. "We have an hour before our first all-hands-on-deck meeting."

I unbutton his shirt, running my hand over the tight curls on his chest and smiling when he groans. "We should be a little late. I can't show up on time like a nerd anyway—have you forgotten who I am?"

"Not for a minute."

Acknowledgments

I'd like to thank my editor, Erika Tsang, who patiently waited for this book and who always believes in my ability to get the job done even when it seems doubtful. Her kindness, feedback, and friendship have been so important to me, and I'm both proud and lucky to have spent so much of my career in partnership with her. My agent, Lucienne Diver, for her unwavering support, helpful feedback, and for being a genuinely great human. And to Alli and Pete for putting their faith in this story, and in me.

Thank you to all of the people behind the scenes who've helped usher this book out into the world, including: Alessandra Roche, May Chen, Kaitlin Harri, Beatrice Jason, and Camille Collins. Particular thanks to Rachel Weinick and the production team, who transformed an unwieldy manuscript into a beautifully laid-out novel.

This book would have never been finished without my co-working crew, whose friendship and presence made the many hours spent wrestling with this novel way more fun. To Erica and Kellye, who have been there for so much of the epic journey toward "The End": THANK YOU. Courtney, Bree, and Donna, as well as the dozens of writers in the London Writers Saloon Zoom sessions I joined, were also instrumental in getting this done.

Shout out to Rebekah, Leona, Kate, Sarah, and Rose, and all my friends who supported me with encouragement and commiseration and by being their wonderful selves.

Love and appreciation to my husband, Nicolas, who dealt with being married to a writer locked in existential combat with a never-ending book. Merci beaucoup à Seb pour son soutien, aussi.

Lastly, I'd like to give so much thanks to Calion Winter, the DID accuracy consultant for this story. His early advice about potential plot missteps and insightful feedback later in the process were invaluable, and I deeply appreciate both his expertise and his kindness. I hope that I was able to write a book that portrays a realistic DID experience, but note that any issues on that front are a result of my words and not Calion's advice.

About the Author

ALYSSA COLE is an award-winning *New York Times* and *USA Today* bestselling author of thrillers and romance novels (historical, contemporary, and sci-fi). Her books have received critical acclaim from *Library Journal*, BuzzFeed, *Kirkus*, *Booklist*, Jezebel, Vulture, Book Riot, *Entertainment Weekly*, and various other outlets. Alyssa currently lives in France with her husband. When she's not working, they can usually be found watching anime or wrangling their many pets.